PRAISE FOR *CROVER ISLAND*

"Reminiscent of the action-packed ensemble thrillers of Crichton and King, J.M. Kelly's Crover Island is an immersive reading experience with characters readers can believe in, cheer for, and—sometimes—cry for as well. As intense and unrelenting as the storm in the book, the propulsive plot will leave those same readers breathless until the very last page. And maybe even beyond that!"

—PATRICK BARB, author of *Night of the Witch-Hunter*

"J.M. Kelly's latest novel, *Crover Island,* pits the legend of Loch Ness, a storm of the century, and creatures that have survived for millennia in underwater sea caves against the local inhabitants of a lonely island off the coast of Scotland. This is a real page-turner filled with characters you hope are able to fight off the existential threat they face from the horror that relentlessly stalks them."

—ERIC J. GUIGNARD, multiple award-winning author, including *That Which Grows Wild* and *Doorways to the Deadeye*

"They say the monsters in your dreams aren't real—but J.M. Kelly begs to differ. The creatures of Crover Island lurk in the mist, ready to haunt your nights and keep you far from the water forever. A chilling horror story that will thrill and terrify, *Crover Island* ensures you'll never sleep soundly again."

—CONNIE FROMAN DAVIS, author of *Death Writes Itself*

"Where [*Crover Island*] unquestionably triumphs is its dense, suspenseful atmosphere … Kelly's novel, like all good horror stories, firmly establishes its setting … [and] maintains a sense of mystery surrounding the creatures' origin, which makes the unknown beasts even scarier. The story's frenzied final act leads to an ending most readers won't see coming."

—Kirkus

"J.M. Kelly's *Crover Island* is a page-turning read, weaving together all the elements that produce shivers in lovers of this genre. Even the storm that starts the book is infused with an eerie intention. The fact that the characters in the book are trapped in their situation with no means of escaping the hordes of creatures seeking to feed on them creates a desperate urgency. This tension carries us to the surprising ending, leaves us wanting more, and causes us to stay up way too late finishing it!"

—Margo Bowblis, Hoffer award-winning author of *Walking with Two Shadows-Real-Life Stories of Love, Loss, and Reunion from Beyond the Rainbow Bridge* and *Walking with the Shadow of Love*

CROVER ISLAND

J.M. KELLY

DEDICATION

To you, dear reader, who will willingly join
hands on a journey into horror.

CHAPTER 1

MOTHER NATURE

Hurricane season promised to be interesting: it didn't disappoint. A large, rapidly growing storm, promptly named Mitch, was anointed to take his place among the honored destructive forces of nature as defined by NOAA. It barreled off the west coast of Africa, garnering high interest in the United States. Mitch then surprised everyone by curving left across the Gulf of Mexico, only to blow himself out while crossing the Yucatan Peninsula.

His demise exposed the tempestuous evil that followed, as he passed the baton to a zealous little upstart named Nora. Hurricane Nora raced across the Atlantic in the backdraft of her forerunner, as if in a hurry to make herself known. She was birthed, like most, from the easterly winds of the Sahara Desert. They blasted across the hot, dry expanse of sand, which then met with the cool, moisture-laden winds of the sub-Saharan coast of Africa. The resultant clash pushed unstable waves of wind over the warm Atlantic towards the heated waters of the Caribbean. Every step along the way, Nora garnered strength, gaining the kind of power that, once Mitch was out of the way, caused the people who watch such developments to describe her as "alarming."

Nora hit the Caribbean packing sustained winds of 160 miles per hour and headed straight for the Dominican Republic. When close enough, she zigged and battered the Bahamas, then zagged and laid waste to Cuba. She turned an angry eye at Key West, but, instead of paying them a visit, decided to catch her breath by resting in the Gulf of Mexico. She stayed almost still, spinning and drinking in vast amounts of warm, moist air, getting poised for a sudden strike. No one had ever seen a hurricane behave like this. Where would she go next? Texas? Alabama? Her CAT-5 size and wind threat conjured memories of Katrina, so the smart money was on New Orleans. The TV pundits continued to prognosticate, whipping themselves into a frenzy. Nora merely whirled, daring her predictors to lay detail to her direction. Then she moved.

She crawled her way east and, like Sherman's march to the sea, followed a scorched-earth campaign across northern Florida. She drew a straight line of devastation across the Sunshine State, destroying Pensacola, Tallahassee, and Jacksonville, before easing out into the Atlantic. Once there, she slowed again, picking up strength in the Gulf Stream as she snaked her way north along the eastern coast of the United States. All the while, she was now pushed by 180-mile-per-hour winds, the kind of winds that accompanied 2019's Dorian.

Where now? Charleston? Myrtle Beach? The Outer Banks? Once again, this hurricane defied the experts to define her. She slowed her pace, taking a tour of the Eastern Seaboard, always from a threatening distance. With each passing of the usual suspects, there was great relief to have dodged such a dangerous and wily bullet. But no one dared get too cocky. Given Nora's quirky demeanor, the coastal cities were none too sure she wouldn't turn in their direction for a closer look.

Instead, she meandered, mocking her potential victims as she crept north. She relinquished a great deal of wind and rain to them all, but kept the bulk of her strength in reserve, at least for the time being. She posed an ever-present threat to the coastal cities she skirted. Richmond quivered, as did Washington, DC. Those on the Delmarva Peninsula quaked. The Jersey shore population moved inland, still smarting from Sandy. Those on Long Island hunkered down for a fight, always conscious of the enormous, almost impossible amount of time and effort it would take for the island to evacuate.

But Nora fooled them all. She shot up the coast just offshore, eventually gliding past Providence, Rhode Island, guided by the invisible hand of a high-pressure ridge that dropped down from Canada. Like a pinball, she spun out to sea, and the entire east coast of the United States blew a sigh of relief at her departure. In a heartbeat, they were no longer concerned with Nora, as she no longer affected them. Away she went, forgotten for the moment, but still a powerful and dangerous force not to be defeated nor denied.

Ever-turning, ever-moving, Hurricane Nora now raced across the North Atlantic on a direct path to northern Scotland. Usually, a hurricane that took this path would lose strength and downgrade into an extratropical cyclone, still deadly, but with less punch. The expected storm fatigue that would have weakened her strength, however, never happened. The water in the North Atlantic was unseasonably warm. And, as she slipped below Greenland, the warm water made Nora stronger. She was still packing wind gusts of 180 miles per hour and rainfall amounts of an inch an hour, with the slow-moving potential to last at least forty-eight hours if she made landfall. The Outer Hebrides took notice and braced for impact.

Again, she fooled them. Nora skirted the Hebrides, but obliterated the Orkney Islands, before banging head-on into a historic high-pressure system in the oddly warm waters of the North Sea. There, the two systems twirled in a dance of death, sending wind, fog, and rain southward, down a tunnel path into the Moray Firth, and simultaneously east towards the coast of Norway. The experts told Norway to get ready.

As Hurricane Nora sat, patiently deciding which way to go next, Mother Nature showed she had more in store. Earth, with its countless natural mysteries, revealed yet another—one that had been created close to four hundred million years ago. The Great Glen Fault Line stretches north to south through a section of Scotland, carving an ugly scar below sea level, allowing for the formation of many deep lochs, the most famous of which is Loch Ness. The northern section of the fault splits Inverness down the middle and continues through the Moray Firth, passing directly under Crover Island. It has only been recognized as a major fault zone in more recent times, but one with minimal impact on the area. While earthquakes were rare in that part of the world, they did occur sporadically from time to time. Even so, they were usually minor in nature, with scientists taking little interest, and the general population not noticing at all.

As Nora idled in the North Sea, leaning east towards Norway, the Earth yawned and stretched. The Great Glen Fault, often compared to the more active San Andreas Fault in California and the Anatolian Fault in Turkey, effected a major slip of its fractured surface. The tectonic plates on both sides of the fault slid past one another, causing stronger seismic waves than ever recorded. A shock wave ran up the northern half of the fault line, up and under Crover Island, causing that land mass to shiver.

Those on its surface could feel the movement acutely. It was noticeable for the first time in hundreds of years that the ground walked upon by Islanders was not quite right.

But what happened below the surface is what really mattered. In a few, brief moments, several fissures opened between the depths of the underwater sea caves that hugged the underbelly of the island and the bottom of several still and silent lochs on the island's surface, creating portals between the two. Portals that now served as a conduit, a means of travel between one realm and the other.

There were thousands of things that lived in that lower realm. Things that had existed for millennia and had long ago adapted to their constricted environment far below the surface of the island. They were things that could only see in darkness, eating the many wayward fish inadvertently swept through the crevices of their confines by the shifting tides. Things that seemed half fish and half human, boasting the powerful jaws of a great white shark, with multiple rows of sharp, pointed teeth. Things that had a hooked claw on their webbed hands for opening hard-to-crack mollusks, or shredding larger fish that drifted into their confined space. Sometimes they would use those claws to kill their own kind: those that challenged others for dominancy, or those that served as a meal when food was scarce. They were things that evolved in a vicious Darwinian survival-of-the-fittest hierarchy over eons.

God only knows from which branch of the evolutionary tree they grew, only to be trapped under the sea and develop slowly, separated from most the rest of the natural world. But now, in the blink of an eye and a twitch of the Earth, all that changed.

Their never-ending search for food to quell their insatiable appetites now led these creatures to the surface of Crover Island through newly created portals. A surface that would be breathable to them through the gills that fed their lungs with oxygen. A surface that was open to them due to the darkness and the rain and fog that coated their bodies with moisture.

A surface, they would soon discover, that was full of new things to eat.

CHAPTER 2

ROBERT CAMPBELL

"Damn leg," Robert said, rubbing his right knee. "A bad day to be out on a boat." He scrunched his forehead in a spasm of pain brought about by the white-capped tumbling sea. Bryan Brown, his good friend and fishing partner for the day, merely grunted in response. Robert wondered, not for the first time, about the growing pain in his legs and whether or not it would ever get any better. He knew he was getting on in years, and, as what happens with men his age, had begun to think about his own mortality.

"A storm out there, just sitting, as if minding its own business," he continued. "Bad one, according to the Maritime and Coastguard Agency."

"They say it's headed for Norway," Bryan said.

"Hmmm." Robert kept his steel-gray eyes focused on the baleful, black horizon. He was never one to trust the "official" weather prediction. Instead, he relied on his old leg injury to let him know when bad weather was heading his way.

"Too dark for my liking."

Fierce, turbulent winds whipped them about, blowing Robert's hat into the churning sea.

"Blast!"

The rising swells swallowed his hat after it bobbed from crest to crest.

"Are we heading back anytime soon?" Bryan asked hopefully.

"I suppose we should. But not because my leg hurts. It's just a bad day to fish." Robert's voice quivered. *There's something strange about that storm*, he thought as he stared out to sea.

"And we're safe on this old tug, are we?" Bryan asked with a smirk.

"You're a funny one, you are," Robert said. It was a running joke between the two of them. Fishing vessels in Scotland were required to be properly registered with the Registry of Shipping and Seamen (RSS). They must also have a license. Robert's boat had neither. Not that this surprised anyone. His innate individualism and natural rebellion against authority were legendary, which was ironic since he was the de facto lord provost for Crover Island.

Robert powered up his engines, which barked with assurance and spewed a column of black smoke for good measure. He turned his nineteen-meter fishing trawler towards Blackpool Harbor on the eastern side of Crover Island with the winds at his back. He rounded the harbor and finally chugged his way into the marina in an hour and a half. The winds abated as they entered the bay, allowing for a much calmer approach, and they were able to dock without difficulty.

"You okay with tying off the boat and seeing to her needs while I get up to the pub?" he asked Bryan. "I've got a meeting with a few blokes. Something important, they said." He paused. "And they were very mysterious about it."

"Oh?" Bryan asked.

"Yes, which means if you're too far behind me, I'll fill you in later."

"Right, I'll be up after a few minutes."

Robert shook his head, then limped his way up the slight incline that was Main Street in Blackpool. Bryan, anxious to hear all about the big mystery, tagged along a short time after.

***

Robert pushed open the heavy door of the Royal Oak Pub, which was owned and operated by Bryan. The pub had been built by a wealthy shipping magnate to serve as his base of operations, social and business—or so he had thought. His company went bankrupt and he committed suicide, but the pub endured, much to the delight of the locals who continued to inhabit the island.

"This door gets heavier every time I push it open," Robert sighed.

He wiped his brow and let his eyes adjust to the dim interior.

"Maybe it's the Buloke, eh?" John Stewart said, who was already seated at Robert's favorite table.

"What?" Robert asked.

"The Australian Buloke, mate. Don't tell me you don't know the story." John frowned, as if everyone knew the old folktale.

"I'm not one for myths, John, so humor my old age and retell it for me," Robert said.

"Well, legend has it that the Buloke, an ironwood tree native to Australia and the hardest wood in the world, supposedly came off a ship bound for Edinburgh that blew off course and shipwrecked in the North Sea. It was picked up by a Crover fisherman and brought back to the island, where it was swiftly repurposed to accommodate the pub, which was being built at the time. According to local lore, when asked about it, all the fisherman would say was, 'Finders, keepers.'"

Robert laughed. He pulled out a chair and plopped down at the pub table, its scratched surface imparting messages from a different time.

Robert nodded at Billy Thomson and Michael Anderson, John Stewart's shipmates. Like most Islanders, he knew them well.

"Gentlemen, what can I do for you?"

"Hold your tongues, boys," Bryan said as he entered. "You can't have a meeting without a glass of scotch to start you off." No one objected, so Bryan poured.

"Where's Marie?" Bryan asked on the whereabouts of his daughter.

"She said she had to run an errand, so we said we'd cover for her until you got back from fishing," John said.

Bryan blew an exasperated breath and rolled his eyes. "That girl will be the death of me," he mumbled as he served the scotch.

"Down to business," Robert said.

All three leaned forward as if they were about to whisper something critically important, sacred even. John was their spokesperson.

"Robert, we appreciate your time and hope you'll give us your best advice on an angle we've been working on for some time now. It's a grand idea we've come up with to bring more revenue into town as a whole, and our pockets in particular." Michael and Billy nodded for emphasis.

"I'm all ears, lads." Robert never dissuaded anyone from trying to increase their lot in life. He folded his hands under his chin and continued. "Carry on," he beckoned.

The three shifted in their seats, knowing they had Robert's ear.

"As you know, we're not all that far from Inverness, the Loch Ness, and all that rubbish about the Loch Ness Monster."

Robert didn't answer, just let his thick eyebrows signal he was still with them. Of course he was aware of the beast called Nessie. Who in the world wasn't? Stories of Nessie ranked up there with Bigfoot sightings and UFO abductions. They were great for the tourism industry, but had no basis in reality as far as he was concerned. No sensible Scot would take those sightings seriously.

"The thing is, they've got a gold mine, down there, don't they? The business opportunities of all the towns along the Loch . . . towns like Drumnadrochit, Foyers, and Fort Augustus . . . they can't help but pull in money by the bucketful, all because of that legendary prehistoric beast. Someone fakes a grainy photograph of it in the 1930s and the world goes crazy, bringing legitimate science expeditions and tourists alike to spend their money on hotels, restaurants, and ridiculous trinkets."

A pregnant pause ensued and seemed inevitable. It hung in the air, begging for an acknowledgment of the obvious. Apparently, Robert missed the obvious.

"And?" Robert asked.

"And," John said, "we were thinking . . ." He glanced at Michael and Billy. "We were thinking we should be making money on that idea as well and have come up with a way to do so."

Not waiting for Robert to inquire about their venture, John unfolded a map of Scotland.

"Look here," he said.

John's finger found the dot that represented their island, settled in the Moray Firth inlet just north of Inverness, about midway between Cromarty to the west and Nairn to the east.

"Here we are," he said. This time the obvious was, indeed, obvious. He drew a line with his finger, straight from their island to Inverness. He was gathering steam now, like a strong headwind on the horizon that brought high tides and the threat of heavy rain. An omen?

"What you may not know," John said, "is that Loch Ness is connected to the Moray Firth by the River Ness and the Caledonian Canal."

Robert began to see the light that was illuminating this story, but maintained the frown of a skeptic.

"We could make a plausible argument," continued John, "that Nessie goes back and forth between Loch Ness and our island. We could even claim this is where her home base is, that she is often seen around one of the many sea caves we have on the western side of this island, and may even be living in one."

Now, the pregnant pause seemed full term. Robert had to admit, it wasn't a bad idea.

"Go on."

"We've had good fishing these last five years, and me and the lads have been saving our money. We've done so well we actually cut back on our fishing this year and spent more time on the mainland. We concluded earlier in the year that we were going to invest in a large boat to take tour groups around the island in search of the beast, with an embarkation and disembarkation point right here at the Blackpool Marina."

Bryan Brown had caught the fever heating up at their table. He was continuously wiping the same spot on the bar as he pretended not to eavesdrop. The more he heard, the faster he wiped, showing a keen interest in this promising outlook. He saw good things ahead for the Royal Oak.

"Aye, lads, it sounds like you've thought this through, and I must say, it's a grand idea indeed, and there's much more to be said about it." Robert stared into space, not at anyone in particular—perhaps at the future?

"We'd have to give some thought to the construction of a proper waiting area for tourists wishing to board, signage for it all, market-ing, and the like, but I don't see anything that could prevent us from making this dream a reality," Robert said.

"We already have, Robert. We worked out the details for all of it. Some of it can wait until we get this enterprise off the ground, but we have a sign maker on the mainland all set to send us what we want. It only needs your approval to make it happen."

Robert cast a pensive eye at John.

"You *have* given this a great deal of thought. And what about this tour boat of which you speak, as if I couldn't guess?"

John hesitated at first, not wanting Robert to think he was work-ing behind his back.

"No one could accuse a Scot of not being a good businessman, Robert. So, we invested in the right kind of boat earlier in the summer. It should be due any day now."

Robert grinned. He liked John and was impressed with his attention to detail. He then sat still as the night and closed his eyes. He needed to think, mumbling as he did so.

"We could find the money for some of those other things, as long as they benefit everyone. Perhaps I should present your idea at a special town meeting for approval. Some people may want to set up their own tour boats, or tend to some other private business related to your proposal."

The moment they were waiting for had come. Would Robert give his full approval? John and his mates wanted Robert's consent, but secretly, they had moved ahead with key investments and purchases already.

"I say, go ahead then. Make your plans, but make sure you keep it to yourselves for a while, and don't make a fuss about your boat purchase until I've spoken to all our residents. Then we'll see what other ideas people may have, who may need help getting set up and all."

The importance of brevity made its mark on these people through trial and tribulation long ago, so John, Michael, and Billy stood, shook hands with Robert and left. Now that they had Robert's approval, they knew he would not go back on his word. That was better to have than not, no matter how far along they were.

Robert let out a lungful of air he seemed to have been holding since the meeting began. He glanced up at Bryan and motioned for him to sit at the table. Bryan hurried over, scraping the hardwood floor as he pulled out a wooden chair and plopped.

"Better be thinking about a makeover," Robert said half in jest, acknowledging Bryan's long-eared interest in the conversation.

"I've already started thinking about it," responded Bryan. "And it sounds like the marina will benefit from this plan. But, I suppose, as a silent partner in the ownership of the marina, that never crossed *your* mind."

Robert chuckled. He knew instinctively the idea would be popular among the people of Crover Island. Despite the freedom and independence associated with the spartan life they chose to live, there was never a shortage of needs that lay just out of reach for most everyone. Fishing gave them a living, but often the vagaries of weather and sea conspired to keep them from ever getting too much of a break. Simply put, everyone could use a financial boost. Robert was sure the townsfolk would buy this proposal hook, line, and sinker.

As the sun dipped below the mountainous terrain to the west, Robert drove his battered 1972 Range Rover up to his home on the hill behind the pub. He smiled at the thought of the bottle of twelve-year Macallan and the crackling fire waiting for him. Little did he know that mother nature would soon conjure a monster far more real than Nessie would ever be.

CHAPTER 3

TIM AND MARIE

Tim Kempson wondered if he'd ever be able to eat again. That thought alone brought up the bile that sat in his gullet, waiting for a quick invitation to make an appearance in his lap or on the floor in front of him. Another wave leapt from the sea, grabbed the bow of the rusty tub he was on—that allegedly passed for a seaworthy vessel—and nearly flipped it on end, the sea-spray reducing visibility through the already grimy windows. He gripped a dirty, white plastic bait bucket under his chin with both hands, dry heaving with each meteoric rise and fall of the boat in the troughs of the dark and angry sea. He'd emptied the majority of his stomach's contents long ago, but was still unable to curtail the incessant retching that accompanied him on the rest of this ill-conceived voyage.

The ship Tim was on, *The Lady Grace*, had originally been bound for Blackpool on Crover Island from the port city of Aberdeen. Her captain was fishing in the North Sea when his ship was battered by a coming storm, forcing him to take refuge in Aberdeen.

Tim, a student of science at the University of Edinburgh, was spending several days around the Aberdeen port, speaking with various ship captains, asking all manner of questions about the type of fish they caught, how far out to sea they went for it, and what the weather conditions were like. Tim found himself relaxing in a local pub wondering where to go next, when he met the captain of *The Lady Grace.* Both men were standing at the bar when Tim struck up a casual discussion about the weather and fishing. Captain Edward Jones, like any seasoned fisherman, was only too happy to engage in a discussion about both subjects.

Jones also spoke favorably about his home, Crover Island, and its many interesting geological features, such as the numerous unexplored sea caves that existed underneath the island. By his third ale, Tim had enthusiastically agreed to accompany Captain Jones on his return voyage and investigate this island for himself. After very little sleep and a rushed breakfast in the dark hours of early morning, the travelers boarded *The Lady Grace* and left the calm harbor behind. Excited about the stories told over several pints the night before, Tim failed to inquire about the conditions enroute to their destination until they were too far along in their journey to return. A huge storm now rested on the horizon north of the island and it was threatening their journey with unstable seas to cross. Tim could not have been more miserable. He was sitting on a rock-hard, wooden bench bolted to the floor, hugging a foul-smelling bait bucket, the dead fish odor baked into its core. The captain whistled a jaunty tune as he wrestled with the wind, the sea, and the ever-present danger of the sinking of his ship.

Conditions did not improve until they rounded Fraserburgh and headed west towards the Moray Firth. Soon they upgraded from worst to just bad. The Firth was a carpet of chop, but it was a pleasure cruise compared to what they had endured to get there. They made it to Crover Island in one piece, and once the ship was secured in the Blackpool marina, Captain Jones half carried Tim to a public bench, hosed down his ship, then returned to his limp passenger. Hooking one of Tim's arms around his own neck, Jones grabbed his passenger's duffle, then dragged him to the Royal Oak Pub at the top of the hill.

"Here we go, mate," Jones said as he hauled Tim into the pub's front entrance. "I think you could use a pint."

It was the weekend, and the pub was bustling.

"Cheers, mate," Bryan said when they entered. "Who's your green friend?"

"Gave him passage from Aberdeen. We met at the Salty Dog Pub. He said he's some kind of scientist and wanted to come here, so here we are."

"He looks a little peaked," Bryan said.

"Aye," said Jones. "He's a nice enough fellow, but for a scientist who studies the ocean, he doesn't seem to take to it too well."

"Maybe a pint of brown will fix him up, eh?" Bryan said.

"What's wrong with you two? He doesn't need ale, Da," Marie said while drawing a draught for another customer. "The man needs coffee. I'll brew up a pot and we'll get it in him quick enough."

Bryan and Edward carried Tim over to a side booth, laid his head on the table and left him to drool on its surface. He was snoring loudly before Marie could bring him the coffee.

"He'll sleep it off and then he'll be fine," Bryan assured everyone and went back to his bar duties.

****

Tim awoke at dawn, dazed, confused, remembering very little. His pants were neatly folded, lying on a blue settee at the foot of the bed. His shirt was treated likewise, his shoes and socks shoved under a nearby chair. Dim light sifted through the thick, cumulus clouds outside, parted the lace curtains on the small window, and rested on his placid face.

Tim stirred. *Where am I?*

It was very quiet. Scattered thoughts came slowly to his addled mind, like ghostly wraiths tiptoeing in the night. His stomach hurt. His throat was sore. His head throbbed like a tommyknocker struggling to free itself. *The sea,* he remembered. *I drank too much,* he faintly reasoned. *The boat ride, vomiting, being dragged up a slight hill to a pub, and passing out on a table . . .* it all came to him in a rush. He tried sitting up. The room spun like a whirligig. He leaned forward, placed his head in his hands and took slow, deep, cautious breaths.

"You're up."

Ah, the girl. "Oops!" Tim scrambled when he saw her hovering in the doorway, grabbed a pillow over his lap, and gauged the distance to his trousers.

"Not to worry, mate. Who do you think tucked you in last night?" Marie asked with a smirk.

Tim, now a deep shade of scarlet, was at a loss for words.

Marie laughed, and Tim thought it the sweetest sound he'd ever heard. "Come to breakfast when you're ready," she said. "I suspect you're fairly empty, at least from what Edward tells us."

Tim nodded and Marie closed the door with another chuckle. He arose slowly, as if speed would be the end of him. He made his way into the bathroom, splashed cold water on his face, and brushed his teeth with supplies already laid out from his own kit. The fog that cradled his mind began to lift. He dressed and actually felt presentable.

Tim made his way down the tight, winding staircase. Customers were busy eating, and only Bryan and Marie looked at Tim as he entered the room.

"Morning, everyone." He sheepishly waved.

"Greetings, lad," Bryan said, then moved on to help deliver food.

Marie stepped closer, openly appraising him as he slowly made his way into the room.

"Not bad, after such a jumpy arrival," she said with a broad smile. He couldn't help but notice her, either. She was a petite five-foot-five perhaps, slim, with cascading auburn hair that radiated under the overhead lighting. She had wide, blue eyes, and full lips he couldn't resist staring at.

"Want some breakfast?"

His stomach growled at the suggestion.

"Yes, but black coffee, first, if you please." He took a seat in an empty, cushioned booth. Marie had caught a full view of him as well. He stood tall at six foot, strong build, and dark, wavy hair. She served him his coffee, then sat across from him.

"Remember much?" she asked.

"No. Especially how I got into bed. I think I would have remembered that."

"Well, I confess I had help from my father and Ed getting you up the stairs and into bed. But they had other things to do, so they left me to get you undressed and under the covers myself. Not an easy task, at your height. Seemed like I was wrestling with an octopus for a while."

"I am so sorry," Tim mumbled, not entirely displeased with the thought.

She laughed, a full-throated, hearty laugh. The kind that sticks with you throughout the day. The kind you wouldn't mind hearing more often.

"I wasn't at all worried," Marie said. "You were in no shape to untie your own shoes. I'll get you some breakfast. Nothing too greasy, then we'll see what kind of shape you're in to explore some of the island. Ed says you're interested. I've got the day off after breakfast, so I'll be your tour guide. Expect a hardy day of walking."

Tim finished his breakfast, surprising himself by eating more than his customary oatmeal and berries. Marie watched with amazement as he ordered, then consumed, a three-egg cheese omelet with a side of bangers, tomatoes, baked beans, toast, and nearly a full pot of coffee.

"Ready to go?" she asked, as he slurped his last drops of coffee.

"Enjoy the day," Bryan said before they headed out the door. "That big storm, Nora, is out there. They say it's heading for Norway, so we needn't be too concerned, I should think, but be wary all the same." Marie nodded and accompanied Tim outside. They left the pub through the basement doors, as it was the only rear exit to the spot where the van was parked.

***

There was an uncharacteristic nip in the air. Islanders generally enjoyed a warm breeze and good weather in the summer months, even this late in August. Today, however, as it had been for several days now, the sea was dark, the wind biting, and the skies angry, a portent of something worse to come.

"I'm usually not skittish about the weather. We've had our fair share of nasty wind and rain every year," Marie said. "But there's something about this storm out there." Her voice trailed as she said, "I don't know about this one."

Tim looked her over again. "You're properly fit for it, though, so no worries."

Marie was bundled in a Barbour Classic coat and neck scarf, and Tim had stored a wool fisherman's sweater in his pack, so both were prepared for the damp chill.

"I suppose you're right," she said and smiled.

They climbed into the pub's well-worn Ford Transit used to pick up guests at the marina. It was more of a wish than a reality, as there weren't that many visitors to their island this late in the year, and their four guest rooms were often empty. Marie got behind the wheel.

They left the pub in a cloud of dust and began to climb out of the village and into the hills along Central Road, the main thoroughfare along the spine of the island. On their end, Central Road ran down from the hill behind the pub, then hooked south around the adjacent building, and joined the top of Main Street. In the direction they were now going, it stretched all the way to the western edge of the island.

"Besides Central Road," Marie explained, "there is South Shore Road, which ties into Central Road, and North Shore Road, which ties into the bottom of Main Street, just down by the marina."

"Hard to get lost with only three roads, I guess," Tim said.

"You'd be surprised. There's a web of smaller dirt roads that interconnect at various spots. Tourists think they can hike and camp without a map, but they get lost all the time."

"They do? On such a small island?"

"Our island is about sixty miles long and twenty miles wide. We only have a little over two thousand people living here year-round. That leaves plenty of open space to explore in peace. Or get lost in."

"How do you explore a place you've known for your entire life?"

"You'll see." Marie glanced at Tim and smiled. He smiled back, and let it linger.

"Here," she said, when they reached the area known as the highlands. "There's a scenic overlook where we can view the coast." Marie pulled the Transit to the side of the road, and they got out. They walked over to the edge of a steep lookout and gazed at the horizon.

"Wow," Tim said. "That is breathtakingly beautiful."

To the north was the Moray Firth reaching into the vast North Sea. They could clearly see the huge spinning storm the news reports referred to as Nora out on the horizon, as if watching their island and trying to decide where to go. All other directions gave views of the diversity of mainland Scotland: to the west, the Northern Highlands, to the east lay the Grampian Mountains, while the Central Lowlands fell off way to the south.

"That's funny," Tim said, curiously. He looked all around, confused, staring at the sky.

"What is it?"

Tim dropped his gaze from the sky to the ground. "There are no bird sounds. Nor insect chatter, either. I wonder why."

Tim paused, a look of concern forming. He could hear the wind howl, as if laughing at his inability to fully grasp what was happening. He shivered and suddenly felt small and insignificant. He held his breath, afraid the wind would grab any words he uttered and toss them about like a bag of confetti.

"Did . . . did you feel that?" he asked Marie, his sense of unease overtaking him.

"No," Marie said, looking at him with concern. "Feel wha—"

Then it happened again, harder. The ground didn't shake so much as grumble, physically rumbling and shifting underfoot; a tease from the gods of the underworld, showing the humans above who was really in charge.

"We don't have earthquakes here," Marie said, as if trying to convince herself. "But I think that was one."

"No," Tim said. He stood stock still, legs spread apart, worried he might be thrust off into the distant sea by the broad sweep of an unseen hand. "I make it my business to know these things, and I agree. You don't have earthquakes here. There may be a couple of hundred quakes a year in Britain, but they're so small they largely go unnoticed. But you're right, that did feel like one."

They stood still and waited for it to happen again, but it didn't. In a few minutes, they were left with the sensation of a fading memory, a dream interrupted, a moment of certainty one minute that dissolved like morning dew the next, and wondered if it had happened at all.

"Maybe we were mistaken," he said, not quite believing it.

"Perhaps."

The two got back into the car, both trying to rationalize what they thought they felt and what might have been the cause. It was a common fallback argument employed by those unwilling to accept the reality of their experience. Then they embraced the final refuge of the willfully doubtful; they chose to simply ignore it and continue with their day.

From the rolling hills of the highlands, they were able to see incredible vistas between numerous spired hilltops. The spectacular views soon lulled them into the comfortable pace of any two sightseers out to enjoy the scenery, all thoughts of unexpected earthquakes nearly gone from their day's experience.

Halfway through the highlands Marie made a right turn. There were various dirt roads branching off to the left and right of Central Road, then other, more minor paths crawling out from them, like ever-growing spider veins. Marie knew the roads, large and small, quite well.

"Down that road to the left is a church. The pastor is the Reverend Henry Knox, who I'm sure you'll meet if you're here a while," she said. "He's a bit of a Bible thumper, always reading negative signs in nature that point to the apocalypse lately, but his heart is in the right place."

"He's got a growing number of scientists in his camp, I'm afraid."

"What do you mean?" Marie asked.

"Since we first crawled out of the trees, man has been in a never-ending battle with Mother Nature for dominance on this planet. And some scientists believe man is losing."

"There's a cheery thought," Marie said. "Let's hope we make it back to the pub before that happens."

Tim chuckled. "I think we have some time."

Marie continued down a long, winding, dirt road, then turned left near a sign identifying their destination. She pulled right into a pebbled parking lot and switched off the vehicle. Tim had no idea where they were, but Marie had driven with the surety of a seasoned resident.

"Welcome to Loch Crover, named after the man who first ventured onto and explored the island. He liked what he saw and convinced a group of people to inhabit the place, which is our history in a nutshell."

Tim enjoyed the placid scene. The loch was like a dark mirror, sharply reflecting the moody sky and surrounding scenery like a somber picture postcard. There were mountains ringing the far end of the loch, which blocked the winds coming up from the sea. There wasn't even a ripple on the smooth, glass-like surface.

"This is gorgeous," Tim said.

"It is, isn't it. There are other lochs that are larger and easier to reach, so this one tends to not get as many visitors, since it's a wee bit off the beaten track." Marie grabbed a basket off the back seat.

"I thought we'd have some lunch here. But after your breakfast this morning, you might not be hungry for at least a week."

"Try me."

They left the vehicle and walked to an old picnic bench near the sandy edge of the loch. They enjoyed the surroundings as each had a bottle of water and shared a roast beef sandwich.

"It looks so mysterious," Tim said.

"Yes, it does," Marie said. "And the lochs go quite deep, many of them. There hasn't been much of an interest to explore them by the locals, though, especially this one. People here are too busy scratching out a living. But, even so, some people believe the lochs connect with the sea caves along the western edge of the island, that perhaps below this island is a warren of connected caves and lochs."

"Hmmm. That's a fascinating premise," said Tim, "but I doubt it's true. These are freshwater lochs, are they not? How could they connect with the ocean? And the sea caves? They're miles away, aren't they?"

"True," Marie said. "But Loch Ness on the mainland eventually connects with the sea by a canal and, some say, by a very deep crevice in the bed of the loch. So, if it can happen there, it can happen here, I suppose."

Tim smiled at Marie. He hoped he wasn't being too obvious, but he was clearly pleased to be with her.

"What exactly are you studying at the university?" Marie asked after a pause.

"Marine science."

"Marine biology?"

"Not quite. Marine biology is a subdiscipline if you will. Other areas of study for me are marine ecology, marine chemistry, marine geology and the like. I study how these other areas of expertise affect the biological organisms of the area, mostly by looking at the climate, tides, currents, and geological features."

Marie yawned.

"I'm sorry," Tim said. "I'm boring you."

"Oh, no, I'm sorry." Marie reached out and grabbed his arm. It sent a mild shock wave over Tim's skin.

"I'm just relaxed for the first time in a while."

"Tell me about yourself," Tim said.

"There isn't much to tell. My parents moved here when I was three. I qualified for the University in Edinburgh when I was seventeen, went there for two years for a degree in math, then returned when my mother passed from cancer. That was three years ago. My father is getting older and needed me at the pub, so I stepped in to help him run the business."

An awkward silence sat between them.

Marie finally spoke. "Well, I guess we better clean up." As they both reached for the trash, their hands brushed against each other. Neither withdrew, instead they looked at each other, recognizing an attraction neither was quite ready to admit to the other just yet.

They gathered their supplies and placed them in the rear of the van. Distracted, neither noticed that the stilled surface of the calm loch was broken. Puzzling bubbles burst from an unknown source and depth, disturbing its naturally peaceful plane.

CHAPTER 4

THE REVEREND KNOX

"Repent now, before it's too late," the Reverend Henry Knox of the strict Evangelical branch of the Church of Scotland bellowed. He stood tall at the pulpit of his large, whitewashed clapboard church, and gazed down at his unenthusiastic congregation. It was Sunday, the day of the Lord, and by God, despite the low turnout—there appeared to be a total of twenty people, if he was being generous—he gave them what he thought was the justified wrath of God.

Henry loved the pulpit. It placed him above everyone else, a position he relished at least once a week. To deliver the word of God from a lofty height simply felt right, as if the Lord of Hosts Himself was looking down upon his subjects, bestowing His teaching to those in need of hearing it. He knew it was hubris to think this way, but he couldn't help it. He rationalized his behavior by convincing himself that gaping down on the poorly assembled crowd like this energized his delivery.

"The end of days is nigh!" he shouted, an all-too-familiar theme of late. The reverend had been on edge for a while, disturbed by any number of things that, to him, pointed towards the coming Armageddon.

His pronouncement was meant to be a revelation, a strong statement of unequivocal fact, and it was more important than ever for his sheep to understand that. To make it, he scrunched his considerable black unibrow, the folds of his forehead gathering like furrowed ruts on a dirt farm road, and raised his voice with a passion he felt deeply in his heart. He only succeeded, however, in waking up the last two rows of worshippers in his personal house of the Lord.

"The signs are clear," he crowed. "We can see it in the appalling behavior of humans everywhere. The poor continue to go hungry, the homeless remain without shelter, the sinners without punishment. We can read it on the wind as if it were a newspaper sent to us from God Himself, and how it sings to us of the sins of man. The devil himself, my friends, walks among us."

This he knew, and he could not fathom why no one else did. Why weren't they getting it? Didn't they see the signs he had been seeing?

His flock, however, were getting tired of his negativity. Those who did show on Sunday were present more out of guilt than glorification, more out of fear than faith. In any religious enterprise, there were those who fancy themselves the true believers, even though they long ago lost whatever semblance of pleasure joining church services could bring. They were the "in" group, those who would be saved first, simply because they faithfully attended. When the bad stuff hit the fan, as it eventually would, their God would come to their rescue. Of that, at least, they were convinced. If for no other reason, they dragged themselves to this exercise in verbal flagellation every week—a hedge, of sorts, on their religious bets.

"Revelation tells us that catastrophe is coming," the reverend said. "Evil will stalk us, the Earth will cough up its vilest creatures, and we will pay with unimaginable pain as we approach the End of Days!"

Reverend Knox showed so much conviction, even those who were still awake and had heard it time and again shuddered a little under his reproachful gaze. It wasn't always that way. The reverend used to preach about hope, peace, and love for his fellow man, and more of his faithful had attended those services when he did. But his doom and gloom stance as of late had resulted in increasingly dwindling numbers.

The church social room in the basement was too often quiet. There was no regular Sunday morning repast after service anymore, no gentle camaraderie over buns and coffee. No regular Bible classes, as there used to be. No one, it seemed, cared to share their deepest thoughts or even a word of warm friendship with Henry Knox, since he became so gloomy. They couldn't abide another Bible-inspired tongue lashing, especially if that meant singling them out in public, to the rebuke and relief of their fellow congregants. Instead, they marched out like a chain gang, heads low, eyes on the floor, feet shuffling as if burdened by the weight of the reverend's words. The only times they truly enjoyed amassing at church anymore was for the monthly potluck dinners, which brought out many more of the faithful than any regular service could. Those gatherings held much importance in their daily lives, as it allowed them to socialize under the banner of religion without the bonds of heavily laden scripture.

Henry watched them go with a mixture of anger and pity. *They'll thank me, one day,* he thought wistfully. *When the devil demands his due, I'll be there to support them, and then they'll see.*

Henry knew he was off his game, that he wasn't connecting with anyone at all. That's because he knew with complete certainty that things were not what they seemed in the world, and it was his job, at least as he saw it, to warn his dim followers that danger was afoot. He could see it when he ate his spartan meals alone and listened to the evening news, dwelling on the international state of affairs. He could also see it when he hiked the countryside alone, deep in thought, completely absorbed in the quiet time he so enjoyed; a time he used to speak to God directly. He knew he was mocked for doing so, that many talked behind his back and whispered stories about him.

"It's okay to talk to God," they'd say to each other, when they thought he couldn't hear them. "Just worry if he starts to talk back."

Silly fools. He knew God didn't speak to man in his own tongue. He conversed in other ways. He showed His pleasure with the abundance of natural beauty we could see with our own eyes, and smell with our own noses, and behold with our own presence of mind. Conversely, He disclosed His considerable anger through the many horrible natural disasters He sent our way, like hurricanes, earthquakes, tsunamis, and the like. It is these latter phenomena Reverend Henry Knox learned to read more precisely than he could read the divine messages in the Good Book. In those hard-to-read signs, God showed us His truest revelations. And if we all only paid attention to them, we'd know what God was thinking, what He was trying to tell us. And, most importantly, we'd be able to head off catastrophe by atoning for our too-often-overlooked sins.

Knox accepted this heavy burden with equanimity. *They really are weak and ignorant sheep,* he thought of his followers. And it was his duty, his mission as a servant of God, to enlighten them, to show them the way, to educate them about the impending doom before it was too late.

The signs, he could plainly see, were gathering. Most notably, the weather had been nothing short of freakish lately, all those dark clouds on the horizon, just sitting there waiting. No storm for days, just a growing army of black clouds, as if Lucifer's gathering forces were gearing for a death blow. And that shaking of the earth he'd experienced—what was that about? When had that ever happened before? It wasn't strong, nor did it last long. But it had happened. And he'd noticed it.

There was something else that raised his hackles. Reverend Knox knew with abject certainty that very soon, the son of perdition himself would make his presence known to them all. And he would do his best, as a servant of the Lord, to figure out how he could prepare for the coming battle.

Yes, he thought again, *my flock will thank me for those efforts someday. And that day is coming soon.*

CHAPTER 5

THE CAVES

Marie was about to open the driver-side door when Tim reached out, placed his hand across the door, and blocked her. He stammered, trying to find the right words.

"Marie, I feel we had a moment back there at the loch, but I don't want to presume anything. And I don't want to create any awkwardness between us." When Marie didn't respond, Tim dropped his arm and lowered his head at first, then looked her straight in the eyes. "Was I wrong?"

"No," Marie said. "I felt a slight tremor as well, and it didn't come from beneath the earth." Marie offered a gentle smile, leaned in, and softly kissed him. "But let's take it slow if that's all right with you. I like you, Tim, but at some point, you are going to go back to school, and I don't want to be left behind with the thought that you took advantage of the local girl before you fled the island."

"I'd like that, and I fully understand," Tim said. He put his right hand on her cheek and kissed her back. He opened the door for her and shut it after she got in. He climbed into the passenger side to continue their journey.

Marie pressed the pedal and drove. She made her way back to the main road, then traveled the island's backbone in leisure, admiring the various points of interest along the way.

"Where are we heading?" asked Tim, finally.

"We're on our way to the most intriguing part of the island, in my view."

"Your place?" asked Tim, not without a little hope.

Marie cast a wary eye at Tim. She decided this was part of Tim's charm, so she played along.

"As interesting as you would find my place, I don't just let anyone see it. In fact, I'm pretty sure you don't qualify."

This time it was Tim's turn to cast a wary eye, along with a forlorn look.

It wasn't that he was unattractive, thought Marie. In fact, quite the contrary. She found herself instantly drawn to his rugged good looks and easy-going manner. He reminded her of a young Harrison Ford, especially with his winsome smile. But she was cautious. He was not the first island interloper who found her desirable. Several had led her to believe they were very interested. That is, until their holiday was up, and it was time to leave. It eventually dawned on her that they were of a type. They were usually off on an exploratory jaunt, hiking the many trails on the island, and wooing the local beauty was an island-tour bonus. But in the end, she was placed in a box labeled "vacation memories," along with their hiking experiences. Despite how she was feeling about Tim, she wasn't about to let that happen again.

"We're on our way to the caves. There's some hiking involved to get to them, and if we have enough time, we may even do some spelunking."

"To the caves it is, then."

They pulled off the road for a quick view several more times on the way. Soon, they crested the highlands and began a gradual descent towards the western coast. When they came to a full stop at a stony, uneven car park, Tim hopped out of the van and stared at the horizon.

"The sky is awfully dark, and it looks like a thick fog is lying on the ocean like a rolled-up blanket. Especially on the line where the water clasps hands with the sky."

"Yes. Da says it's Hurricane Nora heading for Norway."

"I have to say, I don't like the look of it. It's just hanging out there, as if waiting for the order to unfurl towards the island."

"It does look odd. But I wouldn't worry much. We rarely, if ever, get fog out here this time of year. No serious storms, either. But just in case something is brewing, let's get going," Marie said, changing the subject. "The trailhead where we'll begin our climb down to the beach is just to your right."

Tim continued to stare at the distant cloud formation with a nagging concern born of a scientist's interest, while Marie opened the back of the van. She called to Tim, and they checked their hiking gear. They made sure they had binoculars, trail food, flashlights, cell phones, and a flare. They took off their coats, slipped into their backpacks, and began the long climb down to the shoreline.

It was mid-afternoon when they reached the small, sandy beach near the entrance to the caves.

"Ruggedly beautiful," said Tim, looking to his left and right, taking in the fractured coast that looked like a set of bad teeth.

"So, as you can see," Marie explained, "there is a long row of caves all along the coast out here. Some are above the water line, and most of those are accessible by foot. Others are either partially or fully underwater, and not accessible at all."

"How far in do they go?"

"No one knows for sure, really," Marie said. "Some have been explored to their end, maybe about a mile or two, but very few, and only those not hindered by the incoming sea. Some people believe that those caves go as far back as some of the lochs on the island, but no one has bothered to explore them thoroughly, as it is not easy, nor worth anyone's time. Most people come here to view the coast, take photos, and leave."

Tim stared off into the distance, nurturing an idea. He had some graduate field work coming up and thought this may be an interesting subject to follow. If those caves did connect with lochs, or perhaps other geographic anomalies on the island, they might harbor select marine life adapted to that specific environment. His excitement at the idea grew as Marie spoke.

"To explore them properly," Tim posited, "you wouldn't necessarily have to go through the cave entrance, though, would you? I mean, with the proper gear, someone could scuba through some selected lochs and look for fissures that may give them access to something deeper on the island, which might eventually lead them here."

"Who would do that, and why?"

"It could fulfill a requirement for my studies, as well as provide an opportunity to pursue other items of interest on this island." Tim turned toward her. "For purely scientific reasons, of course."

Marie leaned in and gave Tim a longer, deeper, and more passionate kiss this time. They separated, then she put a finger to his lips and said, "That's all for now." She grabbed her backpack and headed to the cave's entrance.

Once there, stones of all size crunched loudly underfoot, despite the competing, crashing surf on nearby caves. The tangy murk sprayed them with each surge of the ocean, coating them in fine, salty droplets. The rushing wind cooled their skin, fanning goosebumps in its path across their bare arms. They marched forward and were soon swallowed by the blackened maw of the cave's entrance. Inside was a mixture of hard sand and rocky outcrop, making progress slow and deliberate. They used their flashlights to guide the way, which caused dark, enigmatic shadows to lurk behind giant rocks and leap out at them as they passed. The muffled sounds of crashing surf could be heard in the distance. Otherwise, except for the hurried sounds of their strained breathing, it was dead quiet.

After a mile of picking their way through the bumpy bottom of the darkened cave, they heard a loud crack, like a reverberating gunshot. The ground shuddered once more, only worse this time, like a soldier trying to shake off bad memories. Tim and Marie lost their balance and bent over to brace themselves against random stalagmites. It lasted only a few seconds, but it was enough to rattle their confidence in continuing forward.

"Let's go back," Tim said. "This may not be safe."

With a brief nod, Marie followed. They moved faster this time, scrambling over jutting stone and tripping in unseen ruts, but still hurrying back with steady progress towards the cave's entrance. In silence, they made good time and soon heard the surf smashing against the entrance to nearby caverns. Tim thought it was louder than before. Perhaps that was a trick of the ear, the sound ebbing and flowing with the tide, from loud, to muffled, to loud again. His nagging subconscious told him it was more than that.

They saw daylight coming from the cave's opening, and the sound got louder still. There was the strident shush, like a lit sparkler at a fireworks festival, that came with the rapidly receding surf, followed by a thunderous boom as the ocean rushed into nearby cave entrances, hitting the inside walls and pushing back out with the force of a dozen demons.

"That's definitely louder," Tim softly said. He stood there at the entrance, sprayed by the salty mist of crashing waves, unmoving and lost in thought as only a scientist can be.

"I agree." Marie grabbed his upper left arm and gave him a gentle tug. "Tim," she said, "we should go."

As they turned away from the caves, casting one last glance at the natural phenomenon they were witnessing all around them, they heard an ear-piercing screech, like a frightened hawk, that froze them where they stood.

"Did you hear that?" Marie asked.

"I sure did," Tim replied.

Marie tugged harder, and this time Tim needed no further encouragement.

CHAPTER 6

THE MEETING

The night crackled with excitement. It was a Sunday, a day of rest, so many people came to the pub for the meeting that evening. It wasn't often that their titular provost sent out a personal request for the citizens of Crover to assemble at their monthly meeting. There wasn't much in the way of what passed for news, apart from what happened on the mainland, so neighbors shared whatever speculations they harbored as to why. And they had plenty, ranging from the need for an expenditure of local funds (which most opposed on principle), to the possible death of a fellow citizen. Not many subscribed to the latter, as they would have heard such news through the grapevine long before being informed by anyone of an official nature. Headlines like that traveled like a fast-moving brushfire on a hot, windy day.

The MacDonalds were the first to arrive. Jeffrey MacDonald was a Scotsman's Scot. He was an independent, proud man, a farmer and sheepherder who lived out on the Highlands section of their island. He and his wife Ella owned 1200 roods, or 300 acres, of prime real estate, and acted the part. Called Mac by his family and close friends, he gave a stern look and gruff hello to others, many of whom called him Mr. MacDonald. His was one of the original families to settle on this island three hundred years ago, and, by his demeanor, he let everyone know it.

Proud of his heritage, he was equally proud of his ability to handle any crisis, man-made or otherwise. He was known to have stared down Cyclone Xaver, otherwise known as the North Sea Flood or tidal surge of 2013. While it wreaked havoc across Northern Europe and caused damage on their own island, Mac resisted repeated entreaties by the provost that any of the island's inhabitants in need could seek shelter at the Royal Oak Pub. Instead, he chose to stay firmly put at his home, insisting his full-time daily workers also stay in his living room and under his protection. At one point, as the story goes, in order to gauge the storm's strength, Mac walked out to a nearby cliff at the hurricane's height. As told by his employees, he stood resolute, with arms folded, smoking his pipe, staring at the turbulent coast as the wind whipped his mackintosh and the driving rain stung his face like a swarm of angry bees. After he uttered a guttural noise, he spat at the storm and returned to his staff, only to proclaim to a scared and huddled group that it was nothing to worry about, to enjoy the scotch he provided from his private stock, and insisted they play cards until it was over. In the end, he sustained minor wind and rain damage, and sent his workers out to do the repairs. His status grew, depending on how many drinks one had, with each telling of that story.

The MacDonalds were soon followed by Angus McLeod, the Taylors, the Clarks, and the Youngs, who, despite their arrival time, did not travel together, and, in fact, did not even live near each other. They acted as various spokespersons for selected neighborhoods, allowing for them to report back to those who chose to stay home.

Inside the pub, Bryan Brown was drawing draughts of dark ale and topping off drams of scotch at a rapid pace. The collective pub chatter picked up as more families arrived, as well as a handful of single fishermen who were there to represent and report back to certain villages. The island temporarily boasted two American hikers. They came for the show, thinking it would be a great example of local color. They also harbored thoughts that someone would be interested in their presence and buy them a drink.

It did not take long for elbows to bend in quaffing, and the din of conversation to rise, along with the fragrant pipe smoke that hung from the ceiling like a low cloud bank. MacDonald sat with a pint in front of him, holding it like a shield, looking regal and unapproachable, while most others were animatedly engaged. The two hikers were looking desperate in their unsuccessful quest for a free drink when the door opened. Marie and Tim entered hand in hand.

"Here we go again," Bryan mumbled, referring to his daughter and her new conquest. *Should have seen this coming*, he thought.

"What's that?" Robert asked.

Bryan nodded at the pair.

Robert took note and smiled. "Aye," he said, as if that said it all. Robert looked around and decided that there was enough of a crowd, and he didn't want to hold anyone too long, as some had a wee drive home and might decide to leave early. He stood, picked up his mostly empty ale mug, and rapped it hard on the pockmarked table in front of him, droplets splashing like blood spatter. After three tries he was able to squelch the gossip to a level he could speak over.

"Mates!" he shouted. The crowd, now in good humor, gradually quieted.

Robert always knew to start off any speech with a bit of humor. If it worked, it never quite mattered what else followed. The joke itself would put people in a good enough mood, and that was what he hoped to accomplish. *At least*, he thought, *I'll have their attention.*

"Does anyone here know the difference between a Scotsman and Mick Jagger of the Rolling Stones?" Robert paused to ensure they were all listening.

"Jagger says, 'Hey you, get off of my cloud,' while a Scotsman says, 'Hey McLeod, get off of my ewe."

A moment of pin-drop silence was followed by utter raucous laughter. There was much pointing at and backslapping of Angus McLeod, who probably laughed the loudest. The American hikers looked at each other confused. After a few wipes of the eyes and calls for another round, Robert knew he had their attention and raised his hand to acknowledge he was about to get to the heart of the matter.

"I asked you here for two reasons," Robert said. "One concerns the weather." The smiling faces he commanded a moment ago morphed into a group who looked like they smelled bad cheese.

"Now, now," he said, hands raised in supplication. "I know that you know more about the weather just by looking out your windows than from any reports you'll get from your TV or radio. And I know that you know how to deal with it."

He visually surveyed the room and noticed that the crowd was leaning slightly forward, their ears tilted up like broken satellite dishes, anxious to hear what he had to say, despite their skepticism.

"Which makes what I'm about to say all the more important. You may have noticed there are some very dark clouds out on the horizon, in a place that, at this time of year, they shouldn't be."

A few murmurs could be heard wafting over the audience.

"And you've heard, I'm sure, that the experts are counting on that storm to go and pester the Norwegians. But I have to tell you, my bum leg has been shoogly like a fish on the dock lately, more so than most."

Everyone got quiet. Locals put great faith in Robert's ability to decipher the mystery of weather prediction, so, no matter what the so-called experts said, when Robert spoke, he commanded attention.

"With that kind of movement, I'm not so sure the storm is going to visit the Vikings. If I were you, I'd make plans for a whopper. I've also been in touch with the mainland authorities, who have given me specific information that I need to relay to you."

It was a risk mentioning "authorities," as anyone with that title, present company excepted, was colored in doubt, like eating yesterday's fish.

"And you know I wouldn't bring them up unless I had a very good reason." A few nods of agreement. "They're getting a bit nervous on the mainland." A comment that brought a few chuckles, as mainlanders were always seen as more frightened of the weather than islanders. "They're saying we may also need to worry about those accompanying clouds we've seen on the horizon, which continue to get closer to us here on Crover Island. There is a concern that the strange looking fog out there may disrupt communications, making it impossible to reach anyone on the mainland." That brought a few murmurs, but not a great deal of concern, as the locals did not generally turn to anyone but themselves for help anyway.

"And, they say, that this storm may not only rival, but surpass Cyclone Xaver of 2013, which I know you all remember well."

Jeffrey MacDonald slowly raised his chin, knowing that all eyes were on him.

"Which brings me to the conclusion on this point. If something is going to happen, and my leg tells me it will, it will happen rapidly. Make sure you are well supplied, and know that the pub is available to you as shelter should you need or desire it."

"Now, moving on. One more critical issue. We all know that there is no better businessman on this earth than a Scotsman." Half-hearted nods all around. They knew the truth when they heard it, but they also didn't trust flattery. To them, as the saying goes, "Flattery and insults raise the same question: What is it you want?"

Robert knew his audience, and since he was about to appeal to their self-interest, he knew they would listen.

"Some of our lads have come to me with a proposal that will not only benefit them, but all of us, so I wish to share it with you now."

Robert continued, skillfully, to lay out the plan to partake in Loch Ness Monster tourism first proposed by John Stewart and his mates.

He downplayed the emphasis on their personal gain and highlighted what it might do for the entire community.

"It means extra jobs, my friends, as well as a financial boon to our common, public coffers. Work for those who need or want it. Work that will pay well and provide for those who could use a financial break. We all know there are things we would like to have but can ill afford."

Everyone there knew Robert did not need the money. There were many present, however, who did.

"So, my friends, I'm asking your permission to develop a plan of action to make this idea happen, while being careful in protecting everyone's interests. Careful financial records will be kept, as usual, and open to all for inspection. I would also suggest you begin thinking of how you may, as an individual, profit from this collective enterprise, and as long as your idea does not infringe on your neighbor's, we can all benefit. Hopefully, once the threat of a storm is abated, we can meet again in a week or so to go over developments."

Robert took a moment to survey his captive audience. It was time to wrap up.

"And now, I need a vote of approval. All those in favor say 'Aye.'" The room erupted in a loud, singular, positive response.

"Those opposed, shout 'Nay.'"

There were no negative responses, which Robert knew signified it was time for closure. "Thank you, my friends," said Robert. "And for your trouble in traveling here tonight, I will buy the next round, and I bid you a—"

"Wait a moment, Mr. Campbell," shouted Marie.

Absolutely no one was pleased about having their free drink interrupted, especially the hikers. All eyes turned to Marie, and immediately she became self-conscious.

"I . . . I'm not sure where to begin," she said. "Something strange happened today."

"I'll say," Bryan said. "Why don't you start by releasing your tether."

Marie realized she was still clutching onto Tim. She released his hand to a smattering of chuckles.

"I'm not sure I can accurately describe it, but maybe Tim, here, can explain."

"On a first name basis already," Bryan mumbled, as attention shifted to Tim.

"My name is Tim Kempson, and I'm a graduate student at the University of Edinburgh, studying to become a marine scientist."

"Cheers to you laddy," someone shouted, holding up their pint of ale. Everyone laughed and resumed their individual chatter.

"Wait," Tim said. "That's not the point, that . . . ." Angus McCleod, now getting impatient, started to pick up and leave, as did some others. Tim blocked the door. "I said wait! You all need to hear this." His gesture was perceived as rude by some and dangerously close to a threat to others, now filling the air with unwanted and unwelcomed tension.

"I'm sorry," Tim said. "But please listen. Marie and I discovered two natural anomalies today."

"I'll wager you did, lad," someone shouted from the back of the room to great laughter, but Tim continued by raising his voice.

"Twice, while we were out to the western side of the island, we experienced an earthquake, or at least that's what it felt like," he said. "It happened when we were exploring one of the caves. You all should know, that doesn't happen here. Soon afterwards, we noticed a change in the water flow into and out of the cave next to us. It was an increase in intensity and it happened so quickly, it was queer at the very least. We then heard a loud, shrill, eerie scream coming from the cave."

MacDonald chose to speak, hoping to put an end to this nonsense. He loudly cleared his throat and the room quieted. "You witnessed something that around here we call high and low tide, Mr. Scientist, and you heard the ocean cause a noise as it drenched the cave's interior, then rushed back out to sea. Now, my friends, I say goodnight, and haste ye back! And laddy, you best not be in my way when I get to that door."

Tim went to speak again, but Marie pulled him aside. They moved to let the MacDonalds pass, and others took their cue and left as well. They had enough excitement for one evening, and many decided it was time to start their long ride home.

"Well, thanks you two," said Bryan to Marie and Tim as the pub emptied quickly. "You managed to drive my customers away with your senseless blather. I hope you're pleased."

Robert chuckled, and noticed that John Stewart, Michael Anderson, and Billy Thomson, along with a few other residents, remained perched at the bar, waiting for that free round of drinks he'd promised.

"Robert," said John, "a word, if you please."

CHAPTER 7

NESSIE BUSINESS

Having previously laid out their case to Robert, John Stewart, Michael Anderson, and Billy Thomson had anxiously looked forward to the day *after* the meeting in town. They had entirely stopped fishing the week before and took rooms in the town of Inverness on the mainland to confirm and finalize their plans. They wasted no time gathering the signs and banners they had ordered months ago.

They took ownership of their new boat, which had been housed at a local marina since May. It would carry tourists to the coastal caves on the west side of Crover Island and return them back to Blackpool. They had christened their boat—in a bold attempt at changing the Nessie narrative—*The Nessie, Crover's Creature*. It was an extra-wide boat with an even keel, state-of-the-art stabilizers, plenty of indoor and outdoor seating, and all of the required safety items as per the country's regulations. The boat was designed to handle all types of weather conditions, which they knew they would need in the waters around their island.

They spent an entire day at the Registry of Shipping and Seamen, ensuring their vessel was registered for legal use and that they had all of the necessary paperwork in hand. They were taking no chances and had spared no expense to ensure their success. They picked up their order of snack-like food items with a long shelf life and bottled water, which were the only things they would allow on board. This way they could control what was eaten, not have to provide a cook, and encourage people to dine at the pub or other eateries in Blackpool. They planned to eventually sell ad space on the inside of the boat to those eateries and thereby establish a stream of inflowing cash as well.

They had, in fact, planned everything down to the last detail long in advance of the town meeting. If the locals approved their idea, they knew Robert was going to drop some heavy advertising the day after this all-island meeting, but even on that score, they had gone ahead with some plans of their own when they first mentioned the idea to Robert. They worked with the same agency Robert had secured and paid handsomely for some video and print advertising to be sent to the best tour operator in Inverness who specialized in Nessie detection trips, weeks before the meeting in Blackpool. Their brochures outlined their own claims of Nessie sightings, bragging how Nessie makes her home along the coast of their island, and how interested parties needed to book now for their maiden voyage set to take place, not so coincidently, the day after the big town meeting. While in Inverness, they checked in with the tour agent. He confirmed his booking of at least thirty enthusiastic Nessie fans, who would be ferried to Crover Island for an eleven o'clock tour, at the tour operator's expense, for this once-in-a-lifetime event.

Special maiden voyage caps with the message, "Don't Messie With Nessie," as well as other souvenirs, ordered long ago, would be free to all participants on this first trip only. The phrase, which Billy Thomson came up with, encircled a caricature of the elusive beast sitting atop the number one, which signified their maiden voyage.

Future hats would keep the design, the number one signifying their tour was the first and the best. John and Michael weren't keen on it, but Billy was the slowest mentally of the three, and they wanted him to feel like he was a necessary part of things, so they gave him his due.

They knew it was a crapshoot to have spent a lot of money this past summer to make their dream a reality. John, however, believed in the axiom that in order to make money, you have to spend money, and they all thought they had spent it wisely to encourage business. In fact, as the all-island meeting date got closer, John received a call from their tour agent asking if they could handle forty passengers instead of thirty, as he had been swamped with last-minute requests.

Securing customers, especially overflow clients from other operators based in Loch Ness, proved easier to accomplish than expected. There was a never-ending supply of researchers, tourists who hadn't made firm plans, and just plain gawkers who were intensely interested in getting a sighting of the evasive legend.

"Yes, but hold it at forty," John said, "and start selling combination ferry and tour tickets for once-a-week voyages on Saturdays at one. In time, we'll assess how well we do and make our adjustments accordingly," he added.

They had taken a great risk in making these arrangements. If Robert failed to convince people of the need for this, there would be great local opposition to them making it happen at all, especially for doing so much planning without any kind of approval. They banked on Robert's promise to sell it, however, and were all-in on making this enterprise successful. If the meeting went well, they reasoned, they'd be starting their new business with a maiden voyage on Monday, followed by regular tours every Saturday thereafter.

They were relieved. The meeting had gone very well indeed.

Now that the meeting was over, the three tour entrepreneurs slid off their bar stools and sauntered over to Robert, Marie, and Tim. Everyone, that is, except Bryan, who took the time to gather the glasses left all over the bar, then took a seat at the table.

"Yes, John," Robert said, "what can I do for you?"

"The lads and I wanted to catch you up on our progress."

"Aye?"

"We didn't want you surprised by it, but we've done a fair amount of legwork this past summer in preparation. Earlier in the summer we had purchased a boat that will suit our needs for our tour business. We got it registered, bought supplies, put out the word with some brochures, and hired a tour agent to start booking long before this meeting."

"My, you have been busy," Robert mumbled. He leaned to the left and cast a wary eye at the trio. "And what might be your target date for taking on tourists?" he asked. The way he asked, it was if he already knew the answer.

John responded without hesitation. "Tomorrow," he said.

The silence was deafening.

"And what, may I ask, is the rush?" Robert asked. "Did we not settle on a plan of action here that involved more than just the three of you?" Michael and Billy were looking anywhere but at Robert. John, however, had thought this through and had no problem laying out his case.

"Aye, we did. And I wouldn't argue with you if you're a touch angry with us. I think you've done a magnificent job in convincing people tonight of the obvious benefits of our idea. And I also don't think any one of them is going to wait until you come up with a plan on how to spend town money before deciding how this will be profitable to them. Many are probably talking about making their own plans on their way home tonight, and, if they can, will be putting them into place before you meet next. Since it was our idea in the first place, I thought it best if we put our touring plans out there before someone else did so."

Moments dragged. Time stood still, as if everyone was immobile, and nothing could be heard but the beating of hearts. Robert knew what John said was true. No one else was going to wait, so he couldn't really blame John and his crew for their actions.

Finally, he spoke. "All right then," Robert said. "There's nothing to be done about it, so, onward we go. What are your plans for tomorrow?"

John filled him in on their special, one-day-only maiden voyage and the number of tourists that would arrive.

"As I said, be wary of the weather tonight, John. Things are getting dicey and the water is churning up. After sitting out there and teasing us for days, I think that storm is going to turn towards us and come in fast, despite what the so-called experts say. There's also that strong fog about, and I have to tell you, I've never seen anything like it."

"We may have some sick tourists at the end," John said, half in jest. "But we're good fishermen and have handled rough water before. It's important we get this first trip in, even if we have to postpone others on account of the storm. People will remember our name and use us in the future. Besides, it's just too late to cancel."

Robert didn't like it. Something was definitely wrong, and he could feel it in his bones. But John was determined to move ahead, and he could make his own decisions.

"Then I wish you well tomorrow, John. But again, it won't be an easy trip."

"I never have, and I suppose I never will understand the attraction of that Loch Ness legend," Marie said as John and his mates left the pub to make last minute preparations.

"It's a strong one, that's for sure," Tim said. "A quarter of all Scots believe it to be true, that such a creature does exist—anything from a Plesiosaur, like in a Jurassic Park movie, to a giant eel. They've even run scientific tests to see if there's DNA in the loch that could help."

"Did they ever find anything?" asked Marie.

"Yes, a lot of eel DNA. But that just means there are a lot of eels in the loch, not necessarily a giant one, so, the jury is, scientifically speaking, still out."

As if in response, the wind crept through the imperceptible cracks in the walls and around the windows, howling at the group and rattling the shelved glass. Conversation stopped as heads turned to the eerie keening that whistled through the building.

"It's like a warning from the banshees," Marie said.

CHAPTER 8

THE HIKERS

Doug Johnson and Dave Barry, college roommates at Boston University, were spending the summer between their sophomore and junior years backpacking through Europe. They breezed through parts of the continent, staying in various youth hostels and enjoying the sense of freedom that accompanies two young men traveling without a firm plan.

They'd heard about Crover Island while in Paris at a hostel in the 4th Arrondisement, not too far from Notre Dame. Four young hikers from Germany regaled them over dinner one night about the gorgeous scenery they witnessed on an island in a bay off the coast of northern Scotland. They couldn't stop talking about the fun they had getting there on their Britrail passes.

Doug and Dave were hooked.

When they arrived on Crover, they heard about a local meeting at the Royal Oak Pub in Blackpool and went directly there, curious to get the inside scoop on the island. After the meeting, they joined the ranks of the locals who were vacating the pub. Once outside, Doug took a risk and shouted, "Can anyone give us a lift anywhere close to Loch Crover?"

The outdoor chatter dropped to a whisper. Angus McLeod looked them up and down, opened the back door to his Kia Sportage, and tersely said, "Get in." Doug and Dave waited a second to make sure they'd heard him correctly, then jumped into the back seat.

"I'm driving about five miles past the road that takes you down to the loch," McLeod said. "I'll drop you there."

"Sure," Dave said. "We're backpacking, so we'll find a nice spot to bed down for the night, then have a short hike in the morning to get to the loch. We've heard it's beautiful and we shouldn't miss it while we're here."

"Aye." That was all the conversation they were going to get out of Mr. McLeod.

***

"That guy was an odd duck," Doug said after they had arrived at their destination, gave thanks for the lift, and waved goodbye. Dave grunted and looked about for a good spot to camp. He spotted a tuft of brush off to the side of what passed for a road on the island, walked over, and said, "This is it. We'll bed down here."

They had heard of the storm and that it was going to head to Norway, so they felt comfortable sleeping outdoors. They unrolled their bivy-sacks and bedded down with a light blanket cover. The clarity of the dark night sky allowed them to admire the stars before nodding off to a sound sleep.

Doug and Dave were sleeping soundly when a thick fog silently crept up the sides of the island, cresting the highlands and hugging the damp earth. When light rain began to drop, coating their faces with a cool mist, they awoke, winced, and climbed into their watertight bivy-sacks. The wind, gusty at first, developed more steadily over time, driving the rain under their meager shelter. They crawled out of their sacks, bunched them into a ball, and looked for a site with more cover. They hustled over to a location behind and under a crop of trees that would, at least, act as a windbreak. They'd barely drifted off to uneasy sleep when the beasts came.

Somewhere in his restless slumber, Doug could hear their approach, and it became part of a disturbing dream that made him toss, turn, and mumble in his sleep. Something was coming for him. Something dangerous. It sounded wet; it was a viscous entity, moving slowly, with a slapping sound accompanying its approach. It gurgled to communicate, like a man in the last throes of drowning; a loud, muffled sound, like two people shouting at each other under water.

Doug stirred. He could feel a subconscious fight or flight reflex taking hold, but he didn't wake. He slept on. *Wake up, Doug,* his mind whispered. *This isn't right, Doug! You're in deep trouble, Doug! Wake up!*

Doug struggled in the gauzy twilight between sleep and consciousness. He could sense the peril, but he was too groggy to grasp the reality of it. He sat up and tensed, wrapped in fear and a wet sleep sack. The ground was coated in a thick fog, and the wind and rain made seeing difficult. He rubbed his eyes and looked about. He saw the outline of dark figures standing all around them. *What the—?*

He slipped on his glasses. At first, he thought they were people from town. *Come to check on us, maybe?* That was the instant conclusion drawn by his over-fatigued rational mind. The monsters in our dreams aren't real, we tell ourselves. They fade away to nothing as we awake. Don't they? Mostly that's true. But sometimes the mind plays tricks on you, then dares you to try and figure them out.

The dark figures took shape and became clearer. Doug's mind registered every frightening detail in under a minute.

There were at least a dozen of them, and they were tall, maybe seven feet, and lithe like a swimmer. Their thin, sinewy arms were bent at the elbow, hands (if you could call them that) like two wide fans, webbed and open, with long sharp talons for digits. And, oh God, the teeth. They were bent downward, sharpened to a point, protruding from a face that housed two large dark orbs for eyes, embedded in a sloped head with open holes where ears should have been.

His logical brain recorded all of that and played it back to an unbelieving consciousness in horrific detail. In another instant, he realized the things were real and not part of a dream at all. He screamed for Dave, but was barely able to utter his name when they pounced, whipping and slashing with their knife-like hands and gnawing on body parts with their razor-sharp teeth as they tore the two hikers apart.

Dave never knew what hit him—a flash of intense pain and confusion, followed by a dark and empty nothingness. Doug was all too frightfully aware of what was happening to them, desperately clinging to a slim thread of sanity, when one of the creatures dove its head into his belly, ripping out his intestines.

Shock finally overtook Doug. His blood pressure plummeted. He became confused and disoriented, and then gratefully succumbed to the warm embrace of blessed death.

CHAPTER 9

THE MAIDEN VOYAGE

The weather had shifted overnight. To the northwest, massive clouds roiled with muddy surf; whites, browns, and grays tumbled over one another like dirty laundry in a rumbling washer.

By the time John and his crew arrived at the marina, the rain had begun in earnest. The storm was now a clear threat to Crover Island, not Norway as the weather experts had incorrectly predicted. A blanket of dense fog had crawled over the island during the night, like a layer of thick cotton, rapidly spreading everywhere in abundant, undulous waves. By the time John and his crew were prepped for their maiden voyage, the foul weather was no longer just a possibility. It had announced itself with intermittent rain, seas boiling in anger, and winds that punished anyone who dared to venture outdoors.

Good fishermen always watch the weather, but they don't always follow its cautionary message. Reports of bad weather all too often serve as a personal challenge rather than an excuse not to fish. To an experienced fisherman, waves were meant to be crested, winds confronted, and thunder viewed as background music to accomplishing critical, often life-sustaining tasks.

John Stewart, Michael Anderson, and Billy Thomson were sensible Scots. They knew they were not venturing out to sea to haul for a much-needed catch. They had often risked much to do so, including their own health and safety. It was a hard life they lived, but despite its challenges, they passionately embraced its demanding lifestyle. And while it made no sense to needlessly risk life and limb on such a thing as a tour in search of a legend, the fact that it was their maiden voyage and the launch of their new business enterprise bestowed upon it a level of importance on par with the sacred rite of fishing.

John was notified by phone that some of the tourists who signed up for the trip bailed out due to weather, leaving them with a difficult decision. John looked at Michael, his first mate, with a blank face.

"We're down many of our passengers," John shouted over the wailing wind. "Although we still have about fifteen people coming over on the ferry, including kids. What are your thoughts on what we should do?"

"I say we go," Michael said without hesitation. "This may be our only chance to establish ourselves as the first and the best. If we wait, we may have competitors right out of the starting block."

A loud silence ensued while John struggled with making a final decision. As captain, it was his ultimate responsibility, his decision to make.

John's second mate, Billy, also weighed in. "It's nearly ten thirty. Whatever we're doing, we've got to do it soon."

John's usual stoicism while making a hard choice wrestled with the inner turmoil he now confronted. "Right, then," he said. "It's a go. Let's finish up before they get here. Michael, you get the boat started and warm her up. Billy, you finish organizing those snacks, then give me a hand putting up this welcome banner. The ferry with our customers should be here within twenty minutes."

Billy went up to John and leaned in so John could hear him.

"This wind is strong, John. And the caps are high." They both looked at how choppy the water had become, even in the protected marina.

"Good thing we packed all those extra vomit bags, eh?" John said, in an attempt to lighten the moment. Billy didn't laugh. "No worries, Billy," John reassured him. "I'll be going around the island on the south side to avoid the chop and foul weather. They'll think they're on a pleasure cruise until we get to the caves on the western end."

"And what about when we get there?"

John was pensive for a moment. "I'm a good sailor, Billy. Put your worries aside, now, and help me with this banner."

They hoisted and secured a large, ten-by-twenty-foot banner over the entry to their dock, which read, "WELCOME NESSIE LOVERS," then got to their boat just as the Inverness Ferry rounded the eastern part of the island and headed for the protected cove of Blackpool.

"Here they come," Billy said.

The Inverness Ferry bounced around the Moray Firth like a tennis ball on a trampoline. The IF, as it was called, enjoyed an enviable reputation, as it had never, not once, had an accident while in service. Its captain, an old salt that had seen plenty of challenging seas over the years, was determined to keep it that way as he guided the vessel around the protected cove and directly into the marina. Despite the rougher than usual waters in the cove, it was a dream compared to what they had just come through to get there.

Billy positioned himself at the end of the Inverness Ferry dock with his new Nessie hat on backwards, while Michael stood at the entrance to their own dock.

Both sailors guided the pale-looking passengers as they stumbled their way from one boat to the next. They appeared to be a mixed bag of Nessie voyeurs: some college coeds, a few old-timers looking for a sense of adventure to recapture their distant youth, a backpacking kid who wanted to check off *the Nessie* visit on his ever-loose itinerary, a few parents trying to keep up with their running kids, and a smug-looking, nose-in-the-air character who was either a scientist, professor, or what the locals called a true believer. Billy found it fun to guess who they might be and why they came on this trip. He smiled at everyone and greeted them with the cheery, customary, "Welcome aboard!" despite their dismal pallor.

An elderly couple approached Billy, and the woman stopped to look at the town.

"Oh look, Allan," the woman said to her husband. "How quaint. Let's do some shopping." She then moved in the direction of Main Street.

Her husband grabbed her by the elbow and steered her towards the *The Nessie.* "Not now, Margaret, we have to go on another boat. This way, dear." He then looked apologetically at Billy and said, "She gets confused sometimes."

Once the crowd left the ferry, John went on board to see the captain, someone he knew well.

"What's it look like, Thomas?" John asked.

"Not good, John. I have to say, if it were me, I'd not be taking these people out for a tour in this. When I get back, I'm done for the day. We already cancelled the afternoon ferry. What's your plan, anyway?"

"I'm heading around behind the island on the southern side."

Thomas squinted his left eye and bit his lip, deep in thought. "You may be okay, there. But hug the coast as much as possible. These winds are not normal, blowing about every which way, causing the sea to behave in very odd ways. And when you get out to the western side by the caves . . . well, I just don't know."

"I'll give them a ride for their money, that's for sure," John said with a confidence he wasn't truly feeling. The two shook hands, and John departed for his own boat as a light rain gently, but steadily, fell.

John walked through the crowd, smiling and giving them assurances that all would be well as he made his way to the bridge console. Some of the people on board looked downright ill. His first thought was he hoped no one would soil his new boat. His second, as he looked out the rain-splattered window, was that more than one person would do so. He picked up the intercom, shook off his nerves like an actor about to go on stage, and spoke.

"Good morning, ladies and gentlemen. Welcome aboard *The Nessie, Crover's Creature*. To simplify, you can just call her *The Nessie*, especially since that is what we are in search of today. You are brave souls indeed, and we are on this journey of a lifetime together." John read his well-crafted speech from a sheet of paper spread out on the dashboard in front of him. Out of all the preparations he and his mates had engaged in prior to today's event, this speech had caused him the most concern. It had to be perfect and set the right tone, or it was all over.

"I envy you," he continued. "You have placed your faith in a legend that we here on Crover Island have come to know as fact. Nessie exists. And, my friends, she exists right here on our western coast, which is our destination today."

Excited murmurs could now be heard drifting through the small crowd.

"Are we going to see monsters?" asked an excited ten-year-old.

"I don't doubt it," said a doubting parent.

"Her legend goes back centuries," John said. "Many who have seen her in Loch Ness have wondered, after the sighting, where has she gone? Well, today we answer that question. We know for a fact Loch Ness is an open waterway to the Moray Firth. You may fact-check that in any geological or geographical reference. And we also know for a fact that Crover Island is on a direct line from Loch Ness to the North Sea."

John never viewed himself as a public speaker. He always liked to keep things short. But today, he was infused with the spirit of this new venture and was warming up to this new role he had carved for himself.

"And today, my friends, we will explore the mysterious sea caves along the western coast of our island together, and search for what we believe to be the home base of our beloved Nessie. My friends," he announced as he reached his crescendo, "are you with me?"

If they pooled their memories, John Stewart and his mates, First Mate Michael, and Second Mate Billy, could probably only recollect one or two times in their lives when they felt truly exhilarated, and it likely occurred in relation to fishing. However, when they were met with a loud, enthusiastic, and gleeful cheer from the intrepid souls on board, they felt a sense of euphoria like never before.

John pulled out of the marina, headed for the edge of the protective cove of Blackpool, and turned right to scoot around the south side of the island. At first, it was anything but smooth sailing. The rain was light, but it was steady and proved to be a nuisance. The boat's wipers worked frantically to move the constant wet from the bridge window and create a good visual for the captain. The wind played tug-of-war, pushing the boat west when it needed to go east. It also swished the firth, moving it about with competing whirlpools and creating a heavy chop that was hard work to overcome. The adrenaline John felt pumping through his system, caused by the positive vibe of his enthusiastic passengers, kept him in good spirits as he battled the elements.

It took longer to round the eastern end of the island than it should have, and it put them behind schedule right away. John thought he could make up time along the southern coast, thinking the island itself would serve as a block for the foul weather.

It didn't.

Even though the rain lessened, and the chop diminished, they were met with the strange, heavy fog that encircled the island, one that impeded their vision and therefore their progress. John's choices were to push away from the coast and go slowly through the thickest part of the fog, the end of which they could not see, or hug the coast and be especially wary of known and unknown rock formations that appeared and disappeared along with the tide, causing him to go even slower.

Michael approached him while Billy manned the snack station.

"I know I said we should go, John, but I'm not liking this fog," Michael said, gazing out the large window where he could only see twenty feet in front of him.

"Aye, it's causing me some concern also, Michael. How are the troops?"

"They're doing surprisingly well after that dull speech of yours."

John grinned, as he was used to Michael's dry sense of humor.

"They think the fog adds to the mysterious atmosphere of the trip, as if you made it happen this way on purpose. Some of them, and they're not all children, think Nessie is going to jump out of the water right next to the boat."

"I won't tell them differently if you won't. I'm going to go through the thick of it. I don't like relying so much on radar and sonar, but we need to make time, so stay positive, my friend. The early signs aren't favorable, but my goal is to beat the worst effects of this storm as it currently stands and get back to dock before it truly hits us in force."

Michael merely nodded and went back to give Billy a hand.

Time dragged, and it gave John a false sense of security, as he was now getting used to the slow, methodical way they moved along the southern coast. It didn't last long. Although the wind helped to dissipate the fog, providing more in the way of visibility, it also served to increase the chop. They rolled with the rough seas as they rounded the western edge of the island towards the caves. The wind suddenly wrested control of the boat, and things went bad in a hurry. John had immediate and critical issues with steering, cresting the wind-swept waves, and maintaining their balance while being tossed like a caesar salad. Normally common tasks became difficult at best. He blessed the day they spent the money to purchase a boat with state-of-the-art stabilizers installed, but even with the aid of such technology, they bounced on the water mercilessly.

Unheard of wind gusts battered the western coast, grabbing *The Nessie* and tossing it like a toy in a tub full of toddlers. John nearly lost control of the boat at one point as it spun a full forty-five degrees from a combination of the wind and current. An audible, universal gasp escaped from the tourists aboard, not to mention Michael and Billy.

John wrestled with the wheel trying to gain control and right his boat, while passengers quickly tightened their life jackets. Waves swirled and moved the boat forward, despite John's panicky attempts to turn her around and head back the way he came. He'd been in rough seas many times, but never experienced the elements like this: totally wild, unpredictable, and uncontrollable. *The Nessie* suddenly swerved from the rear to the right, then swiftly to the left, all while continuously moving forward. It was as if a mutinous maestro was guiding the boat towards a demonic crescendo. The fog was thick on this side of the island as well, and the crazy wind shear was tearing it apart, throwing it helter-skelter until it resembled manic ghosts dancing on the tips of turbulent sea caps.

Fifteen pale, frightened faces reflected off the ship's side windows. The stunned, desperate passengers gripped the armrests on their seats with white-knuckled fists until their hands ached from the task. They were too afraid to speak, too shocked to do anything but stare, mouths agape in a silent plea for mercy. The boat behaved as if guided by an unknown hand, propelling it towards the crusty coast, which was punctuated with spires of rock and intermittent sea caves.

What the hell did I do? John thought. *How could I have brought people out in such weather?* He was a good sailor and he'd been in rough waters many times, but it was his own life he risked when he'd done so. Was this maiden voyage that important? Did he really have the right to risk the lives of so many trusting people for this business enterprise of his? In the flash of a moment, he saw something hopeful and made a desperate grasp at its promise. There was one cave ahead with more of a beach than some of the others. It was being swamped by the sea, sure, but if he could drive the boat ashore, he might at least be able to save their lives.

John turned his rudder to the left, hard, steered the bow into the wind as best as he could, caught the crest of a wave, which lifted them up high, and gunned the engines. He grabbed the mic and shouted, "Hold on, everyone!" as if they needed to be told. The wave pointed them directly at the beach he wanted, but the weather changed yet again. He was no longer at a right angle to the shore, but tossed again sideways, and thrown to the right, then to the left, until he wasn't sure where he was exactly. Right in front of him, rising out of the sea to his left as the water dipped, was a massive two-spired rock formation that seemed to instantly grow from the ocean floor. It was clear to John, or as clear as anything could be in that moment, that they were going to crash. He no longer had any control whatsoever.

"Brace for impact!" he shouted.

The current, wind, and waves lifted the boat and smashed it against the rock. It was a sturdy ship and well-built, so it didn't break apart. Instead, the tempestuous sea thrust it between the two spires, where it wedged itself and rested, as if nestled comfortably in a two-tine fork.

Passengers were flung in every direction the instant the boat connected with rock. Arms and legs were intertwined as bodies were flung in opposite directions, like a mass of humanity dropped in a blender. Screams, moans, and cries of fear and pain filled the cabin. John picked himself up and rubbed the growing bump on his forehead. He had banged it hard against the console when they hit. He tried the radio several times in rapid succession without success. Perhaps his cell phone would work—nothing but dead silence. He cursed and stumbled into the main cabin to survey the chaos. People were hurt. Whimpers echoed from every corner. Michael, miraculously unhurt, was tending to the injured, but Billy was nowhere to be seen. John looked out the side window at the rock. It appeared to him they had a pathway down the back slope of the rock formation they were wedged into. *If we can negotiate our descent safely*, he thought, *perhaps we can take shelter in that cave, just off the beach.*

One of the older passengers, a college professor of sixty-five with a bloody forehead, grabbed John roughly by the shoulder.

"What the hell were you trying to do? What kind of captain are you? And what are we doing out here if the weather is as bad as it is?"

John pushed past him and went up to Michael. "What's the damage to the passengers?" he asked.

Michael shook his head and spoke softly. "A few with bad bumps and contusions, but fortunately nothing looks too serious."

"And Billy?"

"In the back, looking for ice."

John bowed his head in relief. "Listen, we've got to get these people off this boat, and fast. Who knows if it'll hold in this position. In this sea, we could get a rogue wave that knocks us off this perch and back into the drink."

"Sure, but how do we do that?" Michael asked.

"Follow me."

John showed Michael the path out through the right front exit and onto the rocks. It wasn't wide, but there was a walkway of sorts that led down to the beach, and then to the cave.

"In calmer times, I'm sure it's used by hikers and photographers to climb up the rock for a picture, so there's a somewhat well-worn path already."

Michael agreed, and John went back to the mic and made an announcement. "Ladies and gentlemen, we are going to exit the boat and enter that cave over there to your right. We need to do this in single file and without baggage, so you'll have to leave your bags behind. No exceptions."

"I have an expensive camera in my bag," the professor said. He jutted his jaw towards John and scowled. "And I'm not leaving it behind."

John flipped off the mic and turned to the professor. "It's too slippery out there on the rock, and we can't risk people losing their balance because of baggage and dragging others down with them."

He then turned the mic back on and continued. "Michael, who is standing at the front right door, will lead you all off the boat and point you down to the sandy shore. I'll bring up the rear. Just take it easy, ladies and gentlemen, move slowly, and take one step at a time. Do that, and we'll all make it down safely." He switched off the mic and people moved swiftly to the exit.

The professor lifted his hand and shouted, seeking attention.

"And no questions," John added, looking directly at the professor. "Unless you want to wait here until the sea wipes us off this rock."

The professor put his hand down.

Michael was already positioned at the doorway. He stepped out onto the rock, turned, and reached out a hand to the first person in line, an elderly gentleman. "My name is Allan. My wife, Margaret, is behind me," he said. "I'd like to guide her down, please."

"The best thing you can do, for the both of you," Michael said, "is to step down carefully and meet her at the bottom. It's less risky that way, believe me."

Allan hurried to the bottom and looked up to his nervous wife with concern.

"See, that was easy," Michael said, turning to her and shouting above the howling wind.

"I'm not sure I can," Margaret said.

"What's your name, dear?"

"Margaret."

"Sure you can, Margaret. Hold onto the doorway here, and take a gentle step down to the first rock, just as your husband did."

Margaret drew a deep breath and nodded. She took a step out and was slapped by the wind, intent on hurling her off the precipice as she fought for control of her footing.

Michael grabbed her arm and steadied her. "Now, take one step at a time, don't try to rush it, and you'll be down before you know it." Margaret did as she was told and made it down without further incident into the outstretched arms of her anxious husband.

Everyone followed suit, even those with a sore limb. Some, especially the sure-footed children, had an easier time of it than the elderly, but all made it down faster than expected. When John reached the beach, the others were already gathered at the cave entrance. John was set to address the group when a massive wave smacked into the side of the perched boat. It sat still for a quiet moment, then moaned long and deep, sounding like a dirge from an enchanted choir, melancholic and full of woe. John felt the pain deep in his heart as he watched the boat slide off the ridge, get pulled out to sea, then fall back again against the rocks, thrust by the turbulent water. It exploded into a thousand bits of lost dreams, as if mashed by a massive hammer of fate.

"Hurry," John said as the remnants of his aspirations rapidly disappeared under the churning sea and the swirling fog. "Everyone into the cave."

Michael led the way, trying to keep up with the few kids who insisted on running ahead. Once inside, they moved forward about ninety feet to a group of scattered rocks and halted. They could still see the entrance to the cave, so they still had a modicum of dim light, but were far enough inside to avoid the harshest of the elements. The thick, mysterious fog that accompanied the storm drifted across the gaping entrance like an ethereal curtain. The dispersed outcrop of rocks in the cave provided an opportunity for the weary passengers to sit and rest. Most were exhausted from their ordeal and simply collapsed.

When they were settled, John spoke. "Everyone, please listen. My mates and I are going to discuss our next steps, and we'll get back to you shortly. Please use this opportunity to rest."

John, Michael, and Billy stepped away from the crowd, far enough so they could speak in private.

"I wasn't able to send an SOS and summon help back on the boat," John said. "Nothing worked. Not the two-way marine radio or the emergency locators, from what I could see. Not even my cell."

"So, I guess we just sit here and ride out the storm," Michael said. "Someone's bound to notice when we don't show up back in Blackpool."

"These people are injured, tired, and they're going to get hungry. Some of them don't look to be in the best physical shape, either," John said. "We can't wait out the storm without knowing how long it will last."

"We can't go deeper into the cave," Michael said. "Not without more lights and proper equipment. Besides, no one knows where it leads. And I don't think anyone is in any shape to venture outside and seek a trail up the slope. It'd be too steep and slippery in this weather."

John chewed the inside of his cheek, deep in thought. "I think one of you ought to make the climb while the rest of us stay here. With any luck, you may see someone who can call or radio for help."

"Who would we possibly meet up with who'd be out in this?" Michael asked.

"I don't know, but it may be our only chance to get out of here, or at least notify Robert that we are here," John said. "If this cave starts to flood," he added, "we're going to be in real trouble, so time may be of the essence."

"I'll go," Billy said. "I'm the only one of us that qualifies as a climber. Remember a long time ago, John, I got a certificate for climbing one hundred trails on the island. Robert gave it to me himself."

"Yes, Billy, I remember," John said with a smile.

"So, it's best if I try, right John?"

John thought for a moment. He had to agree. Billy was an avid hiker and had been all over the island. He knew he also needed Michael to be with him in case things got ugly. "Okay, Billy, you're our man."

"And John," Billy added, "I know you said no bags, but I managed to throw a bunch of snacks into three bags and smuggled them down in my shirt. I thought you'd need them."

"You are a lifesaver, Billy." Billy was pleased that he was going to make another important contribution to this expedition.

"Here, Billy," John said. "Take a few candy bars yourself and head out quickly. People are going to lose patience pretty fast."

Billy grabbed two Cadbury's Chocolate Dairy Milk bars and stuffed them into his pockets. He gave John the rest of the food and headed for the cave entrance. John and Michael stood still and watched him go. They kept eyes on him until he turned left at the entrance and disappeared into the peculiar fog.

After distributing some of the candy, John and Michael sat away from the group. They didn't mean to fall asleep, but the pressure of the previous few hours wore them out. They didn't get to sleep very long, however. John awoke with the professor kicking the bottom of his shoe.

John wiped the sleep from his eyes. "Yes?"

"I came here today at some expense, as I flew up from London. I've been investigating The Loch Ness Monster for decades. I've researched your claims, found them plausible, maybe even probable, and needed this trip to continue my status at the University of London. I needed to make a scientific discovery at best, and at least a sighting caught on camera. You have ruined my slim chance at either. I will probably lose my job as a result. I will not allow this trip to be foiled by foul weather. You will get me a private boat tomorrow and . . ."

A loud, piercing, screech suddenly filled the cavern. It bounced from wall to wall, echoing in every direction at once and making it difficult to pinpoint. It was followed by another, and yet another of different pitch and timbre, as if coming from three different entities.

"What the hell was that?" Michael asked of no one in particular.

The sound faded to dead silence. Everyone was on their feet, huddling, very still and listening intently.

Another screech filled the void, louder this time, and was clearly coming from the entrance to their cave. People tightened as a group, and moved backwards, as if of one body and mind.

"Michael," John said, "get in front of the group and use your flashlight to go deeper into the cave."

He no sooner uttered those words when three spectral figures appeared at the gaping mouth of their chamber. The strange shapes sifted through the passing gray fog, with the dim light of stormy weather as a backdrop. John was able to make out some of their features from a distance. He saw rows of sharp, pointy teeth, vicious claws, and big, wide gills on the side of their heads, which moved in and out as they breathed. Less difficult to ascertain was the rank smell.

The professor, who saw some partially opened bags of candy on the floor of the cave, grabbed one and suddenly ran toward the creatures.

"Michael," John whispered forcefully, "move."

Michael backpedaled to the front of the passengers, took out his flashlight, and snapped his fingers. He leaned into the group and said, "Follow me. Now."

John was rooted to the ground, unable to take his eyes off the creatures and the horrific drama unfolding in front of him.

***

As he approached the creatures, the professor was assaulted by their awful smell, but he was so enthralled by the very scientific nature of what stood before him, he couldn't stop himself from approaching further. He marveled at the creatures' features, which were clearer to him now. Their webbed hands were pointed with sharpened digits, their webbed feet anchored to the sand by a raptor-like claw. Their teeth were truly frightening, with a thick mucus dripping as they breathed through flapping gills opening and closing in a rhythmic pattern matched to their air intake.

"Listen, to me," the professor said. "You are sentient beings, as am I. So, you must know I'm sincere when I say this. I want to know all about you, to know where you came from, how you got here, how you live. I know we can get along, if you'll trust me."

The creatures stood staring with their huge, solidly dark orbs that hugged the sides of their faces.

"You can breathe, therefore I'm sure you can eat," the professor rapidly added, and reached into the bag. He opened several bars of chocolate and offered them as a sign of friendship. If he could get them to understand his intent, if he could only reach them on an intellectual level, he could lead the effort to study them, these new beings, and achieve something unlike anything else in history. If he could do this, he could buy the damn university.

"Please," he said with a shaky smile, "please, take this offering."

The creature furthest from him was holding something odd. It was roundish in shape, like a partially deflated soccer ball. It looked slick and greasy to the touch, and was being held on one end by a crop of loose, wet strands. It was small in the claws of such a huge beast, and it took a moment to focus on it clearly. The professor turned and examined it, drawn by the drip, drip, drip that cascaded from the bottom of the damaged, mishappen sphere.

His hand flew up to cover his mouth in a silent scream of horror.

It was Billy's head. It was nearly drained of blood and now stared at the professor through cloudy, lifeless eyes. The professor shrieked, filling the cave with echoes of his hysteria. The creature closest to him flung his left arm across the space between it and the professor, slicing his head clear off. It rolled across the cave floor, propelled by the brute force of the monster until it hit the side wall with a dull thud. The three creatures then pounced on the professor's fallen body, devouring it in an ecstatic fury, like starving sharks falling upon a sick dolphin.

Amidst the brutal savagery, Billy's head had rolled towards John, who stood frozen by fear and completely dazed. He was able to see the shock and fear in Billy's dead eyes that now pointed at him. He retched, wiped his mouth, and nearly tripped hurrying after Michael and his retreating passengers.

CHAPTER 10

A GRUESOME DISCOVERY

"It works like a barometer, John, I assure you."

On the morning of John's maiden voyage, Robert had met with him at the dock to issue one final warning. Robert's leg was giving him the most pain he'd ever experienced, and to him that was a crystal-clear message. Trouble wasn't just coming. It was already here.

"You should not be going out there today, John. The sky is black and the seas are much too rough, even for an experienced sailor such as yourself."

"It'll be a challenge Robert, to be sure, but one I'm well equipped to handle. And besides, I'll have the boat back in port before you know it."

The fog, in a preemptive strike, had swept over the Moray Firth the previous evening, creeping up and over the island like a silent, stealthy plague. The rain followed, slight at first, but picking up, along with the screaming winds. All were a harbinger of death and destruction. To Robert, it was an opening salvo in the never-ending battle between man and nature. He tried his best to convince John of that, but it fell on deaf ears.

Robert had watched *The Nessie* ease out of the marina and into the rough waters of the cove from the safe confines of his car before he retreated to his cozy home on the hill behind the Royal Oak. He tried to work his radio to get a weather update from the mainland. All he received was a steady stream of crackling static punctuated with a few garbled, indecipherable words.

Robert's landline rang, its tone jarring and insistent in the quiet confines of his study. It made him jump. He yanked it up and said "Hello," almost afraid there'd actually be a response. "Slow down," Robert said. "I'm sorry, I can't . . . Oh, dear God . . . tell me what happened . . . Okay, lock yourself in the car, I'll be there soon."

When Robert terminated the call, he was white as a sheet. He made another quick call while his phone was still working.

***

Bryan was pounding on the door to Tim's room.

"Tim! Marie!"

Marie dashed to the toilet. Tim rushed to pull on his trousers and stumbled to the door. He creaked it open, and Bryan stood there, ashen faced.

"Hi," Tim said, embarrassed by this uncomfortable situation.

"Robert called. He wants you to meet him at his house up the hill. He said to tell you that he needs your science background to assess a . . . a situation."

"Did he say wha—"

"No, just to hurry. He sounded desperate."

"And, uh," Bryan added, "I don't have a great deal of control over what Marie decides to do or not do, but Robert recommended she not accompany you. I'd like her not to go, based on the tone of his voice and what little information I do have."

Tim nodded, closed the door, and resumed getting dressed. Marie came out of the bathroom and asked, "What was that all about?"

"Your father. I have to go up to Robert's. There's been some kind of emergency, and he's asked for my expertise."

"I'll hurry and get dressed," Marie said.

"No," Tim said. Marie looked surprised. "He asked that you not accompany me."

"He doesn't tell me what to—"

"I agreed, out of respect for your father's wishes."

Marie looked at Tim, picked up her belongings, and left the room without saying another word.

"That went well," Tim said.

He finished getting ready, grabbed his knapsack, and went down to the pub. Marie was already tending to customers and refused to look his way. Bryan nodded, handed him a set of keys and whispered a quiet "Thanks." Tim left the pub, got into the Ford Transit, and drove up the hill to Robert's house.

When he arrived, Robert was outside, waiting out of the rain under his portico. Tim swung into the drive and left the motor running, while Robert climbed into the passenger seat. They took off without even a hello. This was clearly not a pleasure trip. Robert, stern-faced, stared out the windshield as if looking for something. *Answers? What might the questions be?* Tim wondered. He suspected he would know soon enough.

"I got a call a short time ago, after I saw John and his mates off," Robert said, breathing heavily between each sentence. "It was from Reverend Knox. He was hysterical. Going on and on about the end of the world, how the apocalypse was here, how evil was upon us, and all the time quoting the Bible. He kept repeating the phrase, 'Vengeance is mine, saith the Lord.'"

Tim had questions, not the least of which centered on the reverend's sanity.

"When he finally calmed down to a reasonable delirium, I told him to tell me in a few words what happened. 'It's a slaughter and they're dead,' was all he would say at first. I told him to go to his car, lock the doors, and wait for me to get there."

"What did he mean by 'It's a slaughter?'"

"I'm not sure. But his voice shook and cracked, and he mumbled a great deal."

"And where is 'there?'"

"Out in the Highlands, along the ridge, near the road that takes you down to Loch Crover. I managed to get that out of him before he stopped talking altogether."

"I know the place. Marie and I stopped there for a view before heading down to the loch."

It took another hour of silent, contemplative driving to reach their destination. When they arrived, it appeared as if nothing had happened. All they could see from their vantage point was the reverend's car. They parked and exited the Transit, then walked through the rain and up to Knox's weathered, 2001 Ford Fiesta. He sat in the driver's seat, gripping the wheel with his eyes shut tight, all the while reciting the Lord's Prayer loud enough for them to hear over the light, but steady rainfall.

Robert rapped on the driver's window several times to no avail. Knox never looked in his direction. He rapped again, then again. Finally, he shouted his name. The reverend slowly looked up at the noise, his lower lip quivering, then opened his door. Robert reached in and removed the keys from the ignition.

"He's slipping into shock," Tim said.

"Aye."

"Is there a doctor nearby? The police?"

"No and no. We have a real doctor who comes over to the island once a week, but every local can handle incidents in need of low-level medical aid. They also carry basic medical necessities in their cars.

In a real emergency, we can call for a helicopter from Inverness, but we've never had to do that. The police are also not stationed here. "

Robert retrieved a blanket from the boot of the Transit and wrapped it around the reverend, whose entire body was now shaking.

"Okay then, let's have a quick look and see what caused this," Robert said.

"Fine, but we'd better hurry. Along with the rain, the wind is getting worse," Tim said.

"This fog is an odd part of this storm," Robert said. "I've never seen anything like it."

"Neither have I," Tim agreed. "And it seems to be having an effect on cell phone service, something I have seen elsewhere."

At first, nothing looked amiss. They scanned the area amidst the fast-falling rain patter, a soft and steady drumroll signaling a pending disaster. A few agonizing minutes rolled by before Robert called out. "Here, Tim! What do you make of this?"

Tim joined him and looked closely at the ground. Robert pointed out a group of odd-looking footprints in a patch of dirt that hadn't yet washed away, but were quickly filling with rainwater.

"That is strange. It looks like a group of scuba divers were here. The footprints, if you can call them that, resemble pairs of flippers."

"Yes, and look here!" Robert leaned over and pointed at several tips at the end of the flipper imprint.

"They look like sharpened points," Tim said. "See how they dig into the earth, here and here?"

They were silent for a moment. There was nothing to disturb the quiet but the falling rain tapping the hoods of their parkas. They stood still, contemplating what it all might mean, but neither could come up with a rational explanation to describe what they were looking at.

"We'd better spread out," Tim said. "We're not going to have much time to explore the area in this weather."

Tim turned to the left and walked towards a clump of trees that further led to an outcrop. From there, the trees descended towards the coast on the southern side of the island. Robert turned right and headed back towards the cars to search the northern side. The wind kicked up, sporadically gusting in all directions at once. A quick glance from Tim confirmed the prints they saw may soon become lost to the weather. He got to the edge of the trees, stopped, and almost turned back. A flash of color grabbed the corner of his eye. It popped quickly, barely noticeable. But it was just enough to make him pause.

Tim peered closer. Was it a piece of clothing? A food wrapper, perhaps? *Please let it be an errant piece of trash*, he thought. He focused, bent towards it, and noticed it was a piece of a red Patagonia puffer coat. *One of those hikers wore a red coat*, he remembered. He pushed further into the brush. More red scraps. Then bits of backpacks and what may have passed for a sleeping bag. It was so shredded, it was hard to tell. He stumbled onward, tripping over clods of brush and bramble, following the trail of material scraps until he came to a small clearing.

Tim noticed the blood first. Enhanced by the rain, there were puddles of crimson connected by rivers of red. Bone and sinew were strewn about like loose kindling, bits of bloody scalp clinging ferociously to them, alongside the battered remains of a bashed-in skull. A torn jacket rested on a clump of innards, with an eyeball resting on a flapping collar.

Tim gagged, covered his mouth, and ran back to find Robert. When he broke through the tree line, Tim tried to call Robert, but his voice was muffled, as if he had swallowed a dry rag and it lay stuck in his throat. His legs wobbled and his head spun like a pinwheel. He managed to choke out Robert's name again, and this time Robert looked up.

"What is it, Tim?"

"It's them. I think."

"Who? And what do you mean, you think?"

Tim started to speak, but then he fell forward with his hands on his knees and vomited. He coughed between streams, but kept going until he had nothing left but dry heaves. He pointed to an area and Robert ran over. He gingerly stepped over the brush until he came to the same clearing Tim had seen. He stumbled out moments later, with a handkerchief over his mouth. He loudly retched and spit.

"Are you able to drive?" Robert asked.

"Yes," said Tim.

"Good. I'll take the reverend with me in his car. You drive the Transit back to the pub. We'll meet there."

"Robert . . ." Tim began.

"I know," Robert said. "We'll talk when we get back. We'll notify mainland police by radio and get some help. We're going to need it."

CHAPTER 11

JACK'S CATTLE

Jack Brodie raised Highland cattle. They were his prized possessions. His wife, Emily, and their two sons, Gavin and Gregory, along with some hired help, aided in the care of his three-hundred head, making his thriving business a true family enterprise. There was plenty of land to graze, water troughs strategically placed to keep them hydrated, and sporadic fencing to keep them away from dangerous cliffs. Their stone and wooden folds, or pens, were placed in various locations in the field, so the cattle had a spot to protect them from inclement weather. They were mostly fenced in by Mother Nature in the form of trees and outcrops that gently forced them back onto open pasture for feeding.

The day after the big meeting at the Royal Oak, Jack had been told Robert Campbell believed the weather was turning for the worse, not the better. That was as good as gospel as far as he was concerned, so he decided to drive around and check on his cattle. It was a foggy, windy, and rainy day, so he and his two boys donned their Macs and hopped in his car to inspect the cattle.

After twenty minutes of driving his ten-year-old, all-wheel-drive Subaru across rough terrain, Jack and his boys came upon their first large group of cattle.

"You boys start here, gather as many as you can, and lead them to the fold. Make sure they're under cover and have enough food for the night. I'll be back as soon as I locate the next group."

Jack started up his old, but highly dependable vehicle and drove off in a cloud of swirling fog. It took him the better part of an hour to locate most of the rest of the herd. They'd been moved onward, driven by the growing wind that swept over the highlands. It was coming from the north, and Jack could see firsthand they were in for even rougher weather ahead.

"Robert was right again," he mumbled.

It didn't take much to encourage the cattle to seek shelter out here. He decided he wasn't going to be moving them into the wind; it would take too much time, and they wouldn't like it. Fortunately, there were adequate folds out this far, along with some excellent tree cover. In fact, some of the herd already huddled closely in the folds that existed. Jack walked up to one of the pens to make sure enough hay was available.

Jack couldn't help but notice that the cattle weren't huddled against the wind so much as crowding together and acting sketchy. If he didn't know better, he'd swear they were fearful of something. *Of what?* he wondered. *The wind?* He patted one of the cow's hindquarters, only to have it skitter away, pushing others into the surrounding fencing.

"That's odd. What's wrong with you, now?" he shouted to the cows.

Jack walked around the structure looking for loose nails, broken boards, anything that might have given his cows reason to be on edge. Nothing. *Was it the coming storm?* he wondered again. Sure, it was windy and there was a strange deep fog building, but they'd been through this kind of thing before. There was always a storm brewing of some sort. They'd always taken it in stride. After all, they were hardy beasts, bred to withstand the elements.

He looked around to see if anything was amiss. He couldn't see anything, but he could feel it. He was picking up on the cattle's sense of fear. Some were pawing the ground, some were snorting, still others were looking about, as if searching for a place of refuge.

The hair on Jack's arms and neck tingled. The wind gusts picked up, giving voice to the Scots pine and juniper tree branches and boughs as they whipped about grabbing for air. Then he noticed there were a few small groups of cattle standing still, as if frozen in fear, eyes wide in terror. The clusters of cattle seemed almost equidistant from each other, forming an arc away from an area with no cattle whatsoever.

It seemed odd to Jack that they should form such a semi-circle, but he found his feet wouldn't move to investigate it. *My gun*, he thought, but then realized he had left it home, not in his car. He swallowed, then nervously forced himself to look. He felt for his keys, and was reassured that he had them handy in case he needed to run. Emboldened, he moved. A tentative step at first, then a more purposeful one.

"This is ridiculous," he said loudly to chase away the fear that squeezed him like a metal vise. He took several bold steps to cross the nearly fifteen meters to the site, then he slowed again. He tiptoed the rest of the way, leaning towards his car, wondering if he'd have to flee. Then wondering if he'd make it.

He approached the area that was carefully avoided by the cattle and picked up a faint, malodorous scent. It was a circular zone, a good feeding area, full of grass. It was sheltered by mostly Scots pine, which gave shade and protection. It would have been a good spot for his cattle to bed down. So why, apart from the smell, did they shun it?

At first, he saw nothing. The area was flattened and disturbed, as if part of the herd had lain in the grass. Then he saw lumps of cattle hair, like thick, unkempt wigs carelessly tossed about . . . and globs of thick red, raw meat and gnawed bone . . . and a sight he wished he hadn't seen . . . then he ran.

When he got to his car, Jack was shaking like a wyche elm in the wind. He trembled so badly he could barely fit the key in the ignition with his unsteady hand. He forced himself to concentrate, thinking of his boys and how he needed to get to them as fast as possible. He thought of his wife, home alone, the rising panic now overwhelming him, wondering if whatever got to his cattle would . . . he didn't dare finish the thought. Finally, the key clicked home and he turned it. The car had barely started when he punched the gas pedal and flew down the road to his sons. What had been an hour-long drive on the way out took him twenty-five minutes to get back.

When he pulled into the pasture where he left his boys, Jack slammed the brakes, turned off the engine, and opened his door, nearly performing all three tasks at once. He leapt from his car and ran, scanning the area in search of his boys. At first, he didn't see them. He licked his lips, found it difficult to speak after what he'd just seen, and tears gathered in the corners of his eyes as he thought of his children.

"Boys," he whispered. He cleared his throat and ran in circles, before he was able to find his voice again. "Boys," he screamed. "Gavin! Gregory!"

"Da!" they shouted. The two had been spreading some hay in a fold, making sure there was enough for the cattle to eat.

Relief hit Jack like a wave at the beach. He knelt, unable to stand, weak from fear. Gavin and Gregory ran to him.

"Whatcha on the ground for?" asked Gavin.

Jack laughed, reached up and hugged the two. "Quick," he said. "In the car. Now." The boys knew better than to argue with Da, especially when they heard the clear tone of a frightened command. They raced over to the Subaru, hopped in the back seat, and strapped in just as Jack bolted for home.

When they arrived at the house, Jack pulled into the drive, left the motor running, and said, "Stay here, with the doors locked." The boys were now so scared they complied without question.

Jack ran into the house, calling for Emily. She responded right away, but it was not without a moment or two of fright that coursed through his veins.

"I need you to grab your coat and get in the car, no time to waste," Jack said. He then ran to the gun cabinet and removed his shotgun, along with a box of ammunition. Although gun control in Scotland was strong, he, like most islanders, had the necessary shotgun certificate and was properly trained in its use.

"Emily, hurry!" Jack shouted, then watched as his wife hurried out to the car. He tossed some ammo into a sack as he heard a noise in the yard behind the house and looked past the living room curtain that framed the sliding door to the rear yard. The weather had worsened since he entered the house. The fog was thicker, the clouds darker, more ominous. The rain was heavy and steady, now. There was that noise again, a loud, sharp cry like a wounded owl. He grabbed the handle on the slider, unlocked it, and slid it open a crack.

The first thing that hit him was the smell. It was like a combination of rotten eggs and a fresh can of fermented fish. He had to catch his breath or he was going to vomit. It triggered a memory of a lingering smell at the cattle site, but how could it? That was miles away. He continued to stare hard into the gauzy haze that surrounded his house, looking for the source of such an odor.

Not twenty feet away stood the outline of four bizarre creatures, tall and muscular. Although they were covered by the fog, seemingly a part of it, Jack could tell, even at this distance, they were deadly vicious. He stood, rooted to the floor, unable to move. Suddenly, he heard the sharp bleat of the car horn, and immediately turned and ran.

Jack yanked the front door open and headed to the driveway. A beast rounded the corner of his house and raced towards him. Jack didn't hesitate. He raised his gun and shot. The beast flew back three feet and landed on the front lawn, lifeless. Emily and the boys flinched at the shot.

Jack sprinted to the car, jumped into the driver's seat, and hurried off his property as quickly as he could. When he hit the main road, he glanced in the rearview mirror and saw three more beings entering the front door to his home. The road, covered in rapidly moving mist, was difficult to see, but it didn't slow him down. Jack drove with abandon, away from the memory of what just happened, straight to the Royal Oak Pub.

CHAPTER 12

LOST IN THE CAVES

Fear coursed through John's veins like a flash flood. His head was thumping from the blood rush. *What the hell? What were those creatures? Where did they come from? And, dear God, was that Billy's head?* He was sure it was. He'd recognized Billy's crumpled new Nessie hat, backwards on the head, the way he liked to wear it. Anger and sadness overwhelmed him. *Why did I send Billy on that errand?* He knew the answer, of course. Billy was a hiker, in great shape, physically, and he really thought he'd given the poor sod a chance to be a hero. As the captain, he had no other choice but to send Billy while he and Michael tended to their passengers, but it didn't lessen the pain and guilt he felt.

His misery was quickly replaced by a sense of horror. The way that creature took off the professor's head . . . the way they all dove onto his body, tearing at his flesh . . . the sounds they made and the smell, that god-awful smell . . . John realized he was shaking.

He had to get a hold of himself. He had too many people depending on him and he had no idea how he was going to get them out of there. As far as he knew, there was only one way out, which was the way they had come in. And that way was no longer an option.

***

Michael wished now that he hadn't turned around to look, but he had, and what he saw shocked him. Those beasts had ripped off the head of that professor and now they were gorging on him. He held down his bile and quickened his pace, encouraging the passengers to follow. He knew John was picking up the rear, so he felt a small measure of security that his back was covered. But as he stumbled forward, he couldn't help but wonder, *What lies ahead?*

***

John caught up to the group as they raced through the darkness ahead. None of them dared look behind them. The fervent feeding sounds pushed them forward. Amidst the cacophony of chomping, slurping, and screeching, they scurried over boulders and picked their way around random rocks dispersed along the sandy floor. Driven to escape from the evil that stalked them, they tripped, helped each other up, and moved forward continuously, trying with every ounce of energy to focus on Michael's bobbing light ahead, and only slightly reassured by John's light from the rear. The elderly amongst them found new energy in their desire to live a few more years together, the parents of children encouraged their young ones to stay near the front for safety, and everyone moved as a trembling mass in one direction, the only one now open to them.

***

Darkness, John noticed, closed in on the group, and with it, their terror solidified. They wore it collectively, like a shared blanket, but their individual problems magnified. John tried to remember who they were and identify the personal issues on the form they had to fill out before departure. Issues that might slow them down now. For Bob Jones, a retired plumber who never did start that exercise program his doctor recommended, breathing was becoming a serious challenge. Every difficult step forward in darkness caused him to breathe faster and with more desperation, tiring him even more quickly.

Christopher Ross and Mitchell Watson, two children who wore glasses, were having an especially difficult time. Christopher had his pair blown off his face while getting off the boat; Mitchell dropped and stepped on his, turning one lens into a web of broken fingers. They struggled to see clearly in the pitch, giving life to things that were only shadow, causing them to stumble over sharpened rock formations. Sarah Tyke, a young mother from Ireland, experienced mini-panic attacks and had to be coaxed back to reality as the group moved forward, one plodding step at a time. Several others could be heard whimpering in the dark, convinced they would not survive this day. But everyone knew no one in the group could afford to stop and nurse their injuries or coddle their fears, real or imagined. There simply wasn't time.

Every few minutes, a loud, shrill scream would reverberate through the cave, echoing in every direction, including their hearts and minds.

"Michael!"

Michael stopped when he heard John call for him and held his hand up for all to stop. Everyone turned to John.

"I think the creatures have fallen behind," John said. "Let's take five."

No one argued. They were too tired to do anything but flop where they stood. Michael walked to the rear of his group, making sure everyone found a soft spot to rest for a few minutes.

"What makes you think so?" Michael whispered so no one but John could hear.

"I've been listening to the sounds these creatures make. They're big so they have a long stride, but they need to be careful where they're walking, just as we do. I've also noticed that the sound of their steps have been getting softer. I can barely hear them now. I think it means they're slowing down."

"I don't know how much more these people can take," Michael said as he looked back at the passengers.

"We need to keep them moving and focused on surviving this. I don't know what's ahead, but we have to keep pushing."

"Well, whatever it is, it shouldn't be too hard a sell to make them face it, knowing what's creeping up behind us."

"Yeah, we better get going."

Michael scampered back to his position, rousting people along the way. As if on cue, a distant cry rang out, reminding everyone of the need to keep moving. The group murmured in despair at the sound, then shuffled ahead, with Michael in the lead once again. Occasionally, a muffled yelp could be heard, the result of a bumped knee, a banged arm, or a slight fall. John, with his light pushing ahead, would sometimes stop to help someone up who had staggered and dropped.

"Can I help you up?" John said when he caught up with the elderly couple propped against an outcrop of rock, hugging each other.

"Captain, I'm afraid we can go no further and we're going to wait here together for whatever might happen. My wife suffers from rapidly progressive dementia, you see, and she refuses to continue. She's very tired, has difficulty walking, and her feet are very swollen. She's fallen several times and now refuses to continue. I . . . I can't leave her alone here, so I'm going to stay with her."

John wasn't going to leave either of them.

"What's your name, dear?" he asked as he sat on the ground next to the woman.

The woman stared into John's eyes, a blank look overtaking her.

"This is my wife, Margaret, and my name is Allan."

"Allan, how long have you two been married?"

"Fifty years. Long enough, I suppose, to have overcome most of the difficulties life throws at you, or at least not be surprised by them anymore, and still be left with an overabundance of love for one another."

"If your wife is that ill, Allan, why did you come on this voyage?"

"Oh, the experience of it all, I suppose. I thought if we could do something like this together, it would help her remember the adventures we shared in our youth. Rather we do that, in these final days for us, than to sit in front of a television set in a rehabilitative home, don't you think?"

A cry of desperate hunger reached them, like a cold slap in the face. It was a merciless howl of pure terror. Allan and John both turned to look behind them.

"Allan, this can't be the end of your journey together. You have to fight. You can't give up, not now. Not to . . . this." John waved a hand behind him. Another hungry cry startled them.

"I'm tired, Allan, and I want to take a nap," Margaret said.

"Not to worry, sweetheart," Allan said. "We'll both take a nice, long nap together, shall we?"

A loud, vicious snarling could be heard this time, along with a distant slapping of the creatures' webbed feet, now hitting the ground with renewed energy. They could smell their prey and were getting anxious.

"Here," John said as he handed his flashlight to Allan. He stood, bent over, slid his arms underneath the petite torso and legs of Margaret, and lifted her up. Then he turned to Allan and said, "Let's go!"

CHAPTER 13

REVELATIONS AND A PLAN

The front door of the Royal Oak flew open and banged the inside wall. Robert and Tim rushed in, soaked to the bone, propping up the Reverend Knox between them. Each one had an arm of the distressed reverend thrown loosely over their shoulders. They dragged him inside, his feet leaving wet streaks in their wake, like two huge slug trails.

Bryan was absently drying glasses at the bar, slightly bored by his chore. Marie was tending to the two lone patrons sitting at the bar, who were trying to ride out the storm by drinking their way through it. All heads popped up like prairie dogs as the saturated trio stumbled inside.

"What's this, eh?" Bryan asked. "Marie, get the door, please."

"We need a room," Robert said.

Bryan scooted around the bar, took Robert's place, and yelled to his daughter, "Pour Robert a dram, Tim and I will take the reverend upstairs."

Bryan and Tim half-dragged Reverend Knox up the staircase to the set of rooms on the upper level. The door next to Tim's room wasn't locked. Bryan used his left hand to twist it open, and they pushed their way through. They plopped the reverend onto the bed and took off his shoes and wet clothes.

"We should prop his feet up and cover him with a blanket," Tim suggested.

Bryan snagged two pillows and placed them gently under the reverend's feet. Tim covered him with a comforter and, once they had him settled, they both slipped from the room.

Bryan and Tim took the reverend's clothes to a washer-dryer, then rushed back to the bar.

"Robert's glass is empty," Bryan said as they rejoined everyone else.

"He's had two already," Marie said. "I don't want to put him to sleep, do I?"

"There's no fear of that, by the looks of it, so pour him another. And Tim needs one too."

Marie looked up at Tim with a slight frown, still upset she was ignored by these two earlier in the day, but the frightened look on Tim's face made her think twice about it. Maybe it wasn't such a bad idea to have stayed behind after all.

"It's the hikers," Robert began. "I . . . we . . . I'm not sure . . ." he stammered, a hitch to his voice.

"They're dead," Tim said in a flat monotone, his hands shaking as he tried resting them on the tabletop. "No," he continued after a brief pause, "they're worse than dead."

All eyes were on Tim except Robert's. His were fixed on the table in front of him.

"In fact, they're beyond dead," Tim said with a blank stare. "They've been eviscerated, decapitated, and eaten. No, not eaten. That wouldn't begin to describe it. They were consumed. Slashed to bloody bits. It was worse than anything I've ever seen, even having observed a fish tank full of hungry piranha."

The whirring of refrigeration and the ticking of the large clock hanging on the rear wall of the pub echoed in the silence. That fearful stillness, the pause before something evil is to be revealed, along with the smell of nervous sweat that leaked from their pores, put everyone on edge.

"It was ghastly," Tim continued, now shaking uncontrollably. Marie put her hand on his shoulder to calm him. "That's an old word, I know, and one seldom used, except in conjunction with some old horror movie. But that's exactly what it was. There was blood everywhere, bits of body parts strewn across the grass, and pieces of shredded clothing that spoke of the pain and terror those poor hikers must have experienced in the last moments of their lives. Those images—I'll never get them out of my head."

"He's right," Robert said. "Ghastly is precisely the right word to use."

"What might have caused such a horrible scene?" Bryan asked.

Tim shook his head in bewilderment. "I . . . I'm not sure. I can only speculate. Some kind of creature, or creatures, that attacked them during the night. It, or they, must have crept up on them while they slept, and then . . ." he trailed off, dropping his head in his hands.

"But what could it possibly have been?" Bryan persisted, now as nervous as the others. "There are no dangerous creatures on this island. As long as I've been alive, there has not been any evidence to suggest a beast capable of something like that lives here."

Robert lifted his head and looked at them all. "Well, there is now," he whispered.

"Da's right, Robert. There's never been anything like this before. So where did they come from? Why are they here?"

"I wish I knew."

"I wonder . . ." Tim said, lost in thought. He scrunched his eyebrows, bit his cheek, and tapped the table with his fingers, something he did whenever he was trying to figure out a seemingly unsolvable problem. "We can only guess at this point, but I wonder if it has anything to do with the earthquake Marie and I noticed when touring the island, and the strange sounds we heard out at the caves on the western coastline."

"It's as good a theory as any, I suppose," Robert said. "But I'm not anxious to meet up with any of those things, wherever they came from."

Marie frowned at this comment. "Well, we've got to do something."

That seemed to rouse Robert. "You're right, Marie. How stupid of me, wallowing in self-pity, worrying about what I saw," he said. Robert tried to shake off his nervous fear by taking control and springing into action. "Bryan, hop on the phone and ring up the emergency phone chain. We need to get in touch with as many people as possible and warn them. And be sure to tell them that by the looks of things," he said softly, with more than a hint of fear, "what we are facing isn't human."

"We can't," Bryan replied. "The phones are dead. Can't get a peep out of them."

"You mean we can't call *anyone?*" Robert asked.

"No, not even the mainland for help."

"It's the fog," Tim said. "The fog and the storm."

Everyone looked at him strangely.

"It's not unheard of," Tim added. "There are examples all over the world of fog alone disrupting land, sea, and air communication. I'm afraid we're probably socked in without a means of communication for the duration of this storm."

At that exact moment, the wind howled, shaking the windows and rattling the door. Everyone jumped as the door flung open once again, driving in rain and wind, along with Jack and Emilie Brodie and their two sons, Gavin and Gregory.

Marie rushed over to the family and ushered them to Robert's table. She tried to move the two boys to a quieter place of the pub, but they were having none of it and refused to leave their parents' side.

"I'll go with them," Emily said, taking the children to the other side of the bar.

Marie went to get them all something to drink, as well as some snack food for the boys.

"What is it, Jack?" Robert asked. Jack tried to speak several times, only to choke on his words in a failed attempt to explain what propelled them to the pub.

"Take your time." Robert placed his hand on Jack's shoulder.

"I saw creatures not of this earth," Jack whispered.

Tim and Robert looked at each other.

"What exactly did you see, Jack?" Robert asked.

"They were huge, Robert. I tell you, they were bigger than any man I know or ever met. Fearsome creatures they were. There was a horrible smell to them, and their claws . . . I . . . my kids . . . my wife."

"Easy does it, Jack," Robert said, hoping to gain control of his own emotions by helping someone else with theirs.

Jack downed the whiskey, and Marie quickly poured another from the bottle she'd placed in the middle of the table. Jack shook his head and wiped his mouth. He let the whiskey settle his nerves and continued.

"They were at least seven feet tall, I'd say. The smell is what hit me first. You couldn't miss it. It was like a bucket of chum that sat in the hot sun for weeks." Jack cleared his throat and continued. "Their hands resembled an oversized cricket glove, with claws that looked like they could easily rip a strong man in half. Their mouths opened, as if to speak, but they only made these strange garbling sounds. That's when I saw their teeth. They were pointed, as if sharpened with a file. Their jaws were wide and powerful, with bulging muscles like a pit bull."

A look fell over Jack, a cowl of terror. Then, in an instant, he exploded with rage. "They killed my cows. They tore them into little pieces and ate them. Butchered them." Jack wiped a falling tear with the palm of his hand and took another slug of a proffered whiskey.

"Is that where you saw these beasts, Jack?" Robert asked. "Out where your cattle graze?"

"Yes," Jack said. "No, wait." He looked puzzled, trying to piece together his jumbled thoughts. "That's where I saw what they'd done to my cattle," he corrected himself. "But I saw the creatures at my home. And that's miles away from where I discovered my cows." Jack looked at everyone. "It looked like a fresh kill, so I don't know how they managed to travel that far that fast." After a moment's reflection he continued. "Dear God, there must be two groups of those creatures."

"Maybe even more than two." Robert proceeded to tell Jack what he and Tim had found.

"So, that would mean three different groups of these things are roaming the island. At least."

"So, I'll ask again," Marie said. "What do we do? What about all the families out there who have no idea about any of this? With the phones not working, how do we warn them? How can they protect themselves?"

No one had a ready answer.

"We all now know what happened out there," Marie said finally. "So, it's pretty clear to me that it's up to us. We've got to get out there and warn as many families as we can before it's too late."

"We can't possibly warn them all," Tim said.

"Marie's right, though. We have to try," Robert said. "There are clusters of homes about the island, whole villages that we can target. One of us can warn an entire group of people in a short amount of time if we're selective."

"What about this storm?" Tim asked. "It's going full blast now, and not likely to let up anytime soon. We'll be lucky if we can even get to a neighborhood to warn anyone."

"Bryan," Robert said, ignoring Tim's warning, "get me the housing chart."

Tim shook his head and joined Bryan, as he scurried over to a pile of loose documents on an untidy shelf nestled on a wall to the rear of the bar.

"What are all these?" Tim asked Bryan.

"A variety of maps we have here on the island. Some are quite old."

Tim leaned over Bryan's shoulder, and one document in particular caught his eye. Bryan sifted through the pile a few moments, finally found what he was looking for, and brought it over to Robert. Tim snatched the one he'd seen, slipped it into his pocket unnoticed, and followed Bryan back to the group.

"We're very informal here on the island," Robert said. "When we need to do any official planning or reconnoitering, we have a few select maps and charts that we rely on. We keep them here in the pub since this is where we make our major decisions. This one," he said, as Bryan placed a big map on the table in front of him, "shows us where all the houses are built on the island. Here," he continued, as he leaned in and pointed to the map, "you can see these little clusters of rectangles, telling us where there are large groupings of homes. There are at least four large areas we may be able to get to and warn the residents."

"If it's not too late already," Jack said.

"And, if we can get through this wicked storm to do so," Tim said.

"We have to try, though, don't we?" Marie said. "There are children in many of these homes."

Tense moments passed. Everyone knew what they were about to do was suicidal, given the measure of the task and the challenging conditions they had to confront to carry out their mission. A crazy notion, foolish to even attempt it, but they all knew they were going to do it. No matter what.

"Okay," Bryan said. "How do we proceed?"

"You, my friend, are going to stay right here, with Emily and her two lads." Bryan started to protest, but Robert beat him to the punch. "No arguments," he said. "I need someone here I can trust, who can hold down the fort if and when people start to arrive. You have a few shotguns here on premises if we need them. Get them ready. And keep the door guarded at all times. You lads," Robert said, raising his voice to address the two local fixtures perched on stools at the bar, who were now scared senseless at what they heard. "That's your job. Make sure you unlatch the door for families in a hurry to seek shelter. But if those . . . things . . . show up, keep it locked and bolted. Now drag your arses over to the door and keep a keen eye out one of the windows to either side of it." The two quickly hopped off their stools and dragged themselves over to the small, shuttered windows flanking the door.

Robert turned his attention back to Jack and the others. "I'm going to warn this group," he said, pointing to a collection of homes about an hour from their current position, located on the south side of the island. "Jack, you take this group here," he said, pointing down the center of the document. "And Marie, you target this group here on the north side."

"Tim . . ." he said, about to give Tim directions, but was unable to finish.

"I'm going with Marie."

"I do not need a chaperone, thank you!"

"Look," Tim said, turning to Marie. "If you and I have to cover two areas, we will. But think of it this way. I don't know my way around the island, and in this weather, I'd be useless by myself. Going with you we can work together to get this done more safely."

Marie was set to argue, but had to admit it would be pointless to send Tim out there alone in this storm. Robert quickly looked at Bryan, who gave him a slight nod.

"Right, Robert said, "it's done. We all have an auto to take. Make sure you have a gun—we have extras here at the pub if you need one. Ready everyone?"

"Just one more thing," Marie said. "We should try to deliver a similar message to everyone."

"What might that be?" Robert asked.

Moments of dead silence passed. Tim broke it. "We should tell them what the science is telling us. We tell them there are creatures in the mist. And that they are coming to kill us all."

CHAPTER 14

RESPITE AND DREAD IN THE CAVES

John silently prayed they were putting distance between his group and the things that chased them. As they all went deeper into the cave, the darkness intensified, making rapid progress more difficult. Their light source was meager to begin with, consisting of one good flashlight and a small, battery-powered flash-lantern, mostly used for camping. And both were fading. *If the batteries fail,* he thought, *then what?* He continued to whisper words of encouragement to Allan, Margaret, and the few people just ahead of him, even as he worried if, in the end, they'd all have to engage in a horrible fight for their lives against these beasts in a darkened cave. Despite their advantage in numbers, he didn't think there was a chance in hell any of them were going to survive.

Allan led the way for John, carefully stepping over rocks, dodging outcrops, and avoiding shadows by using John's flashlight.

"You must be tired, Captain," he said.

"No, not really, Allan, your wife is very light. And please, call me John."

"I am a dinosaur from another age, I'm afraid. I call you Captain as a measure of respect and support for your position. Something I'm afraid you are going to need from many of us before long, given our dire circumstances."

The beastly noises faded yet again, John noticed. He called ahead to Michael to rest the group for five minutes. Everyone sat. Even the children were silent, huddling quietly next to their worn-out parents. Fear can be a progenitor for fatigue, especially when the stakes were high. And the stakes don't get much higher than when you're fighting for your survival. John lay Margaret down on a soft spot of sand. She had slipped into a state of disturbed slumber, restlessly tossing with the demons that played in her mind.

Allan rested his hand on John's shoulder.

"I didn't want to give in, Captain, but I didn't know what else to do. We never would have been able to make it this far on our own, you understand. So, thank you."

"Aren't you afraid of what's coming up behind us?" John asked.

"Yes, of course I am. I'm also terrified of the miserable hell that lies ahead for the both of us if we live. If we ever get out of here alive, what awaits are hospitals, rehabilitation centers, and an endless array of medications. In the end, which is coming sooner than later, none of it will stave off the lonely, isolated conclusion to our lives that we confront. In many respects, I'd rather we both left this earth together, before Margaret slowly, inexorably fades away, never again to even know who I am."

"I'm not in your shoes, Allan, but I think I understand. Let's hope it doesn't come to that, though. Not today, at least."

"John!" Michael said.

John hustled to the front of the pack. "What is it?"

"Come with me."

Michael walked about twenty paces, and took a sharp turn to the left. "I was too hopped up to lay down, so I thought I'd walk ahead to see where we're going. My torch-lantern was acting up, so I stopped right about here to turn it off and on again, trying for a better beam of light. Watch." Michael turned off his lantern and John gasped. There was light emanating from around the bend, about ten more paces ahead.

"Where's it coming from?"

The two walked the remaining distance together, and when they rounded the curve, they were surrounded by the sparkling miracle of nature known as bioluminescence.

"Beautiful, isn't it? I think it's caused by algae," Michael said.

John stood with his mouth agape. Sparkling light, like a room full of fireflies sprinkled the cave walls in a stunning display of natural marvel. "Aye, it is," he said. "And right now, I don't care what causes it. Whatever it is, it's a welcome gift to the spirit." John turned to face Michael. "Let's go and gather our people. And don't tell them what we've seen. Let them be surprised. It'll give their mood a much-needed boost, I think."

They both hurried back to the immobile crowd. They encouraged everyone to get to their feet, it was time to go. Many were reluctant. Some even voiced their mounting frustration and anger.

"What's the point?" one tourist said. "Why are we running away? There are only three of them." John noticed a few heads bobbing up and down. "We should have stayed where we were initially when we were at full strength. We've got weapons. We're surrounded by rocks. If we banded together, we could have stoned them to death. Now we're on the run, in darkness, and we're weak and tired." Buoyed by his own argument, the tourist turned to John, his voice rising in level and tone. "And this is your fault," he said, pointing an accusatory finger at John. "When we get out of here, I'm going to register a formal complaint with the proper authorities."

There were a couple of half-hearted "ayes" in the crowd, but not many. Michael stood by, shifting his weight from foot to foot. John knew he could count on Michael to do whatever was necessary to help him restore order if it came to that.

John looked everyone over in the silence that followed and decided to address his accuser directly, but spoke loud enough for everyone to hear. "What's your name, friend?"

"Charles Clark," he said, sticking his jaw out as if to say, "I dare you to challenge me."

John walked over to the self-appointed mouthpiece for the collective fear and frustration of the group. He stood tall and strong in front of his adversary, taking a moment to look him in the eye and tighten his jaw muscles. "Well Charles," he said. "As the captain of this expedition, I am in complete control, whether we are aboard my vessel or here on land, until this expedition is completely over. As such, you and everyone here will obey my commands and follow my orders to the letter. To do otherwise is mutinous, which is still punishable by death." Those who previously nodded their heads in agreement with Clark now gazed directly at the sand in front of them. "Is that clear?" John finished.

Clark withered under John's stare. He looked around nervously for support and found none. But he wasn't finished. "Then why haven't we at least considered the possibility that we can overtake those . . . things, and bash their heads in?" said Clark, a bit whinier and less forceful than he intended.

John once more assessed the crowd, and knew they had no stomach for a real fight. This time, he addressed everyone. "I'm only going to say this once, so please hear me. There is a way—a respectful way—to bring your captain a suggestion or an idea. This has not been it. I will tell you that we considered such a proposal some time ago. But my first mate and I dismissed it as improbable at best, especially after seeing what those creatures did to our mate, Billy, and the professor who tried to reason with them."

A few murmurs of remembrance shook the already nervous audience.

"We are, in fact, determining the best course of action for your survival constantly, and always with your safety foremost in mind. And you are going to have to trust that."

Now, he turned to look Clark directly in the face. "Is . . . that . . . understood?"

Charles Clark swallowed his pride, nodded, and sat.

"It isn't, is it?" asked Michael, when he sidled next to John.

"What isn't?" John asked.

"Mutiny, punishable by death."

"Not anymore," John said. "But he doesn't know that."

The trailing creatures, suddenly howled in unison. They weren't close, but their cries served as a reminder to the group that they were not safe by any stretch.

"Everyone up," Michael said. No one needed prodding, least of all Charles Clark, who responded to the cries by swiftly elbowing his way forward, closer to Michael. John bent forward and picked up Margaret, with Allan, again, leading the way.

"Is she getting heavy for you, Captain?" Allan asked.

"No, not at all," John said. "In fact, she's remarkably light."

"Yes, she's always been petite. In recent months she's lost so much weight due to her affliction, I think she's wasting away some days. But you have much more than us to worry about."

"Don't you worry about me, Allan, I'm going to get you both out of here."

When they got to the point where they had noticed the phosphorescence, Michael raised his hand. "Gather around," he said to the loose group. Everyone waited fearfully, thinking they were about to get more, bad news.

"We are not out of this yet," Michael said to everyone. "But this should lighten your spirits a wee bit." With that, Michael turned off his flashlight. Everyone gasped and suspended their fears, at least for a brief time. What followed were expressions of wonder and delight. They moved forward as if drawn, slowly and deliberately, filled with the momentary joy of witnessing something truly special.

"Mind where you go," Michael said, "and don't go too far." The group slowly progressed into a large room. The ceiling was double the height of the cave they'd been trekking through, and it was at least three times as wide. The phosphorescent algae smothered the walls and ceiling, giving the impression of standing in the middle of a lit planetarium. Everyone was mesmerized.

When John approached, Michael looked at him and said, "You do know she's awake now, right?"

John looked at Allan, who confirmed. "I'll take her now, Captain," Allan said. John lowered Margaret and placed her feet on the ground. Allan reached over and took her hand, passing back John's flashlight.

"Oh Allan, look," Margaret said. "The stars are all out tonight." Allan put his other arm around his wife and walked her through the sparkling cavern, all the while whispering to her, telling her what a lovely, star-filled evening it was.

For just a brief moment in time, the ragtag band of survivors was at peace. The horror of the natural world that pursued them was briefly overshadowed by the beauty nature could also produce. They smiled without realizing they had done so. They whispered to each other with pleasantries normally reserved for less threatening times, their stress evaporating like summer rain on a warm surface. After an all-too-brief respite, however, John had no choice but to break the momentary spell.

"Okay people," he said. "We need to move. Michael will lead the way again."

Almost at once, there was a collective sigh of regret, a deep and profound sense of loss. Terror marched its way back into their consciousness, making it difficult to move, even to breathe. They trudged along, bent with the burden of fear. Their momentary shot of positive energy had already depleted.

The spell, indeed, had been broken.

CHAPTER 15

DASHED HOPES

With Michael still in front, they walked for the better part of an hour. John had asked him to refrain from using his lantern for as long as possible to allow the group to experience the full effect of the bioluminescence.

The cave was large, and when they reached the end, it presented two plausible points of egress. Michael halted the group and huddled with John, who had once again picked up and carried Margaret. He gently placed her down, left her with Allan, and moved to a secluded spot with Michael.

"What is it?"

"I'm at the end of the cave and there are two ways to go."

"Can you hear anything from either? Feel any wind?"

"No, nothing."

John dragged his hand through his hair in frustration.

"Go left, alone, for ten minutes and see where that takes you, then come back. If it's good, we'll follow. If not, we'll try the other one. I'm cautious of us both leaving the group. That Clark fellow may cause a problem without one of us here, so be quick."

Michael ventured immediately into the passage to his left. John went to the group and relayed their plan. Again, everyone sat where they stood, gathering a modicum of strength from a much-needed rest.

***

Michael clicked on his lantern and covered decent ground, at first. He disappeared around a bend that went further left and was once again swallowed by the hungry darkness. Soon, the route Michael took began to narrow. Rock formations stuck out across the path. The sandy floor gave way to solid rock marred by pockmarks and pitted holes. The cave ceiling got progressively lower every ten yards or so, and Michael feared it would soon become a hindrance to the older members of their group. He had set the timer on his watch for ten minutes, but when it went off, he thought he needed more time. Ten minutes stretched into fifteen, fifteen to twenty. The ceiling had narrowed to a sliver, and only the smallest and most athletic would have been able to continue. It was nothing short of a horrific trap.

Michael scrambled backwards out of the tight cave until he was able to kneel, then stand. He hurried back to the group, trying to make up for lost time.

"Well?" John asked, when Michael returned.

Michael shook his head no.

John checked to make sure no one was listening. He leaned into Michael and spoke softly. "Okay, we don't have time to waste. You'll have to lead us into the other cave. If it's also a bad choice, so be it. We'll have to make our stand when we can go no further."

"Got it."

John turned to Allan and had a thought. "Do you have anything on you that has a strong odor? Some cologne, perhaps?"

"I have some tobacco and a pipe in my pocket. Will that do?" Allan asked.

"That's great, give it here." John rolled the tobacco and pipe in his outer shirt, and tossed it inside the cave just exited by Michael. "Those beasts will get a strong whiff of this and be drawn into this cave, buying us some valuable time, I hope. If not, they'll be right on our tail."

Michael went back to the front of the group. "Okay, everyone, let's go." Each person stood, and no one, surprisingly, argued about the new course of direction, or why the first choice failed. They simply accepted their dismal fate as if they had already been defeated and tramped onward. John carried Margaret, accompanied by Allan who picked up the rear. As they were about to enter through the new portal, the howl of a starving creature pierced the silence, causing both men to stop in their tracks and look at each other. Each recognized the intense fear that lay just below the surface of their gaze. They progressed slowly. Michael shone his lantern light to brighten the landscape ahead and behind him, but the darkness was overwhelming. Many stumbled repeatedly.

Michael halted the group and scurried back to John, who set Margaret down and stepped aside to talk with Michael. "John, the ceiling is getting lower up ahead. If it was anything like that first cave we'll soon have to crawl. And if it gets that bad, we may have to make our final stand against these creatures that stalk us."

Some of the passengers noticed the lowering ceiling as well. Frightened murmurs spread through the group like a deadly virus.

John was the captain. It was his responsibility to do whatever he could to save these people, or at least explore every option to do so. Knowing that it was a life and death decision, one that had to be made quickly, and one likely to end in everyone's horrific demise did not make it easy for him.

After some arduous thought, John said, "Okay, Michael, here's what we'll do. You stay here with the group and keep everyone seated.

I'll go forward and see what lays ahead. If it gets too narrow and there is nothing to do but advance on our bellies, then I'll come back. We'll do our best to hurry back to the large cave and fight the bastards. I frankly think those beasts would carve us up like a holiday roast, but you're right. Better that as an option than the only other alternative."

John and Michael walked back to the front of the group and spoke to the nervous assembly.

"All right, everyone," John said, "stay seated for a while. I'm sure you've noticed that the roof of the cave is getting lower. I'm going ahead to explore further on while you rest a bit to see if that continues. I'll be back as soon as I can to let you know what I find."

Michael didn't mention the only other option they would have if the cave became too difficult to traverse. He didn't think they could handle that kind of debate right now, so he hoped like hell John would find them a way out of there. Unfortunately, someone brought it up before he had a chance to leave.

"And what if you find that we can't go onward, what then?" shouted Charles Clark. Although Clark's was the voice behind the challenge, there were shouts of agreement among many.

John slowly turned in their direction. He stared at Clark for almost a full minute, and even in the dark could see him wither.

"Then you will get your wish to fight these creatures, Mr. Clark," John said.

The noise dialed down quickly when the full impact of that statement hit.

John turned, flashlight lantern in hand, and moved swiftly forward. It didn't take long before he was bent over, occasionally resting his hands on his knees to support his aching back. Soon after that, he crab-walked until that, too, became too difficult. He paused, sweating from the fatigue and frustration of knowing that the ceiling was dipping yet again, and he'd have to make a further adjustment. Once on his stomach, he inched his way between the rock floor and the ceiling until he believed that further effort would be useless. He was overcome with anger and sadness. Angry that for all of his work and effort, he had nothing but scraped knees and elbows to show for it. Saddened that there would soon be great loss of life, especially involving children, and he hadn't been able to do anything to stop it. He lay on the hard rock with his face to the side to catch his breath before inching his way back. As he started to move, he felt something odd.

A breeze. A slight one, but it was there, nonetheless. He closed his eyes and focused. No doubt about it, it was coming from an area just ahead of him. There was still a foot or so of space above his head and he had room to move, so on he went. To his amazement, the ceiling soon rose. Rapidly. He was able to crouch, and was bent forward for a brief amount of time, but was soon walking again. Within minutes, he was fully upright. And with his forward movement came a familiar noise. It sounded like running water, and it was getting louder with every step. He rounded a bend and entered another large cave. He moved his light around its darkened walls that were slick with moisture. On the far end of the cave, his lantern danced in the reflection of a beautiful sight. It was a rapidly flowing waterfall. It gushed downward from an unknown source in the ceiling with the force of a raging river, leading to God knows where. He instantly knew this represented a chance.

John hurried back through the cave the way he came with renewed energy and purpose. When he returned, he was met by a sullen group who believed they were about to be slaughtered by the beasts that hunted them. "Good news," John said. "We have a chance by moving ahead."

John told them quickly, quietly, and efficiently what they needed to do, how difficult it was for a brief time, and what they would see when they finally got through it. Hearing about the large cave and running water gave everyone renewed hope. They saw an opportunity to survive and they were going to reach for it like the brass ring on a carousel. When he finished, John said, "There's no time to waste.

Michael, it's a straight path through, so you lead us on, and I'll once again pick up the rear. And, Charles Clark, I need you back here with me. Now."

Clark, who had shoved his way to the front of the group, hesitated briefly, then moved to the back, still fearful of the captain's threat about mutiny.

"Listen to me, Clark," John said. "You're going to help me get this woman and her husband through the rough spots ahead. You understand me?"

"Perhaps our time is at an end, Captain," Allan said. "We would only slow you down. We could wait here, and I could have a go at those things. Maybe I could . . . distract them for a time, you know?"

John looked at Allan and could see the despair in his eyes, even in the darkness. He knew the future he and his wife faced, having had a parent succumb to the ravages of Alzheimer's years ago. He understood Allan's feelings, but he couldn't allow him to stay behind.

"No way Allan, we're doing this together, and everyone is getting through." He then looked at Charles and said, "And you're going to help, Clark."

Charles looked at Margaret, then Allan, and nodded in agreement, as if he had a choice. At first, they did fine keeping up with the rest of the group, even when they reached the point of having to bend at the waist. It got difficult after that. Allan was still strong, despite his advanced years, and could take care of himself. John and Charles were positioned on either side of Margaret, hauling her forward from a seated position before crawling forward on their own. Because of that, they were slower than the rest. When they had to lay down, they did so on their backs, and moved Margaret with much the same technique. After two tries, however, she panicked and screamed for her husband.

"Allan! Allan!"

"I'm right here, dear," he said, and reached out over John to grab her hand. John and Charles tried to catch their breath, while Allan continued to reassure Margaret.

"There's no need to get upset dear," Allan said. "I'm right here."

"I'm afraid, Allan," Margaret said. "Where are we?"

"We're playing a game, dear, and it's almost over. When we're done, we're going to see a lovely waterfall. Would you like that?"

Margaret calmed at his soothing voice. "Yes, I would. Are we almost there?"

"Yes dear, we're almost there. So, close your eyes and let John and Charles carry you to the waterfall, okay?"

"Well, if you say it's all right."

Margaret let go of Allan's hand.

"Margaret," John said, "let's count when we do this move together, shall we? I bet we can get to the waterfall in less than ten."

"Okay," she said.

John and Charles moved themselves, then grabbed Margaret's arms and moved her. "Two," they shouted. They repeated the move and said "three" together. By the time they got to "five," the ceiling seemed to rise. A few more pulls and they were able to stand.

"Allan, are we there yet?"

"Not yet, dear," Allan said, "but we're very close, just a little bit more."

A few more steps and they could hear voices. A few more still, and they emerged into the large cave. Everyone was resting, including Michael. John hurried to his first mate and huddled for a chat.

"I could hear the creatures, Michael," John said. "They took the bait and went into the other cave, but I'm not sure how far, and it won't be long before they come this way. We have some time, but not much. We need to find a way out of here."

"Right," said Michael. "Let's check out the waterfall and that fast-flowing river near the end of the cave."

John went to settle Allan and Margaret.

"We'll be all right Captain," Allan said. "You go do what you need to do."

"Where's Allan," Margaret said.

"I'm right here, dear," Allan said with his arm wrapped around his wife's shoulders.

"You're not Allan," she protested. "And where are the stars? Allan and I were out for a walk under the stars."

"It's really me, sweetheart," he said, as he buried his head on Margaret's shoulder. "And the sky is dark tonight, you see? The stars must be asleep, don't you think?"

John looked at Allan's forlorn face, patted him on the shoulder, and left with Michael. They hurried to the falls, which gushed from a hole in the roof of the cave, high in a corner that was not accessible at all. It flowed rapidly, like a small and swift river, polishing the smooth rock underneath it, into a smaller, side cavern that contained a good-sized pool of clear water. The pool had a constant eddy that twirled with the promise of movement out of there and into somewhere else.

"That water has to be going someplace, don't you think?" Michael asked.

"Yeah," John said. "But where? It could be a way out, or, it could be another easy path to our death. For all I know, it might even lead us into another group of those things that are chasing us. I'd hate to think of what would happen to us if we had to confront those creatures underwater."

"None of those sound like good options," Michael said.

"Let's search the rest of this cave," John said. "Maybe we'll find something else."

John and Michael walked the perimeter of the cave. It had round, smooth walls, was almost circular in shape, and boasted a twelve-foot-high ceiling. But there was no way out, not even a meager alternative consideration. They were trapped, like bugs in a petri dish. They could run around in circles all they liked, but there was simply no escape.

They dragged themselves back to the pool.

"We have three choices, as I see it," John said. "One, we go back, try to beat the creatures near the opening of this cave. Maybe then, some in the group would have a shot at getting through the melee and making it all the way back to where we originally started. I don't think that's likely to happen, though. And even if they did, then what? They'd never make it up the mountain. Two, we make a stand here. They're vicious, but it will take some time for them to squeeze their way in here. We may be able to pick them off one by one as they come through. Someone might even be able to make it past them in a break to freedom."

"Probably Charles Clark," Michael scoffed.

"And three," John said, "We do a quick exploration of that pool to see where it goes. If it leads somewhere and is swimmable, it may be our best hope."

"But John, what if some of these people can't swim?"

"If it's doable, we can help them through it," John said staring at the pool.

"Who's going to explore it?" Michael asked.

"I am," John said, kicking off his shoes. "I'm a better swimmer than you, and I can hold my breath a lot longer." John looked at his old friend. "Michael, if I'm not back in five minutes, get these people ready for battle."

The men shook hands and shared a hug. John took three deep breaths of air, then eased under the pool's surface. Michael turned the timer on his watch.

"Where's he going?" Charles Clark came up quietly behind Michael, making him jump.

"You shouldn't do that," Michael said. "It isn't good for your health."

"Sorry," Charles said in a way that showed he really wasn't.

"He's risking his life to find a way out of here," Michael said. "And if he's not back here in five minutes, we're going to have to fight our way out."

"How much time left?" Charles asked Michael.

Michael checked his watch. "He's been gone one and a half minutes. A normal person might start to panic about this time, but John is an excellent swimmer and diver."

When four minutes ticked by, Michael started to get nervous. He watched the glow-in-the-dark second hand sweep by rapidly, slowly bringing the minute hand into play. When his watch passed the five-minute mark, Michael scowled, licked his lips nervously, and bowed his head in silent prayer. The next few minutes of explaining their one other option to these people was going to be a challenge.

As he took a step towards the others, he heard a loud splash, and John stumbled out of the pool, breathing heavily.

John looked up at Michael and shook his head no. "I'm afraid I didn't see a way out. There might be one, but I'm just not sure," he said. "I came to a Y-shape in the tunnel and went to the bend on the right which had a stronger current, but it quickly narrowed. We'd never get everyone through it. I had no time to explore the other branch."

At that moment they heard a loud, vicious, angry howl.

"It's them," Michael said. "They must be entering the cave that will lead them straight to us."

Charles looked at the water and saw something. "Look," he said. Both men turned to the pool and saw intermittent bubbles coming to the surface. "You brought more of them here," Charles said to John. "They followed you, and you led them right to us. Now we'll have creatures coming at us from both directions."

He looked at John directly. "Dear God, what did you do?"

CHAPTER 16

RESCUE MISSION

Rain pelted the party of would-be rescuers, hitting them like buckshot as they darted from the pub to their parked vehicles. Robert was drenched before he managed to squeeze behind the wheel of his Rover. Jack dashed to his Subaru, fell behind the wheel, and wondered how in God's name he was going to see where he was going. Tim threw a bag into the back of the old Ford Transit, then climbed into the passenger seat. He and Marie were soaking wet, worrying if their vehicle would even start in this weather.

"What's in the bag?" Marie asked, distracted by the unbearable conditions.

"Some of my science equipment," Tim said. "In case I can get a sample of one of these creatures to analyze."

It sounded reasonable, given Tim's background. But something, perhaps the way Tim sounded when answering the question, gave Marie cause for doubt.

After a shaky startup, all three vehicles pulled away as one. Once at the top of the rise, not far from Robert's home, they drove off in different directions, united in wondering at the impossibility of the task that lay ahead. Roads throughout the island were not in the best of condition, even in fair weather. Paving was a luxury, and the few paved roads that littered the island were riddled with potholes, some sections even pulverized to near dust. Maintaining them regularly was an expense no one could justify, so, over time, they fell into a state of gradual disrepair. Most of the other roads were simply flattened earth, more oversized paths, really. Some were covered with bags of stone where appropriate to mitigate flooding and mudslides. Even though the roads were not in the best condition, and the weather was intolerable, each driver knew every inch of roadway on the island by heart. People would often comment, "I could drive these roads with my eyes closed, while bedding down for a nap." They were about to get the opportunity to test that theory.

***

Robert's path took him southwest to a lower slope of the island that overlooked the expanse between the island and the mainland. There were several clusters of homes, each spread out far enough to make his job foolhardy at best. Within each cluster were homes that could be reached by a short drive. He was in a near panic to get to them, as they were not far from the spot where Jack had seen his butchered cow. He had at least an hour of leisurely driving in good weather, but had no idea how long it would take him now. Since he was traversing the leeward side of the island, he prayed the severity of the storm would be somewhat lessened.

***

Jack drove towards his own home. It was more centrally located off the main spine of the island, along with many other homes that usually enjoyed the fair winds and beautiful scenery that could be had in all directions. Homes there were spread further apart, meaning there weren't as many for him to warn and investigate at a clean sweep, so he hoped he could get help spreading the word from his friends. He would be passing his own property first, and he shook at the memory of what he had seen there. He hoped he'd be able to reach his neighbors before it was too late.

***

Marie and Tim took the road on the windward side of the island. The going could only be described as a slow crawl. The wind howled and buffeted their vehicle hard enough to make their teeth chatter.

"This van is shaking worse than that earthquake," Tim said.

"Right," Marie said, almost afraid to talk, lest it disturb her laser-focused attention to the road.

"Sorry, Marie, I need to talk or my head's going to pop."

Marie nodded, but kept her eyes glued ahead. Tim picked up a roughly drawn map of the houses they were to visit.

"No need for a map," Marie said. "I know every house on this island and where they are, which should help us get there quickly."

Nonetheless, they inched their way along the dirt and stone roads, blinded by the torrential downpour and vicious winds that impeded their meager progress.

***

Robert knew he was close. There was a grouping of Scots Pine that marked the turnoff from the dirt road into a deep vale, which would take him to the homes he sought. He saw the pines bending from the wind, near horizontal to the ground, as if pointing the way downhill.

He crept his way along the curved roadway, meandering slowly over bumps and across scattered ruts. The wind pounded the side of his car, sounding like a herd of cattle trying to get in. Rain fell in sheets, blinding his approach to the gathering of modest homes spread out below him.

As soon as he rounded the downward slope, he gained the protection of the natural bluff, which, although it did not give him complete shelter from the storm, acted as a buffer to the intense winds that chased him downhill. The homes below were nestled along the lower reaches of the massive palisade, shielding them from the worst of the northerlies that accompanied major storms.

He got a break, too, from the blinding rain that sprayed his windshield. It still came in force, but it, too, was thwarted by the natural umbrella cover of the craggy landscape and overhanging precipice above. The geography helped to push the rain and wind outwards, where it hit homes hardest that were built further south towards the shoreline. It fell with such massive strength, and was powered by such incredible winds, those homes could not even be seen from Robert's vantage point.

It took Robert far too long to negotiate the switchback nature of the access road. At this rate, he feared, he wouldn't be able to reach many homes before having to turn back to the pub for safety. Driving under these conditions was risky at best. Under cover of darkness, it would become impossible. Not for the first time, he wondered if this was indeed a fool's errand.

Robert finally reached the driveway of the first house, belonging to the Taylors. Now there was a house in sight he slowed even more, afraid of what he might find. He nervously scanned the area. Jack's description of the beasts refused to leave him, especially as it related to those poor hikers. To think of it filled him with cold, heart-stopping terror. He pulled his car near the front of the house and peered out his windshield. The outer screen door was loose. The wind continuously grabbed it and banged it hard against the house, again and again, whipping it open, then slamming it shut. Robert jumped every time it made contact. At a quick glance, the house appeared dark and deserted. No lights were on. No warm glow from within, or friendly sounds emanating from the living room or kitchen. Nothing at all to reflect there was a happy family safely inside. Robert's hackles were raised as he approached the entry. He grabbed hold of the hammering screen door to silence it. It practically fell into his grasp. The wind had attacked the door so much it was loose enough to come off its hinges. He laid it on the ground, only to have it tumble and blow away in the fierce wind. He paused at the front door, gently placed his ear to it, and listened. He heard nothing. He reached out and turned the loose doorknob. The door opened with ease. He stepped inside and gently closed it behind him, all the while ready to bolt for his car, if necessary. The floor creaked underneath his heavy feet, the sound echoing throughout the silent home, announcing his entry to anyone or anything that may be alive to hear.

Robert shouted into the void. "Hello?"

No one answered.

He crept along slowly, shotgun at the ready. He moved through each room one small step at a time, limping his way to the rear of the building. When he got to the kitchen, he noticed the broken dishes and strewn silverware. There were splotches of water on the floor, and the back door was gone, ripped off its hinge, allowing wind and rain to enter the house unimpeded. A trail of smudged blood made its way out the back door, as if something had been butchered on the kitchen table, then hastily dragged from the house. Robert moved towards the open gap that was once a doorway and peered out into the rear yard.

There were two of them, and they were feasting on the corpses of Ronald and Joan Taylor. At least that's who Robert assumed they were. There wasn't enough of the couple left for the casual observer to clearly identify. He stared for a moment in awe and fear. He couldn't take his eyes off the horrific scene and couldn't make his legs move to get out of there. The slurping sounds and cesspool smell that wafted over him caused his face to involuntarily scrunch in disgust. Still, he could not move.

One of the things paused in its assault on the lifeless body, looked up, and gazed at Robert with hungry eyes. It rose from the ground, blood, guts, and goo still dribbling from its bloodied jaws. It fanned its claws and raised its arms to a ninety-degree angle, all the while staring at Robert. It took two long strides in Robert's direction, its webbed feet slapping the rain-soaked earth with a loud smack. A low, guttural sound fell from its wet, dripping mouth.

The mounting fear that had grown since he'd entered the house fled Robert in a heartbeat. It was replaced by an intense anger he hadn't felt since he served in the Korean War. He had been a young lad in combat then, and he saw many of his mates die in front of him. His mind went completely blank, and any fear of losing his own life simply disappeared. It was replaced by an anger-fueled calm that completely overtook him and guided his every action. His sole focus became one of revenge.

Robert lifted his shotgun and fired both barrels into the center mass area of the creature. The blast lifted the being at least two feet off the ground and planted its dead body flat on its back, where it came to rest atop the red-smeared, wet grass. Before the other creature had a chance to react, Robert slapped two more rounds into the empty chambers, raised the shotgun and blew its head off. He removed the empty shells, replaced them with two fresh ones, and slammed the gun shut. At first, he could only hear his own heavy breathing as it echoed throughout his skull. He caught his breath and reentered the house.

Suddenly he heard a noise. The front door was kicked open and smacked against the inside wall. Robert raised his shotgun and moved swiftly towards the front of the house. He entered the living room and saw the opened door, now hanging on by a thread. Robert heard wet steps in the dining room across the entry hall. They were approaching the living room, where he stood still, straining to hear more. As he approached the front door foyer, Robert placed his hand on the trigger. He took one long leap into the opening, ready to fire.

***

Jack was only one kilometer from his own home when his Subaru hit a deep rut. It teetered on two tires, wobbling back and forth, and he briefly thought he would come out of it all right. He thought wrong. It rolled over twice, kicking up mud and water in its wake. The car spun like a top on its roof before coming to a dead stop in an open field.

Jack was dizzy and disoriented. He hung upside down, held by his seatbelt. Blood rushed to his head, which pounded in sync with each beat of his heart. He did a quick mental check on the pain he felt, as well as any possible injuries he may have sustained. Besides his headache, Jack felt soreness across his chest from the seatbelt, and a numbness down his left arm. One glance at it told him it was dislocated. He struggled to reach the driver-side door pocket with his right hand to retrieve a hand-held safety device that could cut through his seatbelt. He screamed with intense shoulder pain in the attempt. His face was pressed onto the upturned roof and the seatbelt twisted his body away from the door he needed to access. Jack looked to his left and saw that water was pouring into the car from the broken passenger side window. His side of the car was slightly downhill, and the water began to accumulate under and around his face. With a dislocated shoulder and incoming water, Jack knew he was in trouble.

He was breathing rapidly and feared passing out. He closed his eyes and breathed more slowly to try and calm himself. Water cascaded into the car and tickled his cheek. It was cold, and he shivered, sending fresh pain down his left arm. He lifted his head slightly, turned, took air through the corner of his mouth, and stretched his right arm and hand towards the driver-side door. Pain vibrated down his left arm and he knew he had maybe one chance at success. He extended his right arm further, and his hand brushed against a loose object. He screamed in pain, grabbed the object, and swung his body so he rested on his right shoulder. His right hand gripped the device he needed. He wept from the pain that coursed through his body, but there was no time for self-pity. He slid his right hand in front of him and sliced into the seat belt. At the final cut, he fell onto the overturned roof. The resulting pain almost caused him to black out, but the cold water he fell into helped to keep him alert, if only for a few critical moments. Jack crawled on his side towards the broken passenger window and slid out of the vehicle. He stood on unstable feet and bended knees, leaning onto his now useless car.

Jack knew what he had to do next and did not look forward to it. He grabbed his left wrist with his right hand. He extended his dislocated left arm straight out in front of him, and with a loud scream, grabbed it with his other hand and yanked it forward. He heard the pop above his own screaming and knew it was back in place. He immediately leaned over and vomited, but the cool driving rain kept him from fainting. When he caught his breath, Jack took off his belt and made an impromptu sling for his damaged shoulder. He knew exactly where he was and decided to head for his own home on foot. If those creatures were no longer there, he could get some first aid help from his own supplies and retrieve their spare vehicle, an automatic Subaru 4x4 his wife mostly used. He grabbed his shotgun from the car and took off at a fast walk, the shotgun slung over his right shoulder.

Through the rain, wind, and fast-moving fog, Jack soon saw the entry to his drive. He stepped onto his property and the fear returned. He saw no signs of life anywhere. His eyes darted in all directions. The front doors were wide open to the storm, moving wildly with the explosive wind. Jack snuck up to his own house, wary of anything that moved. The wind and rain nearly knocked him to the ground, he was so weak. He leaned forward, scanning the area around both sides of his home. Seeing nothing, he stepped onto the front porch. He tucked the gun's stock into his hip, pointed the barrel ahead, and let his gun lead the way inside. He tip-toed inside with trepidation. He heard nothing, but it was hard to hear anything over the shrill wind and drumming rain, which soaked him to the bone. Each step through the house brought him closer to the idea of facing a creature hell-bent on tearing him to pieces. Given his current condition, he felt he was not up for that battle. The thought of those things attacking his family, however, brought a rise of anger and sense of retribution. He walked more forcefully, listening intently for any sound but the weather. There were clues they had been there. The floor was wet and the kitchen destroyed, with food remnants splattered onto the floor and other surfaces. The rear door was askew, fully torn away from the house in one spot and partially attached to one of its hinges in another. It swung violently in the wind. A quick peek into the rear yard showed no lurking creatures.

Jack turned and made his way to the stairway. He paused to listen. He heard nothing and saw that the stairs were not wet at all. He figured they would be if those things had made their way to their bedrooms. He continued upstairs and into the bathroom. He snatched a bottle of Tylenol and swallowed four pills with a slug of tap water. He then found a lightweight towel and fashioned a sturdier sling for his left arm, wincing from the residual pain. As he came out of the bathroom, Jack saw a shadow cross the front entry.

***

Marie and Tim approached their first house. It was hard to make it out in the whirling weather that tumbled around them, but based on memory, Marie was sure it belonged to the Jenkins family—two parents plus two children, a boy and a girl, ages ten and eleven. The two-story, brick home looked solid. Between flashes of egg-white, foggy mist and wicked, battering rain, they could barely make out the entry. Tim grabbed his gun and went for the car door handle.

"Wait," Marie cautioned. "Something's not right."

"What is it?" Tim asked.

"I'm not sure, exactly." Marie paused. Her forehead scrunched and her eyes remained unblinking. Her subconscious was trying to tell her something. Something she witnessed when they drove up, but she couldn't recall what it was. Her deeper mind whispered caution. "But it's something important," she said. "We need to be very careful."

"Roger that," Tim said.

They both made sure their guns were loaded and on safety. They stayed close together as they moved towards the house.

"Try the front door, Tim."

Tim reached out and gently grabbed the handle. He turned it very slowly to the left. "Locked," he said. Tim tried to peek in through the front window, but the curtains were drawn. He leaned into Marie. "Let's go around back."

They turned the corner at the left side of the house and proceeded towards the rear yard. The powerful winds continued to be a hindrance in their ability to hear one another. They no sooner got a word out than the storm grasped it and flung it into the turbulent atmosphere. Marie squeezed Tim's shoulder.

"Tim, that's it," she said, pointing to a location in the rear yard.

"What are you talking about?"

"When we came in the drive," Marie continued. "I saw something that didn't look right, but I quickly forgot it because the windy fog obscured it from view in seconds."

"What is it?"

Marie pointed into the recesses of the rear yard. "There!"

There was a mass of wind-driven dense fog whipping around the yard, and all Tim could see were pools of swirling mist. The winds shifted, and for a brief moment there was an image of bed linens hanging on a clothesline. It was gone in a flash, a photo slide posted for a heartbeat of a second before being covered over in a white shroud. Tim scanned the area, confused.

"No one would leave their bed linens out in a storm like this," Marie said. "Something is definitely not right."

They both raised their guns and thumbed off the safety. They walked cautiously over to the clothesline, looking in all directions, waiting for danger to emerge at any second. The winds shifted yet again, and this time, they received a good view of the area, which lay about ten paces ahead of them. There were three sections of hanging items. The first two contained bed sheets snapping in the wind, the third, clothing items, all of which any sensible Scot would have brought into the house long ago. Some in the second row, they could clearly see, were covered in streaks of bright red blood.

"Wait here," Tim said as he held his hand out to stop Marie's forward movement. She pushed his hand out of the way and continued forward, shoving sheets aside with the point of her gun. Tim trailed quickly behind her. When she got to the last blood splattered section, Marie used her gun to move one flapping sheet completely aside.

A body, or least that's what she thought it was, was shriveled and curled up on the lawn in front of her. Pieces of the corpse were loosely thrown about the area, mostly inedible bits. It resembled a disorganized pile of rodent roadkill long after the buzzards had their way. Marie suspected it was Marla Jenkins, but her only clue was a blood-stained, shredded housedress. She turned quickly, pointed her gun away from Tim, and moved towards the house, a stark, blank look on her face.

"Follow me," she said.

Strong wind gusts moved more of the fog and showed a clear path to the rear door.

"Oh my God," Marie said.

"What is it?" Tim said.

"The rear door is wide open."

Marie led them over to the back entrance to the house. She peered in, and scanned the kitchen.

"Marie."

"What?"

"I . . . I just don't want you to see the children if they're in there."

Marie stood still for a moment, staring into space. "All right, fine," she said, more softly this time. "I'll stay here at the doorway as a guard, while you search the house. If anything comes out of that mist, I'm going to shoot it, so come running if I do."

Marie watched Tim go through the house and turn to go up the stairs. She dragged over an upturned kitchen table and placed it across the doorway. She then took up position behind it and kept her eyes moving from left to right, looking for anomalies, as she heard Tim climb the creaky staircase.

****

There were three bedrooms on the upper floor. Tim found Sean Jenkins and his two kids on the master bedroom floor, although there wasn't much left to help identify them. It looked like Sean tried to protect his kids with a golf club. Bloodied, bent, and broken, it was lying next to Sean's remains. The attack probably came so fast Sean had no idea what was happening and couldn't get to his gun in time. All of that crossed Tim's mind in seconds. He then flew down the stairs he had come up, and once he hit the bottom floor, he dry heaved until he choked. Marie came running when she heard him clamber down and gag. She patted his back and eased him up. He managed to get to his feet, but his legs gave out and he had to lean on the wall for support.

"It's them," he managed to say. "They're upstairs." Marie started to go up, but Tim said, "No," and grabbed her arm. "You mustn't," he said, wiping the drool from his chin. "Please don't go up, it's too horrible."

Marie shook off Tim's hold and brushed past him. She took the stairs two at a time. At the top she walked right into the main bedroom. Her gasp could be heard downstairs. She came out of the room and to the lower level much slower than she went up. She was pale and lifeless. The appalling scene she witnessed deadened her stare. She found Tim now leaning against the banister. He reached out for her.

A loud animal screech filled the house, and they heard the table Marie had dragged across the kitchen doorway being banged and battered to bits.

CHAPTER 17

A MAELSTROM OF DEATH: ROBERT

Robert heard a soft shuffling noise coming in his direction from the opposite side of the foyer. He dragged his game leg forward, planted it firmly, then held his ground. Whatever was making that noise was only a few moments away. Robert swiftly leaned forward into the open space and came face to face with one of the Taylors' neighbors, Jim Cross. Both had raised their guns simultaneously, holding them up in a firing position. Both had reacted on instinct and placed their finger on the trigger. Both had begun to squeeze gently. Fortunately, in a split second of recognition, both hesitated to shoot, thus avoiding what would have been a catastrophe of friendly fire. Each exhaled, shaking at the near prospect of killing someone they knew out of sheer panic.

"Sorry, Jim," Robert said, wiping his forehead of nervous sweat. "I just dispatched two of those things out back, behind the house. I'm afraid the Taylors . . ." He didn't need to finish.

Jim shook his head, but there was no time for grieving. "I need to see," Jim said. He walked out the back, through the driving rain, and up to the creatures to get a good look. He then saw the pile of human debris that was once his neighbors. He bent over at the waist and vomited twice before staggering back into the house.

"Robert. What the hell are these things? Where did they come from?"

"I don't have a lot of answers for you, Jim, but I can tell you this. They may have come from below the island, perhaps in the underwater sea caves, where the earthquake released them somehow. That's what our scientist friend thinks, anyway."

"How many are there?" Jim asked.

"Too many."

"I heard the gun blasts over here. Nothing else before that because of the storm. I wish I had, though. Maybe I could have done something," Jim said.

"No, you couldn't," Robert said. "You may have been killed yourself just for trying, so don't even think of it, Jim. Where is your family?"

"I locked Barbara and the boys in our house before coming over. We have storm shutters on our windows, so that helps a bit masking the storm noise. Barbara knows how to shoot well and has her own gun. But after seeing what I just saw, I need to get back to them all. Now."

"I'll come with you to make sure all is well, then move on down the line," Robert said.

The two climbed into Robert's Land Rover, shaking off rainwater like a pair of wet dogs. Robert jammed the key home, turned the ignition, and fishtailed across the wet grass towards the Cross residence. He slid to a hard stop not far from the entrance, leaving a fifteen-foot trail of muddy tracks in his wake. Both men jumped from the car and ran to the front door. All looked quiet with no signs of damage. Jim explained he had devised a secret code for knocking on the door that would let his wife know it was him. He reached out with his right hand and rapped: three hard, fast thumps followed by two hard, slow ones.

Nothing. No response. He clicked the safety off his gun and tried again. Still nothing. He looked at Robert and nodded to his left. "I'll take the right side," he shouted over the rain.

There were no signs of a struggle, as yet, and no tracks of any sort, though it would be difficult to see anything in the raging storm. There were no scratches on the outside walls of the house or window shutters. Both men turned the corner and approached the rear of the house at the same time. Guns were up and at the ready.

A wind gust blew off Robert's hat, but he didn't flinch. His coat flapped around him, and the rain soaked his bare head, but his eyes remained steely, fixed on any suspicious movement. Jim held his gun up, but his arms began to shake. His eyes darted back and forth across the yard. He felt his way around the backside of the house to the rear door. Everything looked secure. He was so intent on examining the door for signs of a forced entry he barely noticed Robert come up behind him.

"Looks okay," Robert said.

Jim jumped at the sound. "Yes," he said, relieved that it was Robert behind him. Jim reached out, hesitated for a moment, then rapped the back door with the same code as he used on the front. No response, again. He looked at Robert and licked his lips. "I'm going to try once more, and then I'm going to kick in the door."

He reached up slowly, curled his fist, and paused. The door opened with a whoosh. His wife, Barbara, stood with a raised gun of her own. She quickly lowered it when she saw who it was. Jim and Robert entered swiftly, closing and locking the door behind them. Jim placed his gun against the wall and hugged his wife.

"Where were you? I knocked on the front, but no one answered," Jim said, trying, but failing, not to betray his panic.

His three children—David, twelve, Paul, fourteen, and Nicola—stood behind their mother. Nicola answered.

"We were all in here, Da, and never heard the knocking. Not until you knocked on this door."

Jim blew a sigh of relief. "You're all safe, and that's all that matters."

"Jim, you need to get your family out of here and straight to the Royal Oak Pub in Blackpool," Robert said. "It's pretty secure there."

"Thanks, Robert, but I think we can handle things here."

"There may be a great many of these creatures crawling about, and there's safety in numbers if we're to mount any sort of defense," Robert said. "A few of us are out warning as many families as we can to get to the pub in a hurry. You'd be wise to do so. You've not only seen what these creatures look like, you've seen what they can do."

Jim hesitated, then looked at his frightened family. "Thanks for your concern, Robert," he said, "but we're well-versed in how to use a gun, and I think we'll feel safer hunkered down here at home."

"Alright then," Robert said. "Not what I'd advise, but the best of luck to you. I'm going down the road to the handful of homes that are nearer the water before I turn back. They're closer to a branch of underwater caves down there, and if that's where these beasts are coming from, they're going to need some help."

Jim leaned in close. "Robert, be safe. I'll not be coming with you down there. I'd normally help, you know that, but I must care for my wife and kids, and I'll not be leaving them alone again. Not after what I've seen."

"I understand."

The two men shook hands. Robert nodded to Barbara and the children, then left. He jogged to his car in the brutal rain, hopped in, and slowly drove down the hill to the houses nestled among a grove of Scots pine near the water's edge. Even under cover of the trees that acted as canopy for the road, Robert was pelted by rain and buffeted by wind. He gripped the steering wheel tightly, leaning over it to see through the covered windshield. His wipers were useless. He had to move slowly or he'd run off the road and crash into a tree. Even at the crawling pace he traveled, Robert dodged a few tree trunks that seemed to leap out in front of him, as if of their own accord.

Finally, Robert rounded a bend in the road. Even through the cluster of trees and over the din of the storm, he detected the boom of gunfire. Once he cleared the forest, the houses lay out in front of him in a tight formation as they unfolded like a fanned-out deck of cards downhill to the sea.

People must have been caught by surprise, Robert thought, now able to see the action unfolding below him. Folks were running pell-mell through the neighborhood, darting between houses and bumping into each other in the confusion. In the panic, some were raising their guns and shooting at anything that moved. They would kill two or three of the creatures and try to reload, but then be overwhelmed by the sheer number of the beasts. Blood spurted everywhere from creatures being shot and people being eviscerated. Doors were torn off homes and beasts rushed in. Whole families were attacked in the streets and heads rolled off bodies with the swipe of a broad claw. It was as if he set foot in an insane abattoir where the butchers had gone amok.

Robert couldn't tell how many there were, but he was sure he'd underestimated the extent of the threat. He drove his car to flatter ground and jumped out to help. His leg immediately gave way to a sudden shot of pain. He righted himself and ran with a heavy limp towards a pod of creatures. They were backing a man into the side of a house while he tried to reload his gun. Robert shot two of them in the back, jamming ammunition into his shotgun as he moved forward, then he mowed down two more. The man he tried to rescue was able to fire his gun once more before being covered by two creatures and eaten while he stood, his painful scream a frightening death knell to the gruesome scene unfolding before Robert.

Robert's chest heaved and his heartbeat drummed with an irregular rhythm. He knew he was out of breath. He staggered back and almost fell from the combination of fatigue, fear, and the weakness in his bum leg. One creature and then another turned to face him.

Robert held his ground. If his time on this earth was about to end, so be it. He silently vowed he would go down fighting. He stood tall, putting most of his weight on his good leg, and loaded his gun as the creatures came at him. He barely noticed them through the fury of the storm, how they snarled and dripped with the blood of their victims, or how they opened and closed their claws in anticipation of their next meal. They came at him rapidly, or perhaps he was much slower than he wanted to believe.

They were mere feet from him when Robert, hit hard by the wind and rain, raised his gun and fired. The first one flew back from the blast, a see-through hole punched in the middle of its chest. The second one almost knocked the gun aside as it swiped its claw at Robert's head. The gun went off, hitting the beast in its left shoulder. It swung its other claw at Robert even as it fell to the ground, tearing strips of flesh from Robert's left arm and leaving that appendage immobile, hanging loosely by his side.

His one arm was now incapacitated and bleeding freely from the blow. Robert could stand no longer and fell to the ground. With the little energy he had left, he opened his gun and loaded it with his right hand. He then placed the barrel on his knees while he slammed it shut, aimed it at the creature when it struggled to get off the ground, and calmly blew its head off. He then lay back in the grass, allowing the rain to hit him in the face and cleanse his blood-streaked arm and hand.

Robert was woozy and fatigued, the effects of his injury overcoming him. He feared he would pass out, that perhaps they'd pounce on his weakened body and eat him while he struggled to remain conscious. But he didn't pass out. He was roused by a shrill scream. It was a young girl, by the sound of it, and she was not far from where he lay. He thought, perhaps, he was dreaming, that it wasn't real, that it was a figment of a fevered imagination that would soon expire and blow away, dispersed by the wind. Then he heard the guns again. Guns that were still going off like violent background music to the deadly play he was in.

Robert shook his head to regain his senses. The gunshots he had heard were now fewer in number, meaning fewer people left to fire them. The girl's screams were getting louder. Closer. Perhaps it wasn't a dream. Perhaps it was all very real, and the little girl was in trouble. He struggled to rise. He was in great pain now. He thought of his comfortable porch overlooking the sunset with a glass of McCallan, neat. He could almost taste the warmth spreading through his body, and his eyes nearly closed again at the comforting thought of it all.

Another scream. More urgent this time. He groaned as he pushed himself over to one side and saw a young girl about eight years old running for her life.

Once a soldier, always a soldier, his mind echoed. It was something he was told time and again by his drill sergeant so many years ago.

Get on your feet, soldier, he told himself. He achingly pushed himself up, using his gun as a crutch. He groaned with the incredible effort it took to perform such a simple act. *Focus, dammit!* It seemed like it took forever, but he was soon upright and vaguely aware of what was happening around him.

He was able to make out the young girl, screaming and covered in blood. *Her own?* She came to a stop in the middle of the road, not far from where Robert stood, with her hands pressed firmly on her ears, trying desperately to drown out the horror that enveloped her. Her shrill screams roused him to action. They also attracted several more creatures that were coming around the side of a nearby home, now heading in her direction.

Robert wasted no time. He reached into his pocket to discover he had only one round of ammunition left. Damn, he had forgotten to jam more into his pocket when he fled his car in such a hurry. Once the gun was loaded, he gripped it with his right hand and loped over to the girl, dragging his right leg beside him. One of the creatures was getting close to the girl, but Robert got there first. He scooped her up with his uninjured right arm that also held his gun. The girl wrapped herself around her rescuer like plastic wrap on a glass bowl, burying her face deep into his neck. He raised his gun and fired, hitting the creature nearest them.

Robert ran as fast as his deadened legs would carry him, as if his life depended on it, because surely it did. He ran like the Victoria Cross recipient he was, with a will that pushed him on and a strength he no longer had. For a brief moment, he was back in Korea, running with a comrade over his shoulders out of a village that was on fire behind him. It boosted his adrenaline, and he was able to put some distance between himself and the creatures that followed them.

Adrenaline is easily acquired in combat, but unfortunately easily expended. It can fade as quickly as it came, leaving the host even more tired than before. His Land Rover, he could see, was still too far away. His legs were heavy, his anguished steps plodding, as if his shoes were made of cement. His raspy breathing came in short, rapid bursts and burned his lungs deeply. His bad leg ached with a pain that screamed of the sad reality he approached. He was going to fall hard and soon, long before reaching his car. It was a simple truth that could not be altered. He stopped still and bent over, immediately overtaken with staggering pain.

"What's your name, child?" he whispered as he set the girl down. She had a blank stare and didn't answer. He shook her.

"What's your name, lass?"

The girl rubbed her eyes and responded. "Anna."

"Okay, Anna, listen to me now. I'll hold them off. You run as fast as you can to the red house at the top of the hill and don't stop or turn around until you get there. Bang on the door until they let you in, then tell them this: "There are too many of them, and you have to go to the pub."

Anna stared at him.

"Can you do that for me?" he asked.

Anna nodded.

"Good girl," he said. "Now, run. Fast as you can."

Anna ran up the hill, pausing only when she reached the top of the road, and turned.

Robert gripped his empty gun, squared his feet, and waited. The creatures, many of them, came straight at him. It was their odor that hit him first, and he nearly staggered from the smell. He turned to see Anna waiting at the top of the hill. He waved her on, then turned to face the onslaught.

Once a soldier . . .

Robert stood resolute and faced his enemy. He raised his only weapon and swung wildly killing the first two beasts that rushed him with the power of his swing. His gun splintered from the impact, so he stabbed two more with the sharp points of wood that broke from the stock. When that failed, he used the gun barrel as a cudgel, smashing a couple of heads and faces, even as they swiped at and cut him with their claws, leaving trails of blood down both his arms and legs. He kept swinging until he could no longer hold the barrel, then he dropped it on the ground next to him. His arms were weary from the fight. He could no longer lift them. He fell to his knees as a wave of creatures approached him, snarling, flashing their pointy-edged teeth and flexing their claws. The beasts paused and slowly encircled him. They could smell defeat. One of them stepped up to the prostrate body of Robert. His legs were unable to lift him, and his arms hung pathetically at his side. The beast bared its sharpened row of teeth in a deathly grin, salivating down its chest in anticipation.

Robert, exhausted and groggy from fatigue, lifted his head to face his foe. "Come on, then," he shouted. "You'll find this meat tougher than most, you filthy bastard."

He then smiled the smile of a seasoned warrior, knowing that even as he fell, the girl who needed his help in her life and death moment of need was on her way to safety.

CHAPTER 18

A MAELSTROM OF DEATH: JACK

From the landing at the top of the stairs, Jack watched two creatures enter the front of his home. Their smell wafted upwards, filling the house with a tangible, malodorous discharge that made him sick to his stomach. He paused, holding his breath, and waited to see which way they would go. The more he thought of these smelly beasts wandering through his home, tearing into whatever food was stored in the kitchen, the angrier he got. He knew it was reckless, and, more importantly, stupid, but he moved out further on the landing so they could see him.

He whistled, then shouted, "Hey, you with the smell of shite!"

Both creatures looked up at once and drooled. Jack could swear they were smiling at him. The first one took a long step up, clearing three stairs at once, with its long, webbed feet. It flexed its equally webbed hands, as if it could imagine ripping the intestines from the noisy meal ahead. Jack let it take another trio of stairs and get halfway up before he blew a hole clean through it. It flew back from the impact, banging into the other one, knocking it to the ground as well. The second one surprised Jack, however. It slithered like a snake, moving around, then over the top of the first one, and crawled up the staircase towards Jack, moving from side to side instead of standing upright.

Jack tried to shoot, but his gun jammed. He darted across the landing and into the bedroom. He kicked the door shut, then locked it. He backed his way towards the window and tried desperately to un-jam his gun. The creature smashed into the door at full force, splintering it and causing it to break free from the hinges. Jack glanced at the window. It was locked. He looked at the creature again. He opened and shut the barrel once more and fired. It worked this time, but he knew it wasn't a clean shot. He winged the creature hard, nearly tearing its right arm off. It staggered from the impact, and Jack took the opportunity to spin around, unlock the window with his one good hand, open it, and roll out onto the rooftop. The thing righted itself and pursued him. It reached out the window with its good claw and barely missed rending the skin on Jack's back. Jack was now exposed to the full fury of the storm. The wind howled and the rain fell in sheets, muffling most other sounds, but Jack could clearly hear the scraping of the rooftop shingles behind him, shredded by the frustrated creature trailing him.

Jack slid down the roof to the gutter, grabbed the gutter with his good hand while holding on to the gun with the injured one, then threw his body over the side. He did not dare take the time to look behind him. He swung into space, realized he was about halfway to the ground, then let go. He dropped the gun, which landed on a bush, and fell onto the soft earth with bent knees to absorb the impact. It helped only minimally.

Jack fought through the pain as he grabbed his gun. He could hear the beast on the roof moving towards the edge. More of the creatures on the ground were coming closer. They must have smelled him and screamed to attract others in their hunt. Jack's arm throbbed, his ankle was slightly sprained from the jump, and his adrenaline was wearing thin. He stood with great effort and thought of his beautiful wife and his two boys, Gavin and Allan. There was so much yet he wanted to teach them, things to share with his wife. He lifted his eyes and could see figures moving in the mist, heading in his direction. He briefly thought, *what chance do I have?*

He heard a sudden crash behind him and turned, instinctively raising his gun. It was the one on the roof. It had fallen awkwardly and howled in pain. Without a thought, Jack pointed his gun directly into the face of the beast and fired, killing it instantly. That sudden act of violence shook him out of his lethargy and focused him on what he needed to do to survive. Despite the wind, rain, and swirling fog, he knew his own property well and ran straight for the space where his wife parked her car.

When he reached it, he threw his shotgun in the back seat, jumped behind the steering wheel, jammed his key in the ignition and punched the accelerator. He spun nearly a hundred-and-eighty degrees across his lawn and flew towards the main road, where he banged into two creatures with a loud thud. He dared not stop to check, thinking no sane human would be out in weather like this, then getting the irony of that thought a moment later.

He arrived at the edge of his own property and knocked down the sign that marked the entrance in his wild spree for freedom. He knew he should turn left and make his way back to the pub. He was injured, after all, and wondered if he'd be a help to anyone anyway. But he wasn't raised that way. And these people were his neighbors and friends, people deserving of anything he could do to help. He turned right.

***

Angus McCleod was a widower of five years, prone to bouts of depression over his still fresh and devastating loss of the love of his life.

He and his wife Martha had a storied romance, one built on a passionate love for one another in the pursuit of a happy and successful life. They worked hand in glove, side by side, ever increasing their land holdings and cattle herd through a careful combination of hard work, harder savings, and sound investments. The spirit of his dead wife was in every parcel of land, every cow that grazed there, and every beam of the house they built with their own two hands. He thought of her often and, if truth be known, would frequently sit by the fireplace and openly speak to her. The simple act of doing so would serve to calm him and help him sleep. He never failed to wish her a good night before bedding down for the evening.

The McCleod home was built on a raised bluff overlooking the northern coast and out to the North Sea. On a clear day, he could also look in the other direction and get a view of the distant land mass of mainland Scotland. *Today, is not such a day*, he thought. The wind, fog, and rain made for a wild storm, which made it impossible to see anything clearly, let alone the mainland. It was the kind of day best spent indoors, warming your feet next to a raging fire.

Angus had just returned from an attempted visit to his neighbors to the west. Since they were downhill from him and more prone to suffer the damages of an intense storm, he wanted to check on them. Unfortunately, the road was completely washed out and there was no way to get by it. Not until the storm lessened. So, he returned home with the thought of trying again later. As soon as he got inside, he went to the den and built a nice fire. He poured himself a scotch and plopped into his favorite leather chair.

A shadow passed across the wall as he did, and there was something wrong with it. Angus wasn't really focused, so it wasn't evident at first, but his subconscious simply wouldn't let it go. It became one of those moments that nags at you, needling your brain with an insistent twitch. The kind of thing that makes the hair on the back of your neck stand on end, warning you of danger, yet failing to rise to the surface to tell you exactly what the problem is.

Angus's seat was a recliner, which he pushed back so he could raise his feet to the flames. Soon his body warmed and his eyelids got droopy. He was about to nod off when that nagging part of his brain finally got through. *Wait,* it warned, *that shadow you saw, something was off.*

Angus reacted slowly at first. He tried to clear away the cobwebs and think. In another minute, he sat up, as the realization of what he had seen struck him. Had he been between the fire and the wall, he could have assumed the shadow was his. That was natural, something you learn as a child, something you accept without another thought. But that's not where he had been. He was on the other side of the flames.

"It wasn't mine, was it, Martha?" he whispered to his deceased wife. "And if not mine, then whose?"

Angus shoved himself off the recliner and looked out the window to the rear yard. The curtain had not been drawn, and though there was a storm, some ambient light squeezed through the mess outside. *Was it a cloud,* he wondered, *a trick of the fog, perhaps?*

"No," he whispered again. "That shadow had human shape, didn't it?"

He moved to the gun cabinet, reached into his pocket for the key, and was about to put the key in the lock when the back door crashed inward.

Two monstrous creatures lumbered through the opening, arms extended and ready to slaughter whatever was within reach. They dragged the wind and rain inside with them, making a mess of the immediate interior. Angus looked up with a combination of shock and awe. Long ago, after his wife died, he'd stopped being fearful of anything. As far as he was concerned, he had just been biding his time on earth until he could join his wife, so on this earth there was nothing at all he needed to fear.

"Get the hell out of my house, you smelly bastards," he shouted.

Angus reacted more from instinct than a careful and meticulous assessment of the situation. He sensed he'd never unlock the gun cabinet in time, so he reached down for the fireplace poker and charged. The creatures were ready, and their survival hunting instincts directed their actions. Their reach widened, they bared their claws and fangs, dripping fresh mucus from their sharp teeth onto the already wet floor. With a loud roar they attacked.

But Angus was quick. And fearless. With the metal weapon in hand, he raced to meet the uninvited guests to his home, hoping to send them back to whatever hell they crawled out from. It was only a narrow opening from the back foyer into the living room, giving Angus a slight technical advantage. The first creature to push its way through reached outward with its clawed and webbed hands, then lunged, trying to remove Angus's head. Angus dropped, then thrusted the poker upwards, driving it through the neck of the beast. The force of his movement helped to drive the first creature into the second, propelling them out the way they'd come into his house. They all tumbled to the ground. Angus leaped onto the second creature, burrowing the poker into its face repeatedly until it stopped breathing.

He stood slowly, his breaths coming in a rapid burst, as he gazed through the storm for more of the beastly interlopers.

"Smelly bastards," he repeated once again, then spat on them both. He looked up and noticed the door was smashed beyond repair and that the rain drove in unimpeded. Angus marched over to the shed where he did his woodwork. He hoisted two large pieces of plywood and carried them over to the back of the house. He went back to the shed for a drill, three massive hinges, and a couple of sturdy bolt locks. Once inside the house, he stuck two sheets of plywood together with glue and bolts, hung the massive makeshift door over the gaping hole that was once his rear entry, and locked it.

"This'll keep the rain out, dear," he said, "but I'm not too sure about those things. Any thoughts on what they are?"

Angus never expected an answer to his questions. He wasn't very religious and didn't believe in all that talk of an afterlife, or how the dead walk among us looking after our well-being and all that. He just knew it felt good to talk to his wife, dead as she was, and didn't give a shite who heard him. It helped him to think things through and make sense of the senseless world he lived in. But then, nothing had made sense since Martha was gone.

"Like the red deer throughout Scotland," he said to his departed bride, "I'm guessing, if you see one or two, there's more."

Angus knew he had to get ready for another attack. He didn't know who or what was responsible, but he did know this: War was at his doorstep, and there was nothing to do but fight it. After securing the rear entry, he went to the gun cabinet and took out several weapons. He opened the ammo drawer and loaded each one carefully. He placed three handguns in places he thought he might need them if things got difficult. He had a shotgun he kept at his side, and a hunting rifle, which he rested on the kitchen table. He then went to the front door.

Angus didn't want to box himself in in case he had to escape, but after seeing what those things had done to the back door, he wanted to slow them down should they try to enter from the front. He dragged over a large credenza and buttressed it with a heavy two-seater sofa to give him a few extra moments to react, which might save his life. He turned off all the lights but kept the fire burning. "Perhaps," he said to Martha, "the fire will repel these creatures, or keep them at bay."

He proceeded upstairs to the master bedroom, which had windows on all sides of the house. It had been a dream of Martha's to have such panoramic views, to watch the seas by day and the stars by night. Angus walked the perimeter of the cavernous room, peering as best he could through the dense rain and fog. He paused on the west side and froze. He then ran to the southern side of the house and his mouth opened.

"Dear God," was all he said.

***

Jack was scared, angry, and frustrated. He inched his way forward, barely able to see the road in front of him. The rain pounded his wife's car with a consistent drumroll. Even though he knew the roads, trying to negotiate them with one good arm in a deadly storm was nearly impossible. He kept sliding off the road into the rough, having to stop and get right again. That infernal fog didn't help either. It swirled about so quickly, he thought there were creatures constantly cutting him off. And occasionally there were. Every once in a while, the moving mirage was real. He was fortunate, though. They seemed to appear mostly when the fog was blown away for a second, and he could recognize them for what they were. He'd then hit the accelerator to run them down. He always heard a satisfying thump as he careened over their smelly carcasses.

The trip to Angus McCleod's wasn't long, but it could be tedious in the best of times. The driving was both slow and treacherous. With unnerving regularity, Jack hit the ruts that could normally be avoided with a swerve of the wheel, jarring vehicle and driver alike. Worse, the road was so wet it was slippery as hell, and in some spots, washed out completely. When that happened, Jack was forced to drive on the rough alongside the road, which slowed things down even more.

On one leg of the journey, water was gushing down a slope towards the road ahead. It didn't look deep where it crossed the road, so Jack decided to gun the engine and plow straight through. Just before reaching the water, he dipped into a rut and hit the water at an angle, which spun his car completely around, pushing him into a thicket of tangled brush. He threw the gear in reverse and gunned it again. His rear wheels spun like a pinwheel, but he went nowhere. *Damn*, he thought, *now what?*

Jack crawled from his Subaru and out into the tempest, instantly regretting his decision. He was soaked to the bone before he got to the rear of his car. Shivering from the wet cold, he surveyed the predicament. Fortunately, nearly everyone on the island was prepared for such circumstances. He found two four-foot rubber tracks, rolled up for easy storage, in the boot of his wife's car. He grabbed them one at a time and slid them under the rear wheels, careful that they would catch both tires when he slipped the gear into reverse. He made it inside the car and behind the wheel, but before he could shut the door, he heard the beasts.

He could tell there were several of them by the noise they made fighting their way through the brush to get at their prey. *I smell them,* thought Jack, *they must be very close.* One of them burst through the brush and reached out, a mere foot from the opened door.

***

Angus saw at least a half dozen of the beasts descending on the front door, and about as many closing in on the western side of the house, near the spare bedroom with a double window. *Damn, why didn't I think of securing that window?* As if on cue, he heard the crash of breaking glass. He raced downstairs and was stepping off the last stair when the front door broke in two. One of the beasts was fighting its way through the stack of furniture. Angus raised his gun and shot the monster in its face, slowing the progress of the others that started to climb over the dead one. Angus waited another second and shot the creature behind the one he had just killed, slowing progress even further.

Even though the door was shut, Angus could hear others shuffling through the spare bedroom, just behind the door. He rushed over and threw it open. He saw far too many of the beasts to fight. He shot again and again and again, killing at least three while wounding others. He backed away and he heard the front door furniture being thrown aside. The creatures poured in. Angus grabbed his pistol and fired several times, killing a few more, but soon, the house would be overrun.

Angus retreated to the den and picked up the loaded rifle that rested on the table. He knew it was hopeless to think he could stand his ground. With sorrow, he made a swift and fateful decision. He grabbed an asbestos glove, slid it on, and picked up a burning log. He then backed into the rear of the house, opened the bolted door, and waited just a moment more. The beasts climbed over their dead and converged.

"It's okay, love," Angus said to his wife, a tear cascading down his cheek. "It's only a house." With one last wistful look, Angus lit the opened drapes, tossed the burning log onto the cloth furniture, and stepped outside. He bolted the door from the outside and ran to his shed.

The shed was as sturdy as the house. With the difficult weather they sometimes wrestled with, it had to be, and Angus never did anything half-measure. With fewer windows, it was certainly less penetrable. Angus opened the fortified door to the shed and, before entering, he took one last look at his home going up in flames. He hoped the rain wouldn't put it out before those creatures were good and cooked. He heard them screeching in pain and anguish, then noticed a handful of them rounding the side of the house, heading in his direction. He slammed the door shut and bolted it securely.

Many would die in the fire, he was sure. It went up fast. He could hear them over the rain that patted the roof of the shed. They were in a frenzy, likely caused by the pain of being burned alive, perhaps along with the anger of letting him get away. *Do they feel the need for revenge?* he wondered.

The one window in the shed burst inward. He had foolishly put that in simply because he had an extra window and thought it would help to have a source of natural light. It was not large enough for one those things to climb in, but it did cause a stress point in the wall on that side of the shed. If they picked at it long enough, they'd eventually tear it apart. Of that, he was sure. The creature that broke the window tried to climb through anyway, being pushed from behind by several others. Still more scratched and pounded the bolted door, shaking it and the whole structure with every hit.

Angus walked calmly over to the window stuck his rifle in the face of the unwelcome intruder and fired. It looked like the bullet killed two of them, but two more quickly replaced them, trying like the devil to get in at their quarry. They grabbed the sides of the window hole and began to tear and widen it. Those at the door were relentless, scratching, ripping, and pounding with a singular, manic purpose. Angus concentrated on the window and shot as many as he could. When a few went down, he reloaded and fired again.

He soon realized his ammo was low. He had an extra box in the shed, but soon that would be depleted. The falling of their comrades didn't slow or stop the creatures. They kept coming, kept tearing, kept snarling. Angus looked at his supply. He had five more rounds and there were at least ten of them out there. And that was counting just the ones at the window.

Those at the door were making headway, poking small holes that revealed snippets of the beasts in their smelly horror. He could see the sharp claws tearing away at the wood and wondered what they would feel like going through his skin. As secure as it was, the door wasn't going to be strong enough to withstand such an onslaught, and he knew it.

"I'll join you soon, Martha, my sweet. My time is near," said Angus, and then he smiled.

He loaded the last of his bullets, whistling while he did so, his smile lingering. He backed into a corner, leaned against the wall, racked his rifle, and waited for the inevitable. Splinters were now flying, the holes in the window and door areas both getting larger. The beasts could see through the door holes now, and their madness increased.

Angus raised his rifle for a few last shots and planned to turn the butt end of the gun on them to beat as many as he could to death before being overtaken. Just as he was about to shoot, he heard a boom. Then another. And, after a few moments, two more. The door beating stopped and the window damage slowed. Angus walked to the door and peeked through one of the holes.

"I'll be damned," he said.

***

Jack was so frightened and surprised that he nearly forgot about the handgun his wife kept in the glove box. With no time to spare, he leaned over, grabbed the handgun, and fired two shots through the opened car door and into the creature that approached him. He slammed the door shut, turned the key, hit the gas pedal, and heard more spinning. He cursed and tried again. The other beast had one claw on the engine hood and reached over with his other claw to slam down on the windshield. The tires caught. Jack whirled backwards, shooting the rubber tracks forward and caught solid ground. He threw the car into gear and surged forward at a breakneck speed, not even caring if he was on the road, following a survivor's instinct to get away from the immediate danger of being torn apart. He slammed the brakes and the creature flew from the hood. He punched the accelerator again and this time ran the beast over.

Jack forced himself to slow down and drive more carefully. He was so consumed with his near-death experiences that he almost passed the entrance to the McCleod home. He turned down the drive and immediately realized things did not look good. He smelled the smoke before he saw the flames. Angus McCleod's house was fully ablaze in an all-consuming conflagration. *Won't last much longer*, thought Jack, *not in this rain.*

He got out of the car and could hear the screams of the creatures being burned inside. He couldn't see any other sign of life, so he said a short prayer for Angus, who he presumed was dead, and proceeded to get back into his car. The wind shifted and he saw two of the beasts head for the rear of the house. The next moment, he heard shots. He tucked the pistol into his pocket, picked up his shotgun and went down the west side of the house. He gave wide berth to the burning home, although the fire was already starting to lose intensity.

When he came around to the back of the house, he surveyed the scene briefly. He then approached the creatures tearing at the shed door, making sure he was close enough to cause damage before he fired. He killed at least three with two shots, then pulled his hand-gun out of his right pocket and fired accurate single shots at center mass, killing with each and every one. He hoped Angus was still alive because Jack was going to need some help. He no sooner had that thought, when he saw the rifle stick out through the window, care-fully picking off creatures one at a time. All ten were slain in a few minutes of battle time.

Jack ran to the shed window, shouting. "Angus, it's Jack Brodie," he said. "Don't shoot!"

Angus pulled the empty rifle back inside and stuck his head through the now large hole in the wall. "What do you want?" shouted Angus.

"What do I—?" Jack repeated, incredulous. Then he burst out laughing. Knowing that his friend and neighbor had just faced immi-nent death and was rescued by the skin of his teeth, it made that ques-tion as funny as it was intended. Angus unbolted the shredded door and walked over to Jack. The men hugged, laughed, and gave thanks.

"I'm sorry for the loss," Jack said, nodding towards the smolder-ing house. "I know how much it meant to you."

"It's a house, Jack. It's wood, stone, and a bit of cloth. It can be replaced. Martha is in here," he added, pointing to his heart. "And I'll never let them get at that."

"We need to go."

They hurried to Jack's car.

"Looks like your left wing is in need of repair," said Angus, pointing at Jack's left arm.

"I dislocated it. Care to drive?"

"Not especially, but given the alternative, gladly." Angus hopped behind the wheel as Jack took the passenger seat.

"We need to head west to warn others and encourage them to make their way to the Royal Oak Pub," Jack said.

"You can't," Angus said. "The road is completely washed out. I tried this morning and it's worse now, I'm sure."

"To the pub then," Jack said, after a moment's reflection. "Those poor souls are going to have to fight it out on their own. God help them."

CHAPTER 19

A MAELSTROM OF DEATH: MARIE AND TIM

Marie and Tim raised their guns. They crept from the front of the house towards the inhuman sounds emanating from the kitchen. When they found themselves face to face with several creatures within the house, they froze. The smell brought them to tears. Tim desperately tried to comprehend how such a creature could exist on the same planet.

Marie was mesmerized. She paused on an intake of air, and, at first, couldn't move. Her fear soon dissipated and, prodded by what she had witnessed upstairs, she felt nothing but uncontrollable rage—hot, feral, and dangerous. Her feet found traction and she rushed the beasts in front of her.

She fired two deadly shots into two of the monsters in the kitchen. She leaped over them as they fell, and used her gun as a battering ram, smashing it into the head of the third one until it stopped moving. She ran out the back door into the raging storm, then stopped in the blinding rain to slip two more shells into the empty barrels of her gun.

A group of four more beasts slithered in and out of the mist. Marie walked in their direction.

Tim shouted after her, to no avail. Marie charged headlong into the swarm of oncoming creatures. "Marie, wait!"

But Marie kept moving. She ducked under the wide swipe of the first beast in the group of monsters, stuck her gun into its armpit and fired. She shot the next one in the knee and smashed her gun across its neck, rendering it helpless. She stood still and carefully loaded as two more came upon her, one to the right, and one to the left. The one whose neck she'd broken squealed from the ground. She spun in its direction and shot it in the face, then rammed the butt of her gun into its head to be sure.

Tim caught up and dispatched the one coming from the left. Marie swung her gun to the right and sent its innards splaying across the lawn. Many more approached from a distance, screaming and growling, and soon they'd reach them.

"Marie," Tim said. "We have to go."

But Marie didn't move. She stared into space, as if she were looking straight through the creatures that were coming ever closer. Tim grabbed Marie by her shoulders and shook hard. He shouted, louder this time. "Marie! Now!"

Marie looked at Tim blankly, then led the way back. They raced through the house, leaping over dead bodies, the smell gagging them both. They made their way out the front door and hurried to their vehicle. Marie got behind the wheel and backed out of the drive. She smashed into one of the vile creatures crossing the drive, and kept going. At the main road, she turned and went further west.

"Slow down," Tim said. "Easy does it, Marie, slow down."

Marie gradually slowed the van down until she came to a full stop.

"Marie, are you okay?" Tim said, whispering now.

It took a few minutes for her to respond. Her grip on the steering wheel lessened, her eyes softened, and her breathing became more regulated.

"I . . . I'm fine."

Tim decided to let it go for now. He knew why she went crazy back there and couldn't blame her for her reaction. She had put all of her fear aside after she saw what happened upstairs and charged headlong into the creatures, killing them with a singular driving purpose: revenge. He needed to help bring her down.

"Where are we going?" he asked.

"A change of plan," Marie said, her voice shaky. "I was originally going to head for the MacDonald home, but if there's anyone who can hold his own against these monsters, it's him. There's a community not far from there, a cluster of homes. They are mostly followers of Reverend Knox."

"So, we're going to . . ."

"We're going to the church. If they're in danger, that's where they would go. We'll stand a better chance of getting a group of them all in one place by going there. Then, we'll get the hell out of there and back to the pub."

Tim reached over and gently put his hand on Marie's shoulder. At first, she tensed at his touch. A few minutes passed and the tension lessened. A minute more and she put her hand on his. Marie turned, grabbed Tim, and pulled him close.

They kissed, deeply and passionately. The death, the destruction, and the tension they had experienced such a short time ago gave way to a survivalist's desire to reach out for human contact, to celebrate the concept of just being alive. They locked the doors, left the engine running, and made fevered love as the harsh rain beat down upon the roof of the old vehicle.

***

The trip to the church was agonizingly slow. Rain, along with strong wind, was a constant reminder that they needed to be cautious. The road they traveled was not marked, and Tim now knew for certain that he could not have made it on his own had he tried to do so. He looked at her and stared. He knew they hadn't been together long, but he also knew he was falling hard for her, which made what he was planning all the more difficult to share with her. He had been nurturing an idea ever since they first left the pub. He had stashed a bag into the back of the van in anticipation of his plan, but he knew at the outset that Marie would not approve or be pleased. He wasn't so sure about the plan himself, truth be told, so he decided it was probably best not to tell her until he absolutely had no other choice.

***

The church was situated on a hillside, near the main road. It provided easy access for Reverend Knox's parishioners and served as a bulwark against weather-related dangers that threatened the nearby community. Whenever that occurred, people would leave their homes and spend the entire day at the church. They always made it a picnic of sorts, bringing food, cards, sleeping bags, and camaraderie with them. They never brought their guns, however, not ever seeing the need, especially around the children.

On the first day of Hurricane Nora, people came early, as the weather prediction had been worse than usual. Tables were set up for the food, and potluck was the order of the day. Children set up board games and engaged in contests that resulted in loud laughter and goodwill teasing. Adults talked over the childhood tumult and played their own card games, accompanied by some good scotch to ease the burdens of the day. There were generally more people present on a day like today than during a regular Sunday service. People always found an excuse to not go to regular service, but the threat of a mudslide through one's living room was a very strong motivator to show up during a storm. The reverend was usually present at times like this, enjoying the swelling crowd, not to mention the food, and chatting with the congregation about important soul-saving matters. But today he was not. No one could fathom why, as he usually loved these sessions, but no one was especially alarmed. Most thought he got caught somewhere distant in the storm and would return as soon as he could.

Time passed, and as the storm raged on, so did the level of communal noise. The church windows were high off the ground and rattled with their age in the furious wind. They were made of thick, leaded glass fortified with steel trim, however, and no one feared breakage. The one true noisemaker was the main double-door entry to the rear of the nave. Both doors were made of strong, heavy wood, kept bolted and held tight with a two-by-six solid wood bar. As a result, the strong shaking caused by the wind would be a constant annoyance at best. A couple of men usually took turns sitting in the rear of the church to hear if anyone came banging on the door to be let in, perhaps a latecomer to the storm-directed party.

James Scott, called Jamie by his friends, along with his brother Will, took an early evening time slot to man the rattling portal. They could barely hear themselves speak over the children and adults talking and laughing, as well as the wicked storm that rumbled the windows and shook the doors. The brothers were close in age and best friends. Jamie was a bachelor and had a small farm. He enjoyed living alone, but also found great pleasure in visiting Will and his wife Angela, and their four children. They were talking about how lucky Will was to have such a brood when Jamie perked up.

"Do you smell that?" he asked.

"The least you could have done is warn me," Will said.

"No," Jamie said. "I'm not the culprit."

He scrunched his eyebrows and inhaled, trying to pinpoint the source of the noxious stench. His look of consternation deepened as he sniffed his way towards the entry. Will followed close behind. Jamie turned and looked at his brother.

"It's coming from outside," he said. "Here, give me a hand with this."

Both brothers lifted the solid wood bar from the doors, then released the three sturdy bolts that helped to keep it shut. There was a foot lock on the left door that held one door stationary, but Jamie opened the one on the right, held the door's handle, and peered out. The smell closed over them like a coffin lid. Will naturally stepped back from the odious onslaught, but Jamie leaned forward into the rain, intensely curious about the odor's origin.

Jamie screamed, and Will watched with surprise as his brother was yanked outwards into the elements. A second later, his head flew back in through the opening and blood spattered across the front of Will's shirt. It was Will's turn to scream. He reached for his brother, who was no longer there. One of the creatures grabbed both doors with its two clawed hands to try and pry them open. Will raised his right leg and kicked the monster square in the chest, sending it spiraling down the steps that led to the entry of the church.

Will's wife, Angela, was the first to notice the rolling head as it came to a stop inside the church at the beginning of the first pew. Not knowing who it belonged to didn't stop her from screaming hysterically. Someone had the good sense to grab a blanket, scoop up the head, and rush it out of sight. Three others hurried to help Will at the doors. One grabbed Will and pulled him away from the dark opening. Will was screaming Jamie's name, his desperate plea deadened by the storm as he tried to go after what was left of his brother. The two others, Andrew Morrison and Gerard Young, took hold of the still-opened door and slammed it shut, but not before Gerard got a good look at what Will had kicked.

The creature lunged and banged into the shut door letting out a howl of frustration. Both men put their shoulders to the door and stared at one another in abject horror.

"What was that?" Andrew asked.

"I . . . I don't know," Gerard replied. "I saw . . . at least I think I saw some sort of animal, but not like any animal I've ever seen."

"I saw a great deal of movement beyond it," Andrew said. "It looked like there were more of them, whatever they are. Lots more. More than we can handle."

Neither man said anything to that, but instead pressed harder on the doors, quickly snapping the locks and wooden bar back into place. And none too soon, as the beast resumed its smashing. Only this time, it appeared to have help. To the two men inside, it seemed that now there were three or more creatures banging into the doors, but the entry was holding up well, so they let up a little on their pressure to gauge the force on the other side. Another crash into the two doors showed no signs of the strong metal bolts weakening. Yet.

Andrew, the stronger of the two men, said, "I'll stay here for the moment. You go inside and try to find the words to explain what we've seen."

Gerard nodded and ran into the commotion that was ensuing in the main part of the church. People were crying, some were screaming, and everyone was running about gathering children with a fearful, terrified look. Many turned to stare at Gerard's blanched face, looking for answers to what had just rolled into their sanctuary, and afraid that he might tell them.

There was only one way to get everyone's attention. Gerard wasted no time. He ran to the front of the church and up the pulpit stairs. The microphone was not turned on, but he was high enough for his voice to carry over the panicked crowd. He held his hands up high and shouted for attention. It took several tries, but the melee finally subsided, and he was able to speak.

"Samuel and Rick." He shouted to two men in the very back row. "Go and give Andrew a hand at the doors. Everyone else, please give me your attention."

People huddled in small groups, a look of shock and disbelief uniformly spread among them.

"Listen to me," he said as the murmurs slowly decreased. "We need to act swiftly. Something is out there and just killed a member of our congregation."

"What do you mean something?" came a shout from the rear.

"I . . . I . . ." Gerard struggled to find the right words, but he had no idea where to look for them. He ran his fingers through his thick hair in frustration and decided to tell them exactly what he saw. He had no other choice.

"Andrew and I rushed to the door to see what did that to poor Jamie." At the sound of Jamie's name, their horror became more real, and the crowd cried out in pain again.

"It . . . it wasn't human," Gerard continued. He barely got the words out when howls of beastly fury competed with the wind and rain for attention. Harsh banging on the entry doors, accompanied by scratching and snarling, echoed throughout the old church. The nervous crowd looked to Gerard for answers. Any answers would do, even though they knew he had none.

Gerard pulled himself together. He grabbed the first thought that came to mind. "We need to protect the children," he said. But the crowd still stirred. "Everyone, your attention please. I said we need to protect the children."

The commotion calmed slightly.

"We not only saw what that thing did to Jamie, we saw that there were many more of them outside the church, and they are not human!" Gerard was gaining control of his emotions.

"What do you mean not human?" shouted Murray Reid, one of Gerard's close neighbors. He could not contain his anger, frustration, and horror any longer. This sounded too crazy to him, and he was not alone. Gerard raised his arms to calm the crowd.

"I know, I know," he said. "This can't be happening. It can't be real. But I assure you it is."

Suddenly, more horrific howls and screams with more intense scratching at the doors punctuated his comments. An apprehensive pall settled over the crowd. No one knew what to say or do. A strong, pungent odor blew through the old windows and settled on the fearful crowd like a veil of pernicious smoke.

"Please, my friends, you must trust me. We are in imminent danger. Please do as I ask, as there's no time to waste! Take the children downstairs to the social room. A handful of you remain there as protection. The rest come back up here. I'll be downstairs in a few minutes to give you further instructions."

Gerard was widely known to all, and they trusted his word, no matter how insane it sounded. Even those who still did not want to believe what he said moved with haste. If Gerard didn't convince them of what was out there, the sounds and the smell did.

There was a sudden flurry of anxious activity—people gathering valuables, grabbing their children by the hand, and rushing to the stairwell to the right of the sanctuary that led to the basement below. The downstairs room was designed for social activity: Bible classes, after-service gatherings, committee meetings, and the like. It was wide, windowless, and empty, save for a scattering of long tables and folding chairs. Well-worn Bibles were stacked on the bookshelves that lined the walls on either side of the room. The air-conditioning system that pumped air from vents in the ceiling whirred spasmodically, but at least it acted as white noise to the turmoil overhead. Metal chairs scraped along the tiled floor as people quickly took a seat and held tightly to their children. Everyone was fidgety, nervous, and frightened.

One of the more dogmatically inclined parents, a deacon in the church, suggested passing out Bibles, with an adult at each table leading their group in selected readings. When he was met with far too many blank faces, he said, "Okay, I'll do the reading."

The deacon grabbed a used Bible and opened to a favorite passage. He looked at the assemblage of frightened parents and children, heads appropriately bowed, and gathered his thoughts.

"My friends," he said, "there is no need for us to fear the unknown as we are in the house of God. He will protect us. He will save us. Let me share with you the words found in John fourteen, twenty-seven: 'Peace I leave with you, my peace I give you. I do not give to you as the world gives. Do not let your hearts be troubled, and do not be afraid.'"

In the main part of the church, men and women alike were pulling a piano from the rear foyer to help block the main entrance. Independent and strong folk as they were, once over the initial shock of what had happened to Jaimie, they all rallied. Despite their natural inclination for self-reliance, most people in times of great threat looked to the strongest in their group for leadership. Andrew Morrison was that man.

"Friends," he addressed the crowd when he came in from the vestibule. Everyone quieted down instantly. A loud thump smashed into the door, sending nervous reverberations through the keyed-up assembly. The crowd uniformly flinched, but everyone remained attentive.

"Friends," he began again. "We are faced with an as yet unknown threat. There are . . . beings outside the church trying to get in. I don't know who or what they are. I can only tell you that they are deadly, and they mean to do us harm." Andrew quickly barked out some orders. "Gerard, please go downstairs and tell anyone down there to look for a weapon of any sort." Andrew paused, but knew his next words needed to be said. "They may be the last defense for the children."

Whispers of fear and anguish flew about the room, touching everyone present.

"Nathaniel, Lucas, and Wesley." Andrew pointed to a small group of men standing along the inside wall of the nave, waiting for instructions. "Go to the office and look for the rear door to the outside. Do what you can to obstruct it with whatever furniture you can find."

The men nodded and scurried off.

"The rest of you, check for any kitchen knives, broomsticks, mop handles, and anything else that may pass for a weapon."

People scattered like roaches in lamplight, eager to be able to do something, anything, just to be productive and take their minds off the absurd lunacy of it all. Some, along with Gerard, scoured the basement, aided by those already guarding their own children. Their efforts were only mildly successful, securing a collection of kitchen knives of various sizes, some mops in a slop sink closet, and a few tired brooms leaning into a dark, lonely corner of the kitchen area. After a scan of the furniture, some enterprising soul stomped on the already weak legs of a few of the metal chairs, breaking them off with a sharp crack. By doing so, he created a handful of short stabbing implements that could pose a danger to any living creature, providing one could get close enough to inflict a mortal blow.

Someone raced down the stairs with a hand saw. "Look what I found! It was leaning against the rear door of the reverend's office. He must have meant to take it to the outdoor shed at some point."

"Excellent! Bring it here," Gerard said. He grabbed the proffered saw and began removing the heads off the broom handles and mops.

"Get me a roll of duct tape if you can find one," he said.

The provider of the saw raced back up to the office. When he returned with two large rolls of duct tape, the crew in the basement were already fitting knife blades into slots they created in the tips of the wooden handles. Wrapping them in tape secured them in place. Even so, when they lined them up against the wall, they all noted what a paltry arsenal they had. The frenzy of positive activity in the face of the horrible danger gave way to the depressing reality of their lack of effective weaponry.

The deacon gazed at his dispirited friends and saw an opportunity to impart the word of God to ease their concern. With conviction in his heart and in his voice, he took advantage of the silence to recite Joshua 1:9: "Be strong and courageous; do not be frightened or dismayed, for the Lord your God is with you wherever you go."

Gerard turned to a few people standing near and said, "Pass out what we have." He then turned to the crowd and spoke louder. "When the time comes, grab a chair, a knife, or whatever you can. Whatever beast comes at us, aim for the head or the eyes. If we can't kill these monsters right away, maybe we can blind them and then finish them off."

On his way back upstairs, Gerard passed the deacon. He shoved a broom handle fitted with a knife into his arms, then recited Ecclesiastes 3:8: "'A time to love and a time to hate; a time for war and a time for peace.' This is a time for war, brother." He then raced upstairs to join his companions in the nave.

Gerard found a scene of controlled panic. People were rushing about, looking for or fashioning weapons from whatever available resources they could find. Some of the women had knitting needles, some of the men, pocketknives. Some brought out a handful of items from the reverend's office: a letter opener, large shards of glass from a broken sconce, a handful of ballpoint pens. Some tools were found in the back office, and people were using a large hammer to tear apart some boards from an internal wall in the rear of the church. Next to Andrew, Keith Argyll, an old-timer with a penchant for being a cantankerous loner, put his leg up on the armrest of an aisle pew, pulled up his right-side trouser leg, and unstrapped a twelve-inch Bowie knife that was attached to his lower leg.

"How the hell do you walk with that thing?" Andrew asked.

"Carefully," Keith said.

"And why would you have that in the first place?"

Keith stared at Andrew as if he just spoke a foreign language. "I bet you're glad I have it now, eh?"

Andrew snorted a laugh and moved about the main hall, checking on whatever passed for progress in the tasks at hand, offering his assistance and a word of support for the battle that was to come. When he got near the office entrance, he shouted to those inside.

"Mates, how are we? Need any help?"

One of the congregants stuck his head out the door. "Aye, we're dragging the last bit of furniture over to the outside door. We've placed a large credenza, a heavy oak desk, and a few chairs against it. There's no window, so that's a good thing."

"Any action?"

"The rain and wind cover much of what we hear, but . . ."

"But what?"

"That said, it still sounds like the gates of hell have opened out there, between the loud screams and pounding on the door."

"Afraid?" Andrew asked.

"No, of course not! Maybe just a wee bit concerned, perhaps."

Andrew knew that no one, not a single man or woman present, would admit to being outright frightened. They were too proud and too independent. He also knew when the fighting started, they would fight to the death, no matter what.

Another person came to the door. "Look what I found!" He stuck his left arm out the entry, holding a Browning X-bolt hunting rifle. "It was in a built-in gun cabinet hidden behind a curtain draped along the wall behind his desk. There was a single, half-empty box of ammo to go with it. Unfortunately, it was the only one in there."

"Outstanding. Do you know how to shoot?"

"Sure," he said, then laughed, as if that was even a question. "But here," he continued. "You take it. You're the better shot, and I only need my bare fists. I should probably tie one of them behind my back so those things, whatever they are, would get a fair fight."

Andrew took the gun, smiled, and headed for the main entrance. He ordered a couple of men from the area to take the loose boards, recovered nails, and hammer to the office, and tell those inside it was now time to come out. Then nail the boards across the door to the office itself to help secure that area.

They did so in a hurry, making sure the door would be difficult to open into the worship area. Any extra boards were fashioned into makeshift weapons. All weapons of any sort were collected and brought to the rear of the church and displayed on the floor area between the last pew and the wall torn apart for wood slats. One of the young men collecting the makeshift weaponry paused at Old Man Argyll to collect his Bowie knife.

"You'll lose your hand if you reach for that again, lad, and it'll hit the ground before you know what happened to you."

The young teen, Bobby Bruce, looked unsure at the threat, and not a little gray at the thought. He glanced at Andrew, who smiled and shook his head, signaling Bobby to back off. When all other weapons were collected and laid out, it was a meager sum to use in a fight against an army of unknown beasts intent on killing them.

Every sound they heard produced a spontaneous, physically fearful reaction. The windows rattled with the wind, and everyone looked upwards, mouths open. Loud banging that came from the main entry doors caused everyone to swivel in that direction, expecting something to come bursting through at any moment. When someone dropped a loose board and it cracked on the hard floor, everyone gasped. Andrew knew he had to say something uplifting, and he had to do it soon. He seized the moment to speak before it slipped away, along with his courage. He went up to the pulpit and called for everyone's attention. They paused what they were doing and looked up.

"You all know the definition of the word 'kilt'?" The off-beat question took everyone by surprise, and therefore, everyone hushed to see if they heard him correctly.

"It's what happened to the last person who called it a skirt."

Robust laughter, fueled by anxiety, let him know that there was nothing more powerful than a Scot laughing in the face of imminent danger.

"We're about to fight something that wants us dead," he continued. "Creatures that are extremely brutal." As if to prove him right, an inhuman howl cut through the sound of the rain and wind outside.

"We don't know what they are, but we do know who *we* are, and *we* don't go down easily."

A number of heads firmly nodded, belying the fear that pumped their hearts and gripped their souls.

"Not that we need weapons," continued Andrew, "but you may want to pick up something to make them feel a little pain when the fighting starts."

Andrew looked at his audience, people he'd known most of his life, all of whom were waiting for a final comment from him. Words they could inhale, words that would help them to face the horror that lay ahead.

"That'll teach them to not bother us when we're in our house of worship."

Amidst a riot of "Ayes," everyone bent to pick something up: a knitting needle, a knife, a fork, a piece of wood with a sharpened end, a utensil taped onto the end of a broomstick, along with, perhaps, a little extra necessary courage. The mood shifted. They accepted their fate, whatever it may be, and now it was a matter of following a battle plan.

Again, Andrew took charge. "We don't know where they will come from first," he said, "the main entrance or through the office. Let's form two lines at each entry, those with large weapons in the front, and those with smaller ones, right behind them. The smaller weapon users may be able to finish the creatures off once those with a larger one tip them off balance."

The unspoken fear of the group was that they'd be overrun in no time, no matter how hard they fought. But the thought of defenseless children down below was all the motivation they needed to steel themselves to hold their ground. All assembled moved as a group, taking up their positions without argument or quarrel. Once in position, they paused, each buried in their own thoughts. Some prayed silently. They believed the devil was indeed knocking at their door, and if he got in, they'd show him a bit of God's vengeance. Others had a more secular view, though they wound up in the same place. To them, these were unknown creatures who were trying to kill them. And their job was to kill as many of them as possible first, and this they would do without question.

Everyone remained as still as a graveyard at midnight. The outdoor elements of driving rain and gusty winds battered the old windows, the sharp, staccato noise teasing the fear out of those inside the church. Yet all occupants remained alert and focused, even while intermittent pounding and scratching continued on the main entrance as well as the outside office doors. Howls of beastly frustration echoed throughout the chamber, reminding everyone that something vicious was desperately trying to get in.

A violent crash ricocheted throughout the church.

"It came from the office," Andrew whispered. Those around him remained stoic, locked in a posture of silent anticipation, tightening their grip on whatever weapon they carried.

The pounding resumed, but this time on the office door that stood between the beasts and them. *Dear God,* thought Andrew, *they're inside.* Bits of the buttressed door began flying in all directions as the creatures tore through it. A hole took shape. Claws emerged as the beasts ripped the door to shreds. They now moved in a frenzy. Food was within reach. Soon, a face appeared in the ever-widening hole. Even those adults facing the main entry turned to have a look, then wished they hadn't. Audible gasps reverberated around the room.

Andrew, and everyone else, was frozen in place. It took him a moment to realize he was wasting precious time. He quickly moved to the front of the group. He turned to them and said, "It's going to get loud, I'm going to shoot."

Some covered their ears, while others were still too mesmerized by the sight of the horrible looking creatures to move. Andrew raised the rifle, pointed it at the face sticking through the hole in the door and fired. The boom of the rifle was quickly followed by a strange sound. Andrew thought it must be what it sounds like if you shoot into a body of water. That was followed by even louder squeals from beyond the door. He believed the bullet went through at least two of them, but it didn't stop their advance. They tore at the door opening with a manic fervor, their screeches filling the church with ungodly wails.

***

Those in the basement flinched at the sound of the shooting. Some of the children began to cry. Their parents did their best to keep them calm. *If it comes to it,* some of them thought, *should I end my child's life before those creatures attack?* That horrific thought exited as fast as it entered their consciousness, too appalling to seriously consider. And yet . . .

***

Andrew fired again, hitting more of the monsters. The creatures in the rear seemed only too anxious to take the place of those that had fallen. *I may only have time for one more shot before they break through,* he thought. He raised his rifle again, but heard screams from behind him.

"They're breaching the main entry!" someone yelled.

Andrew ran to the rear of the church and saw first-hand how bad it was. The metal hinges on the door were hanging by a thread, the beam of wood holding both doors shut was seriously cracked, and the space between the two doors was widening. Within minutes this side would break wide open, and they'd be attacked from both the front and rear entries to the church.

"They're almost through the office door," someone shouted from the front. Andrew spun to see the group bent and tense, prepared for battle. A creature pushed its way through a thin, body-length split in the door. Its support boards split in two. It was the most horrible thing Andrew had ever seen. The beast had one arm with an outstretched claw squeezed through the gap and was reaching for the crowd. One leg with a webbed foot was also through, the rest of its body was being shoved through by those behind it.

A woman in the front line, Maureen Murray, one of the bravest souls of the group, let out a primordial scream and rushed the door. She raised the hammer she carried and brought it down, just as the beast broke through. The hammer missed its mark and hit the creature's shoulder. A sharp snap was heard throughout the room. The beast howled in pain and bloodthirsty anger as it swiped its now free claw across her throat, tearing Maureen's head from her body. Her blood painted the wall alongside the door with streaks of bright crimson. Andrew raced to the beast, lifted his gun, and shot it between the eyes as other creatures pulled their way through the thin slot. He only had a couple of bullets left, then all would be lost.

The rest of the front line rushed the office door, half-crazed at what had happened to their friend. Gerard picked up Maureen's hammer and swung with wild abandon. Carl Engers hacked at one of the beasts with a makeshift spear, a sharpened, double-edged knife protruding from the broomstick he carried. Thomas Thomson swung at a creature, his back to another that bared its teeth and leaned in to bite him, taking a large chunk from his neck and killing him instantly. Those who made up the second row forgot all about strategy and raced into the fray, kicking, stabbing, and fighting as best they could.

Bobby Bruce fought hard for a young teen. He used a short, homemade spear, jabbing the blade deeply into the oncoming creatures. It was a versatile weapon. He could jab upwards into one creature and slice downwards, then cut the head off another. He moved so fast, though, he didn't realize he was backing himself into a corner.

He swung left, then right, but kept moving backwards against the wall near the broken door. He found himself quickly surrounded by three creatures, but he didn't give up. He screamed and swung his blade, expecting to die and hoping to take one more of those disgusting beasts with him.

Seemingly out of nowhere, Keith Argyll, the crusty curmudgeon, jumped onto the back of one of the beasts threatening Bobby Bruce and slit its throat from ear to ear. He leaped off and crouched, drawing his sizable blade across the back of the knee of the next creature before stabbing it in the neck, as Bobby disposed of the third with a quick jab to the chest. Both stood face to face.

"Not bad for a young pup," Keith said with a smile.

"You're pretty spry for an old geezer," Bobby retorted, and barked out a laugh.

At that very moment, another creature burst through the door and landed on top of Keith, burying its head into his stomach, eating him alive as he screamed in pain. Bobby jabbed his spear into the creature's back numerous times, even after it was clearly dead, screaming in anguish. He kicked the creature off the now lifeless body of his savior and bent down. He gently pried the Bowie knife from his hand and whispered through his tears to the lifeless body below him.

"I swear to you, old man, I will put this to good use."

His eyes swept the room and he saw his friends fighting ruthlessly, some of them falling in the fray. He ran to their aid with renewed vigor, slicing, swiping, and cutting in a fevered pitch.

***

The adults in the basement were torn. They heard the guns, the fighting, and the screams of pain and anguish upstairs, and wanted to rush upstairs to help their friends and spouses. But they had sworn a silent oath to protect the children in their care to the death. As anxious as they were to help their friends, they stayed put, hugged their children, and prepared for a final stand.

***

To the rear of the church, Andrew shot two more bullets in the growing gap between the two doors, reducing his available ammunition to two more bullets. *Then I'll use it as a club,* he thought in despair.

Those in the vestibule of the church were still trying desperately to hold the main entry doors in place, even as the creatures reached through the gap, trying to grab them. It was a losing battle, and they knew it. A moment of deep sadness arose in Andrew's chest, thinking of what would happen to the children when they were overrun by these things.

What was that? he thought. There was a sharp noise, like a clap of thunder. But it couldn't be that. Then there were two claps, and they didn't linger like thunder. There they were again.

"Hold on mates," he screamed. "It's a shotgun. Someone is out there shooting. Hold on a bit longer!"

With that encouraging news, the frightened and exhausted combatants found an inner strength they didn't know they had and fought even harder. The gap was now closing with their effort. There were more thunderclaps, but louder this time. And it was coming from two directions. Someone was shooting from the front, and someone else from the rear. The main entrance doors were now closing, and activity from the office gradually ceased, leaving a deathly silence in its wake.

Andrew looked around and was stunned by the brutal aftermath of battle. Bodies of the creatures and his neighbors alike lay everywhere. Survivors sported the kind of vacant look only those engaged in violent conflict can possess. Gerard was trying to contain Bobby Bruce, who was repeatedly stabbing an already dead creature with a massive knife.

All eyes lifted to the office as a rustling noise once again returned to the area. The broken door, barely covering the office entry, was fully kicked open, and there stood Marie, a shotgun firmly in her grasp.

"Everyone listen," she said. "We've got to go. Now. There's no time to waste. We killed many of them and drove off the rest. But make no mistake, they will be back. And soon! Get to your cars as quickly as possible and follow us back to the Royal Oak Pub in Blackpool."

Andrew caught Gerard's eye and nodded towards the stairway. Gerard nodded back and ran to the basement. Andrew addressed the group. "Friends," he said. "Gather the wounded. Bring them and your weapons to your vehicles, and double up where you can. We'll travel in a single-file line as a caravan through the storm."

"What about our dead?" someone shouted.

With a pale face and shaky voice, Andrew responded. "We have no choice," he said. "I'll be the last to leave. We're going to have to burn the church."

Andrew was met with looks of shock, fear, and mental anguish. Mostly, though, there were looks of grim acceptance, even understanding. Everyone knew the only alternative was to do nothing, and that would turn their dead into a feast for the creatures once they returned. And return they would. So everyone bowed their heads, grabbed their weapons, and hurried to the main entry to don their foul weather gear, which hung from pegs along the wall.

Gerard led the frightened group up from the basement. Parents shielded their children from the surrounding carnage and hustled them towards the main entry. Once outside in the storm, people ran through the battering rain to their cars and trucks, spooked by the ever-moving mist.

"Gerard," Andrew shouted. "I have two extra gas cans in the back of my truck. Bring them in here, please."

***

Outside the main entrance to the church, Tim greeted those beginning to exit, directing them to get in their cars and wait for the van to lead them back to Blackpool. Marie made her way through the church and connected with Tim outside. They walked to the van together. Once there, Tim opened the rear door and pulled out a well-packed set of scuba gear with a compact spear gun and a duffel filled with several cans of Spare Air that Tim had snuck into the back of the van before he and Marie departed the pub.

"What in God's name are you doing?" Marie asked.

"What I need to do. What I was trained to do."

"Tim, we don't have time for this," Marie said, her voice wobbling. "Is that what you slipped into the van when we left? Why? Put that back and let's get out of here."

"You're right. We don't have time for this. So listen to me, please. When we were back at the pub and your Da was pouring over those maps, I came across an old one that featured Loch Crover and I slipped it in my pocket. It outlined a possible connection to underwater caves that lead to the western coast. It was a diver's account of what he'd been told, and it had a ring of truth to it. I knew we were heading in the general direction of the loch and now see that it's down the hill from here. If I can find the underwater cave, I just might be able to find out what happened to those people on the sightseeing cruise and help them. I have to try, at least."

"Even if it were true, how would you know if they're still alive? How would you know where on the western coast they are? What if you run into those beasts down there?" she screamed, her voice rising in pitch with every question, tears cascading down her cheeks.

"I don't know," he said, hoisting the backpack of gear over his shoulder. "But, again, Marie, I have to try. I couldn't live with myself if I didn't."

"And what are you going to do if you find survivors? How do you plan to get back to the pub from out here? Walk?"

Tim looked a little sheepish. "I guess I didn't really think that part through, other than to look for an abandoned vehicle and cart people back that way."

Marie sighed loudly. "Jesus, Tim." Then, more quietly, she added, "There's an old, white church van in the detached garage behind the church. The keys are usually in the visor. Reverend Knox keeps it there if any of his parishioners need an emergency vehicle, or if he wants to take people on a church picnic."

Tim leaned in and kissed her hard. "I promise you, Marie, I'll come back," he shouted over the wind. "For you! Now, lead these people out of here and get safely back to the pub."

With a shotgun in one hand, a spear gun in the other, and his backpack of gear, Tim fought his way through the force of the storm and loped down the hill in the pitch dark towards the reverend's van.

Marie stood in the rain and watched Tim go until he rounded the church and was out of sight. Suddenly, a loud boom shook her from her worry about the man she'd fallen in love with so fast and hard. Gas tanks exploded inside the church, and the light of the hungry flames reflected in her tear-filled eyes.

Marie ran to the Royal Oak Pub's van she and Tim arrived in and slid behind the wheel. She pulled to the head of the line, flashed her headlights twice, honked her horn, and led the caravan of survivors, twenty-five cars long, out to the main road, without ever looking back.

CHAPTER 20

THE MACDONALDS

Jeffrey MacDonald and his wife, Ella, lived their lives mostly in seclusion on their vast farm.

Theirs was a stately mansion, sitting high on a central bluff overlooking the Moray Firth, with views to the far edge of the North Sea. It was distant enough from any damage that may have ensued from a surging sea or rain-induced mudslide. It was also free from both the curious and the neighborly, as the closest neighbors, aside from those who resided in the workers' bunkhouse on his property, were a good three miles away. That distance, along with the careful planting of trees and shrubs, as well as strategically placed fencing and stone walls, kept the word "private" attached to the word "estate' when describing their home. And that's the way they liked it.

On the night the wicked storm was raging outside, the worst he had ever seen,

MacDonald and his wife sat in their favorite chairs facing the fireplace, each with a cup of tea nesting on the small table that lay squat between them, each cradling a book to hold their interest before bedding down for the night. It wouldn't take too long, as far as Jeffrey was concerned, as his eyes drooped a bit lower with each passing page.

"What was that?" he said, suddenly alert.

"What was what?" Ella asked.

"That noise."

"What noise?" she asked, slowly turning a page. "You're either imagining things, Jeffrey, or it's the storm. Maybe you snorted while nodding off."

"I didn't nod off," he said. "And I don't snort!"

"Jeffrey, you nod off every time we sit down to read. I don't know why you choose those tiresome history books to pore over at night. They seem to work better on you than taking a sleeping pill."

"Shhh. Did you hear that?"

Ella stopped reading and cocked her head to the left. "No, I'm afraid I do . . ." She paused. "Wait . . . I think I did hear something. It sounded like a tree rubbing against the side of the house."

"Except we don't have a tree that close to the house, do we?"

"No," she agreed. "We don't."

They got up from the comfort of their chairs. Ella started to move, but Jeffrey held up his hand for her to wait. He walked to the back of the great room, grabbed a shotgun from the cabinet, and listened intently as he crept further to the back of the house. At first, he heard only familiar, identifiable noises: the split-shot crackle of the fire as it ignited dry tinder, the methodic ticking of the grandfather clock resting tall and stately along the west wall, the buffeting winds that hurled abundantly falling rain against the hurricane-proof windows, and his wife's shallow breaths that now came more rapidly.

"Jeffrey, what is it?"

Jeffrey didn't answer right away. He didn't need to. They both heard the sharp tinkling of breaking glass coming from somewhere on the main floor, definitely on the other side of the house. Jeffrey snapped his head towards Ella.

"Ella, go upstairs and lock yourself in our bedroom. Get the pistol in our closet and load it. Be ready for anything."

Ella knew better than to argue, but she also was not going to lock herself up while her husband took risks on behalf of their safety all alone. She wasn't built that way, but she hustled upstairs to get the gun nonetheless. They kept a spare pistol in the safe that sat inside their massive closet. She knew the combination by heart, dropped to the floor in front of the safe, and rapidly punched in the numbers on the keypad. The door popped open with a whirrr, and she reached in for the pistol. She pulled it out and grabbed a box of ammunition. She loaded it, put a handful of bullets in her pocket, clicked the cylinder shut, and cautiously approached the stairs.

Jeffrey walked slowly through the kitchen towards his office on the other side of the house. The great room, the kitchen, the office, and the dining room were all part of an area that wrapped around the central staircase, which led to the upstairs bedrooms. There were no doors separating the kitchen from the great room and dining room, but there was one on his office along that side of the house, and the office door was closed. Jeffrey crept down the hall with his gun raised. He could feel a strong draft sweeping through the house, cooling and wet, alive with the rage of the storm. Along with something else. Also riding the wings of the wind was an unusual smell.

Dear God, he thought, *what could make such an odor?*

Jeffrey was reminded that one of the drawbacks of living on Crover Island was the lack of a public sewage system. Instead, each home had a septic tank. Once, shortly after the house was built, their system failed. Raw sewage rose to the surface above the tank, and there was some backup in the house pipes. It was the worst smell Jeffrey had ever endured. Until now.

The wind felt stronger when he reached the far edge of the kitchen. He was convinced the wind and smell came from the office, past the dining room towards the front of the house. He heard yet another noise that invaded his home. Heavy breathing now accompanied that abhorrent, loathsome smell. And there was a sloppy, dripping noise, as if someone turned on a faucet and only thick fluid dribbled out, slapping against the hardwood floor with a splat.

Jeffrey tip-toed down the hall, and the closer he got to the office, the more his nose wrinkled in disgust. His brow furrowed and his right eye nervously twitched. His entire face contorted with hateful contempt for the repulsive smell emanating from his private sanctum, the one area where he liked to be alone with his thoughts. Even Ella knew not to bother him when the office door was shut.

The wind now shrieked as he got near the door to the office. Jeffrey grabbed the door handle, twisted the knob, and pushed. The door squealed and lightly bumped into the wall. He peeked into the void, seeing nothing but inky darkness. He reached around the doorframe and felt for the light switch. He found it and pushed the lever upwards. Instant brightness dropped from the ceiling.

Perhaps it was a measure of failed expectations; that what he thought he was going to see—a man waiting to attack him, or someone caught in the act of stealing—simply wasn't there. So, his response was more one of confusion.

What the bloody hell? he thought.

Standing next to the broken double-hung window with wind and rain pouring in, sloshing the floor with pellets of water, stood a . . . thing. A tall, grotesque beast with rivulets of saliva and blood snaking their way from its feet to his office floor. Jeffrey briefly thought that it must have cut itself on the broken window. Then it moved. It screamed in hunger and pain and lunged at Jeffrey, who, having regained his wits before it was too late, raised his gun, blew a hole through the creature's chest, and took its head off with a second shot.

"Jeffrey!"

He turned.

Ella looked past her pale-faced husband and saw the creature, or what was left of it, strewn across the office floor. She screamed.

Jeffrey ran to her, hugged her tightly, and rapidly whispered, "You have to get back upstairs. I don't know if it's alone. There may be more of these . . . whatever this is."

They both jumped when something pounded on the front door. Neither moved. They could hear the storm forcing its way through the broken window in the study, bringing with it the wind with its eerie whistle, and the rain tapping its destructive tune on the hardwood floor. Again, the pounding came, harder this time and more desperate. Jeffrey gently raised his gun and nodded to his wife.

"Open it quickly, and move towards the fireplace," he said.

Ella reached over to the door, unlocked the heavy bolt, and grabbed the door handle. She twisted it to the left, yanked it hard, then hustled into the living room. Jeffrey stepped back, raised his shotgun, and gently squeezed the trigger. He went slack-jawed for a moment, shocked at the sight in front of him. A scarlet coated human figure stood in his doorway, dripping rain and what appeared to be buckets of blood, all over his front portico. Thank God he hadn't fully pulled the trigger.

His wife clutched at her neck when the door swung open and shouted, "Jeffrey!"

Her husband flipped his gun on safety, then screamed at the mysterious figure.

"Get in, now!"

Jeffrey lunged to the doorway, grabbed the figure by the arm and yanked him forward. His hand nearly slid off, due to the sticky layer of blood now coagulating all over the man who shook with the cold and fear that gripped him physically and mentally.

"Mmmmr . . . Mmmmr . . . Mr. MacDonald sir, I . . . I . . ."

"Calm down, man, and tell me, what is it?"

Their unexpected guest, a worker named Jakob, lived in the bunkhouse on their property along with the other hired help.

"Jeffrey," Ella, said again. "Can't you see Jakob's shaken by whatever happened to him?"

Ella fetched a warm afghan she had tossed off her lap at the first sign of a problem and now lay on the floor next to her chair. She rushed it over to their worker and wrapped it tightly around his shoulders.

"Come and sit."

She pulled over an extra chair and helped him ease into it, then ran upstairs for a couple of towels. By the time she returned, she found that Jeffrey had locked the door and was now standing vigilant, as if waiting none-too-patiently for an answer to what happened.

"They . . ." Jakob began. "These things . . . monsters they were. They came at us in our bunkhouse. At first, we thought it was the wind hitting our door. We could barely hear the banging over the storm. Then the doors blew open and were splintered into a thousand pieces. I ran for a window, opened it, and dove out, landing on Stefan's body that had been . . . shredded, I think. That's the only way I could describe it. I panicked. I started to run. I slipped and fell on more bodies. I heard screams and gunshots. It all happened so fast. They were everywhere, and I didn't know what to do. So I . . . so I . . . I ran for help." He then put his soggy head into his blood-drenched hands and wept.

"Get hold of yourself, man," Jeffrey said. He was used to barking orders at this man, as well as the fifteen others who lived in the bunkhouse on his property, which was down his long drive, then off a path into a thickly wooded area. He marched over to the gun cabinet, removed another shotgun, and snatched two bags of extra shot. He gave the surplus gun and bag of ammo to Jakob.

"You stay here and protect my wife and house. And if you don't, you'll have me to answer to. Is that clear?"

But it was Ella who answered. "Yer aff yer heid!" she exclaimed. She was so angry, she resorted to slang to let him know how daft an idea that was. "I'll have none of that," she said. "I'll take care of myself, thank you, and no more of those filthy buggers are getting into this house while I'm here. So go help those men if you can, and take

Jakob with you," she said. She lifted her pistol and waved it at the door. "Come now, off with you."

Jeffrey let a tight smile form, allowing himself to remember why he admired his wife so much, then pointed at the gun cabinet.

"You'll need something more substantial than that toy you're waving about. So, load up, and if they do show, Ella, give them hell." He kissed his wife on the forehead, started for the door, then turned back to her and kissed her long and hard on the lips. "I'll come back before you know it," he said. "Don't shoot me by mistake when I do."

"Oh, it won't be a mistake," she teased. Jeffrey chortled and left abruptly, Jakob trailing close behind.

CHAPTER 21

LOCH CROVER

Tim's eyes were as wide as pie plates as he crept along a dirt and stone trail to the detached garage, down a small hill in the back of the church. The wind and rain continued to soak and buffet any fool who dared to go outdoors on such a night. One gust nearly knocked him flat, and the rain made it impossible to see anything with clarity.

Every unexpected noise made his head swivel. He imagined seeing vicious, salivating creatures ready to attack where none existed. Tree limbs swayed in a wind-driven frenzy, pounding their leaved branches to the ground, as if angry at the world. Rain ricocheted off the metal roof of the garage, sounding like automatic rifle fire. When he heard a loud boom, Tim nearly jumped out of his skin. He turned to see the church go up in flames, mesmerized by how quickly the blaze grew. Sorrow for those poor souls who'd perished inside filled his heart.

He slowed as he got nearer the garage. It was ink-dark, save for the flames reflected on the small garage door windowpanes. He tried to peer through a broken window by sticking his flashlight into the gap and swirling it around. He stood in front of the garage bay that was empty. He noticed an old workbench that was pressed against the rear wall, a couple of pieces of plywood leaning along the side, and an unswept dirty floor covered with dried leaves. He leaned into the window and the room smelled dank. He shined the light across the second bay and saw the van. Marie's description of it as white was a stretch. It looked like it hadn't been washed in a decade. He hoped it wasn't laying in a state of disrepair from sitting still for any length of time.

Tim reached down for the garage door handle. He tugged up and met resistance. "Locked," he said. He almost couldn't hear himself over the fury of the storm. He swung his light to the other door and saw the handle on that one. He shuffled over, reached down, and tugged up. The door moved but not all the way.

"Jesus, didn't he ever oil this thing!" Tim screamed against the wind as if in a shouting match, and he was losing.

This time, he grabbed the handle with two hands, supported his back by bending his legs, and yanked the handle upwards. The metal handle popped off in his hand as the door rolled all the way up. Tim threw the broken piece onto the drenched ground and stepped inside. Raindrops capered across the tin roof of the garage as Tim felt his way around the van to the driver's side door. He expected it to be locked and prepared himself for a wet walk ahead, but was pleasantly surprised when it easily opened. He threw his equipment across the back seat, climbed inside the musty vehicle, and slammed the door shut.

Dust fell from the roof as he did so. He flipped the visor down and caught the key in mid-air. He stuck the key into the ignition and turned it.

"Yes!" he shouted as the engine hummed to life.

He turned the headlights on and there stood three creatures, backlit by the blazing fire. Tim reached over and quickly pushed the door locks into place. He revved the engine, but the creatures didn't budge. So, he let his anger at the death and destruction he'd witnessed at the church guide his action. He clicked on the bright lights, jammed his foot on the gas pedal, and smacked headlong into the trio lining his only exit.

Bodies flew into the tempest. Pain laden screams radiated into the van's cabin as Tim pushed onward and rolled over the beasts that would have gladly torn him apart given the slightest chance. Blood splattered over the engine hood and across the windshield, only to be quickly washed away by the constant, driving rain. Tim thumped and bumped his way to the small road that led to Loch Crover. He turned left, took a deep breath, and hoped he knew what he was doing. He serpentined his way down the slope, hugging the steering wheel, with his face inches from the windshield. In this storm, the wipers served little to no practical purpose.

After ten minutes of white-knuckle driving, the headlights illuminated a big blurry sign. Tim could barely make out the name "Loch Crover" as he crawled into the parking lot. He stopped the van and killed the engine. He retrieved his gear from the back of the van and slipped it on as quickly as possible. He did not have a full wet suit, but he did have a vest. He had also stored one full tank of oxygen, a pair of flippers, a mask, a spear gun and the Spare-Air mini-tanks. He knew he didn't have any time to waste while in the water. He had to try to find the lost group, if at all possible, and fast. He took one more look at the map he'd filched at the pub. If it was to be believed, he thought he might have a chance.

He thought of Marie and how angry she was at his plan. He found it difficult to explain to her, and she would not have approved in any case. But he was haunted by the past and had to try. Long ago, when he was first learning how to dive, his instructor, mentor, and friend insisted on a very specific safety protocol. It dictated that if a diving buddy was in distress, Tim was to check his own oxygen supply first, and measure his ability to get to his buddy before his oxygen ran out.

If Tim couldn't conduct a proper rescue because he might not have enough oxygen, he was to immediately surface to save himself. Then, and only then, was he to attempt a rescue.

"It's bad enough when *one* diver is lost in an accident," his mentor used to say, "but don't ever make it a day when *two* divers don't get back to the surface or their families."

However, his mentor never told Tim how to live with himself when he had to make that decision, and his mentor was the one who never made it up. At the time, everyone, including his friend's family, told Tim he'd done the right thing and he was not to blame. Yet, he never forgave himself, and at times the guilt threatened to drown him on dry land.

Now there was a group of people in distress, and he was going to help them if he possibly could.

Tim leaned into the wind, grabbed his underwater flashlight, spear-gun, and flippers, then trotted over to the lake. Although the slant of the stinging rain obscured his vision, Tim pictured where the lake was from when he was here last. Almost without realizing it, he was ankle deep in the tepid water. *The water should be much colder, around fifty-seven degrees Fahrenheit,* he thought. But this, Tim realized, was seventy-plus degrees. *Must be the result of the earthquake,* he reasoned.

Once he was waist deep in the loch, pulled on his mask, adjusted his oxygen, and submerged. With his light leading the way, Tim explored the area swiftly, searching in quiet desperation for any sign that would be helpful. He soon came to the large hills that rimmed the loch, scanning their underbelly with his flashlight. He kicked with a steady rhythm; his large diver's flippers propelled him along the edge of the solid rock wall that extended downward to the bottom depths of the loch.

His light snatched the shimmering reflection of something moving under water. Tim slowed and made sure the spear gun was ready to fire. As he got closer, he noticed it wasn't a solid physical object at all. It was a steady flow of water, and it was gushing out of a hole in the base of the mountain. His light beam refracted through the fast-moving stream of liquid, which made it look like a creature that lay in wait. A couple of hard kicks brought him to the edge of the large, gaping cavity. He shined his light into the underwater cave and checked his oxygen level. He had enough time to briefly explore, he decided.

He pushed his way against the tide, which wasn't too strong, but strong enough to give him some resistance. Resistance cost him oxygen, so he'd have to be careful and check his levels more frequently. He wasn't close to running out of oxygen yet, but he was using it up at a much faster rate than he'd like. Tim came to a lazy Y-bend in the cave. To bear right would continue swimming into resistance. To bear left he'd swim with the water's current. He went right.

Tim wanted to see if he could find the source of the underwater flow. If he couldn't, he'd at least be able to turn around and let the current take him back to conserve energy and oxygen. He'd just have to remember that when he got to the fork in the Y, he'd have to bear left to retrace his route.

He swam on, looking left and right, fearful something could be lurking in the shadows and catch him before he knew what hit him. Tim looked up and saw something move ahead of him. When he tried to focus on the object, he couldn't see anything. He moved forward with caution, positioning his spear-gun for attack.

There it was again!

One of those beasts, thought Tim as he got closer. *And it's swimming towards a dim, watery light, where it is lifting itself out of the water.*

***

"Everyone, look around. Find a rock to grab, or anything you can use as a weapon," John said. "And hurry!"

Panic swept through the group like a rogue wave. In a moment's time, everyone transformed from a subdued undercurrent of nervous energy to an explosion of terrified panic. Those who could find one grabbed a rock for defense. Some hugged their children and wouldn't let go, as if squeezing them harder could prevent the inevitable. John saw a hefty stone and picked it up, then faced the thing crawling out of the pool of water he had exited moments before.

Parents buried their children's faces in their breasts to hide what was coming. The creature opened its terrible, razor-filled jaws and howled the howl of the hungry. Midway through its cry, as John was about to rush it with his rock, it stopped. Everyone paused. A spear came directly through the beast and rested, half of it sticking out of the front of its chest and half out of its back. Its mouth was open and its eyes wide when it fell dead on its face in front of them.

"I guess I got here just in time." Standing directly behind the now-dead creature, with his spear-gun in hand, was Tim.

John dropped his rock.

"You sure did," John said with a crooked smile.

"My name's Tim, and I came from the Royal Oak Pub to try and find you."

"Tim, I remember you from the meeting at the pub. You were with Marie. I'm John, the captain of this expedition. We're more than pleased to see you, but we'll have to talk later," he said. "Right now, we're desperate for help." An ear-piercing scream filled the void and broke the joyous spell of seeing another person connected to the outside world.

"Now Tim," John said, "how do we get the hell out of here? And I do mean now."

Tim quickly explained how he found them. He stressed that the swim would not be too bad, because the current would help carry them to safety.

"I'm afraid I don't have much air in my tank, and I may have to ditch it halfway back, but I do have seven Spare Air mini-tanks. If we do this conservatively, with a buddy system, we might be able to make it."

"I just did the math, though, and we're short," John said. "We have two crew, nine adult passengers, five children, and you. Even if you rely on your tank alone, we still need eight of those breathers, not seven. So, that's not enough for all of us. Two of us will have to stay behind until everyone is through. Michael and I will stay while you lead everyone out."

Allan came up behind John. "It seems to me, Captain, that there are higher priorities that need your attention than giving a few more days of life to two old, feeble-minded seniors."

"I'm getting everyone out to safety," John said. "You bank on it Allan, and I don't want to hear anything to the contrary."

"But hear it, you must," Allan said. "Triage is always difficult, Captain, but necessary in situations such as these. These passengers need you to lead them, not lag behind and be lost to those . . . things. Once out of here, you don't know what you'll confront. These parents, and most of all their children, need you. You mustn't fail them. You need to get those people to safety, now."

"The man's right," Tim said to John, reluctantly. "I'm sorry, but maybe I've got enough air to get halfway back without any problems, but nothing like this ever runs smoothly. We've got kids we need to get through, and some of their parents don't look like it's going to be easy for them either. When we get out, we'll check to see if there's any leftover breathable oxygen in a few of the minis. If so, someone could bring them back for this couple. But I have to say, the chance for that is slight at best."

A horrible cry, like an animal caught in a bear trap, echoed all around them. Everyone froze in place, rigid with fear.

"Allan," Margaret said. "Let the dog in. Can't you hear her barking?"

"Yes dear," Allan said. "Let's wave goodbye to our friends first, and then we'll see to the dog, shall we?"

John knew in his heart he had no choice. Triage *was* his only option if he was going to save as many of these people as possible. He was a great swimmer. Going and then coming back to rescue Allan and Margaret was the only feasible plan he could see.

"We've got to go, everyone," John said. "I want the best swimmers in the group paired up with the children, now." A quick discussion among the adults resulted in an equally quick match-up. Three parents stayed with their own child. Two did not, asking if their children could go with Michael and John, who immediately agreed. Three other groups were paired adult with adult. Tim, who had a waning level of air in his tank, would lead the way.

"Listen carefully, everyone. Tim will explain how this will go down," John shouted.

Tim explained to the nervous group how to use the tanks and how to buddy-breathe. He told them to let the current take them forward and to not exert too much energy. He likened it to moving slowly in a lazy river water pool. He warned them of the Y in the tunnel, that they needed to stay to the left and follow him, then once they were past that point, it was a few short kicks to the surface. He searched their faces as they kicked off their shoes, and saw the fear resting there. Oddly, the kids were less frightened than the adults, but perhaps they were more anxious to flee their current location, remembering what was chasing them.

Tim and John dragged the dead creature to the side, and Tim led the way into the water. Before donning his mask, he took a moment to calm everyone. "Each couple count to ten," he said, "then go in after the couple in front of you has done so. Take your time and try to relax. I'll be right in front of you, and I promise, it's a short trip and we'll all be on the surface soon, so focus on that." Tim nodded to the couple behind him, turned, and submerged into the pool. Each couple counted and took their turn in succession. Kids hung on the backs of their guide swimmer and let them do most of the work. They were buoyed not only by the swift-moving current, but also by the simple act of doing something to make their escape.

"Not you yet, Clark," said John to Charles Clark, who tried to move ahead after the second group went in. "You get back here with me along with your partner. I'll pick up the rear, but I want you in front of me, where I can see you." Charles licked his lips. John thought he was going to lose his shit, so he lowered his voice and spoke more softly.

"Listen, Charles, it's the same trip whether you're first or last. I don't want you to worry. You and your partner will be behind Michael and in front of me, so you couldn't be in a better place. Try to relax and let the current take you. When you're underwater, count to ten, take a breath on the spare, and pass it to your partner. You'll be out of here to safety in no time. We all will."

Michael and his child partner submerged. John turned to Allan and Margaret and pointed.

"I'm coming back for you both," he said. "Be ready when I do." He whispered one more comment before turning back to the pool.

John expected everyone else except his partner to be gone.

But Charles hadn't moved after Michael went in. Despite encouragement from his partner, he kept twitching, and stood rooted to the lower end of the pool, unable to move forward. Suddenly, Charles grabbed the spare and dove into the water swimming hard, even with the current. John looked at Clark's partner, a twenty-five-year-old bartender from Inverness.

"Are you a decent swimmer?" John asked.

"I'm pretty good," he said.

"Can you take this boy through?"

"I sure can."

"Then here, take this breather," John said, handing him his tank. Count to ten after I go in. Go easy and don't forget to turn left at the fork."

John reached over to his partner, a feisty nine-year-old, and asked, "Are you okay with that?"

"I can do it, I'm a good swimmer too!"

"Good lad," John said.

John, without a breather, took two deep breaths and dove into the water after Clark. He could see him ahead, struggling, even though the current propelled him forward. By contrast, John tried to not use up too much energy by taking long, slow strokes that would drive him forward but not deplete his strength. It seemed longer to John to approach the fork this time, but he was still holding his breath well. He was fifteen feet away when he saw Clark had lost all of his oxygen. He saw the empty canister falling to the bottom of the tunnel floor. The current pulled to the right and the limp body of Charles Clark went with it.

For a second, John thought of going after him. In the next second, he knew he would probably die trying, and it may confuse the couple behind him. At the fork, he went left. He knew the current wasn't as strong going this way, and he had to fight his way up that branch of the flow. He was getting dizzy and knew he couldn't hold his breath much longer, that he was beyond the amount of time he could normally hold his breath. He saw a light shining down and thought he was dying. People who have had near-death experiences often spoke of seeing a bright light as they felt their life ebbing away, coupled with a calming sense of peace. John's lips parted, allowing small air bubbles to float to the surface. He stopped swimming and gently floated, one hand reaching for the light above.

Suddenly he felt a push from behind, then a pull from above. He broke the surface, gasping for air. The swimmer that was behind him had given him a good shove, while Tim had grabbed his outstretched hand and yanked. The last pair behind John swam to the edge of the loch, which was made more difficult in the storm, but neither noticed as they were so happy to have made it to safety. Once ashore, they wedged in with the others into the van.

***

Allan and Margaret stood by the edge of the pool of water and watched the last of the group swim away. John had left his flashlight behind, and whispered to Allan to take good care of it, as he'd soon be back for it. The roar of the beasts came again, closer this time. There was a note of anger and frustration in their howls, like hyena fighting over a mound of carrion.

Allan didn't care for himself. He had lived a long and happy life. He didn't want to die, but if he had to, he would go down fighting if necessary. He shuddered, however, to think of what those beasts would do to his beloved, unsuspecting wife. It's not that she wasn't strong or strong-willed. He'd been married to her long enough to know that was not the case. But, ever since this horrid disease overtook her, it robbed her of her precious memories and her sharp mind. It had snuck in, like a silent thief in the night, steadily removing the things that were most important and leaving confusion and weakness in its wake. She simply wasn't *her* at times, and he already missed her terribly.

"Allan," Margaret said. "I told you. We have to tend to the dogs, they sound awful."

"Yes, my dear, we certainly will. But it's such a lovely night, I thought we would take a brief swim in the pool first."

"Wait," she said. "You're not Allan. Where's Allan?"

Allan paused, a deep melancholy settling over him.

Several beastly screeches filled the air. They were getting closer by the second.

Allan gazed across the water and put his right palm to his forehead. "There he is," he said. "Allan is on the other side of the pool. All we have to do is swim over and he'll be waiting for us both. Look, see, he's waving."

Margaret peered into the darkness, as she had been doing since her diagnosis, and waved.

"Are you sure that's him?"

"Yes, of course. Let's go and join him," he answered with a tear running down his cheek.

Allan took his wife's hand and gently led her into the rushing water.

"It's cold," Margaret said.

"Yes," Allan said, his face now wet with tears. "But very soon, you'll be able to hold your husband again and stay warm forever. Wouldn't you like that?"

"Oh yes, I would," Margaret said.

Allan put his arm around his wife of fifty years for the final time in this life and kissed her gently on her forehead. He then led her into the pool and let the moving current take them.

***

Tim handed John two minis with only partial air left as they tread water next to each other. "It's all I've got," he said, screaming over the noise of the storm. "And I'm telling you, there is not enough air combined for you to make it there and back, let alone you plus two other adults."

"I've got to try," John said.

"John, you can barely catch your breath, now. Here," Tim said, "take this with you as well." He gave John the spear-gun with one spear left.

"You get to the van and keep it warm," John shouted. "If I'm not back soon, get those people to safety."

"I'm not leaving without you," Tim said.

John stuffed the spares inside his shirt and dove with the spear-gun in hand.

Tim shook his head, knowing this was a mistake, but also knowing why John had to try. He said a quick prayer that John would make it, then swam back to the van.

John was fatigued and found it difficult returning. Even though he now knew the way, which was helpful in knowing how much further he had to go before he dared take a breath from the breather, he was experiencing difficulty. He preferred to swim all the way through without using the breather and conserve what air he could for Allan and Margaret, but he wasn't sure if he could manage that.

When he approached the bend in the Y, he saw them. They were hooked on an outcrop, gently moving about with the current, like a flag rolling in a soft breeze. Allan had his arms wrapped tightly around Margaret, and hers were around him. It could even be said they looked calm and peaceful, as they lay in each other's embrace. John knew if he had left them there, floating as they were, the creatures would find and eat them. But he also knew he couldn't take them with him now. There would be no place to put them in the van, especially with the children in tow, and their bodies would be no better off on the beach or a picnic table. He did the only thing he could do.

John breathed in what air was left in one canister, let it go, and turned his attention to Allan and Margaret. *I swear to you*, he thought, *I will come back when I can and bury you properly*. He unhooked Allan's shirt from the rocky knob and let them flow the rest of the way up the dead-end arm of the Y. There they would hopefully rest, hidden, until he was able to return.

John went to breathe the oxygen out of the remaining canister when he looked up and saw one of the beasts. It was coming fast up the canal. They must have gotten through the cave to where he left Allan and Margaret. In a nanosecond, the thought occurred to him that Allan did the only thing he could do, and both he and Margaret would have been torn to shreds and eaten alive if he hadn't. In the next second, the beast was upon him. John dropped the other canister without taking a breath and raised the spear-gun. He barely had a moment to get the shot off. It whooshed through the water and pierced the skull of the creature before it had time to grab him.

John wasted no time to see if there were more, or how far behind they were. He dropped the spear-gun and pushed his feet off the side of the cave in the direction of the Y arm. He grabbed handfuls of water and pushed them behind him as he scissor-kicked his way to the surface. His lungs were burning without that last bit of oxygen, but the adrenaline boost he received from believing there were more creatures behind, helped propel him through the water. He broke the surface and kept swimming until he reached the beach in waist-high water. He ran through the falling rain until he was on solid ground.

"Run, John, run!" Tim screamed. He opened the front passenger side door that was facing John. John sprinted for his life, now knowing for sure that he was being chased. He could hear water splashing behind him, but didn't dare turn to look. He reached the van, dove into the front seat alongside Tim and shouted, "Go, go, go!"

Tim pushed the gas pedal and hit the automatic locks once John slammed the door shut. It was only then, that John looked out the window and saw the thing that chased him. It was moving rapidly across the sandy beach, loping through the storm's fury. It screamed a shrill, ear-piercing howl, full of fury at losing its prey.

CHAPTER 22

THE BUNKHOUSE

Jakob, Jeffrey's worker, and the others in his bunkhouse, had begun their employment as migrant workers from Poland. Once they proved their worth, Jeffrey kept them on as full-time employees, providing room and board, along with a decent salary, in exchange for their hard work and loyalty. Both sides profited from the arrangement. The workers had a steady job that allowed them to send money home to family. Jeffrey, in turn, would do anything to protect, defend, and support them.

In cold anger at what he'd seen so far, Jeffrey, with his gun over his shoulder, weathered the storm as if it weren't there and marched towards his bunkhouse.

"Mr. MacDonald, sir, do you really think we should be going down there?" Jakob asked.

Jeffrey stopped, gazed at the man, and shouted over the din of the storm. "My men are in trouble. Need I say more?"

Jakob withered under his stare, unable to utter a syllable in response. They continued down the rain-sodden lane of his drive towards the bunkhouse, which was lodged in a corner of his wooded property. Once they reached the lighted path that led to the bunkhouse, they could hear the screams, even over the raging wind and rain. Jakob shivered in fear, but Jeffrey picked up his pace. Now that he'd seen his enemy and knew they could be killed, Jeffrey was hell-bent on killing as many as he could. When the bunkhouse came into view he stopped.

"Load up, safety off, shoot on sight," he shouted. "But get close, so you don't waste ammo."

Jakob always did as he was told, but wasn't too sure he could obey that last order. He'd seen them too, and it made his blood curdle. He had no intention of getting too close to those beasts ever again.

There were shadows in the woods. Things were moving out there, figures that were distorted by the wind-whipped branches, blinding rain, and shifting fog. Jackob was turning this way and that, yelping at human-like shapes both real and imagined. At one point, Jeffrey calmly reached over, grabbed the edge of Jakob's gun, and moved it from pointing at him.

"If you accidently shoot me in the back," Jeffrey said, "I shall be very upset."

A figure emerged from behind the curtain of rain, more solid than the wispy shadows that appeared and disappeared with the fog. Jakob screamed, and Jeffrey nearly walked into the beast's open arms. Instead of being caught in a deathly embrace, Jeffrey calmly placed his gun within inches of the creature's chest and blew a large hole straight through it. The monster stood still for a second or two. Jeffrey shoved it with his gun and toppled it over, flat on its back. He stepped over it and glanced to the left and right. More snarling figures emerged from the misty woods.

"It seems that my gunshot has drawn some attention," Jeffrey said.

Cries for help, coming from inside the bunkhouse, increased in urgency and intensity. The angry sounds of the protean storm twisted the desperate pleas of those trapped in the attic into garbled appeals for help. Jeffrey didn't hesitate. He moved swiftly toward the bunkhouse, avoiding the darkened figures that began to surround the building. He kicked in the remaining strands of wood that were left of the entry and strode into the main living quarters.

"Jakob!" he shouted.

"Yes, boss," Jakob said. He was right behind Jeffrey, causing his boss to jump.

"For God's sake, man, you're worse than those things out there. You'll give me a heart attack before they get to me."

Jakob licked his lips, nervously looking about.

"Shoot anything that comes through that entry, understand?"

Jakob nodded repeatedly, stood his ground facing the doorway, and raised his gun. Jeffrey walked to the pull-down stairs that led into the attic. He pulled the hanging cord, and the ladder's feet hit the wooden floor with a loud thump. Jeffrey gazed upwards at six pairs of eyes.

"Do you have any weapons up there?" Jeffrey asked.

"No, sir," came the response. "No time!"

Jeffrey looked around and saw a disheveled room. Chairs were upturned with broken legs, mattresses were bent and slit, their guts pouring out like bloodied intestines. A couple of bodies lay in the same condition. He spied two broken rifles and a coiled rope, rushed to them, grabbed the rope, and then heard a gun blast behind him.

"Jakob, you all right?" Jeffrey asked while turning to see what happened.

Jakob had shot a beast coming through the doorway, quickly followed by another. He shot that one as he backpedaled. Jeffrey joined him and they were both soon discharging their shotguns together. Jakob was out of ammunition first.

"Hurry, up the ladder," Jeffrey said as he shoved the rope into Jakob's hands. Jeffrey moved to the door entry and shot two more beasts coming through. He could see figures amassing behind them. He spun around and shot one that fell coming through the window, its belly split open by the sharp glass left behind. He heard a roar behind him and didn't bother to look, as he too was out of ammunition. He ran as fast as he could to the ladder, took two steps at a time, threw his empty shotgun up first, then dove into the black space above. His workers yanked the ladder up as a creature reached for it, barely scratching the bottom with its claws. Someone turned on a flashlight. Scared, sweaty faces were illuminated in the shadowed light.

"Well, hello mates," Jeffrey said to a round of nervous laughter. "This is a fine fix we are all in."

"Thank God you are here, sir," said a man named Antoni.

"Well let's not thank Him yet," Jeffrey said. "Jakob, hand me the rope." Jakob did so, and everyone got quiet, while Jeffrey outlined their plan.

"We can't risk lowering the ladder, so, we'll have to try and make our escape from the rooftop. We'll tie one end of this rope to the skylight, and drape the rest of the rope over the side of the bunkhouse. It should be long enough to reach the ground. We'll have to move fast, and climb hand over hand to the ground. Once there, we'll race to the main house together."

The tension was thick and palpable, as if it came wrapped in a package. The smell of sweat, tangy on the back of the tongue, hung in the air like a wool coat, smothering them all with the taste of desperation.

They heard a crash below, accompanied by a vicious, hungry howl. The anger and frustration of the creatures caused them to snarl and snap at each other with abandon. Horrible, beastly screams coated the main living quarters. It sounded as if they were tearing each other apart to vent their upset, with more and more of them continuously joining in. One of the workers trapped in the attic started to shake; another, a man named Emeryk, wet himself.

Jeffrey looked them all in the eye.

"Listen to me, now. None of us are going to die tonight. I give you my word. Have I ever lied to you before?" he asked.

After looking at each other, they all shook their head no.

"And I'm not about to start now. Everyone, out the skylight and into the storm, eh? Quickly, lads."

Each of Jeffrey's loyal workers climbed out the skylight and onto the roof one at a time, the din of the raging storm now muffling the excessive noise being carried out below. Jeffrey came last, carrying the rope and his impotent gun. Once on the roof, he turned and tied a loop around the skylight, making it as tight as possible. He gestured to the group to catwalk their way to the rear of the building. He halted the group several feet from the edge, and raised his index finger to his lips for them all to be quiet. He didn't want them to take any chances of being discovered by them shouting over the storm. A strong gust almost toppled one of them who stood too high, and he was nearly blown off the rooftop.

Jeffrey reached out to Jakob and drew him near to speak in his ear.

"If anything happens to me," he said, "you take the group up to my house and get my wife. Take the black van parked near the garage and get the hell out of here as fast as possible. She may resist at first," he said, with a choke in his voice. "But you tie her up if you have to, and you make sure she goes with you."

"But where should I take her?" Jakob asked.

"To the Royal Oak Pub. Now, you promise me!"

"Of course, Mr. MacDonald."

"Good man!"

Jeffrey patted him on the shoulder and slid up to the very edge of the roof and looked over. He scanned the area for a good minute. He wiped the rain from his eyes constantly, trying to discern if tree and shrub movement was caused by the creatures or was a direct result of the squall that surrounded them. Satisfied, he tossed the rope into the storm, and it fell to the ground next to the building. He motioned Jakob over.

"You first. Huddle near those tall bushes to the left and stay close to the barracks. I'll be down last." Jakob nodded, then quickly scooted down the rope like a suicidal squirrel. Once he was safely out of the way, he motioned for the others to follow, one at a time, saving the man who wet himself for last. When it was that man's turn, Jeffrey noticed he was pale and shaking. Jeffrey moved over to him and sat.

"Emeryk, you've been with me about six months, right?"

The man nodded.

"Listen to me, then. There's no shame in being afraid," Jeffrey said.

"But you're not afraid, sir."

"Aye, but I am. In fact, it's the most sensible thing to be right now. If you weren't afraid, I'd think you were daft." Jeffrey looked over at the rope. "I don't want to walk down the side of the building in a seething storm, either. But it's our only choice, since going back the way we came is not possible, and I'm going last."

They sat and stared at each other for a few seconds, then Emeryk crawled over to the rope, grabbed hold of the thick cord, and carefully slithered over the edge. At first, the wind gripped his helpless body and flung him outwards, away from the building. He was then thrown violently back towards it, slamming him hard against the wall, and he nearly lost his grip. Jeffrey leaned over the side, grabbed his wrist, and shouted.

"Put your feet against the building and walk down it. Go hand over hand with every footstep until you're down."

Jeffrey thought his man was going to let go and fall to the earth, but after another attempt, he got the hang of it. As soon as he reached ground, Jeffrey followed, taking only seconds to accomplish the task.

The mayhem inside the barracks, spilled over to the outside. Groups of the creatures were now leaking out into the storm, scuffling with each other. A clump of six creatures were blocking the way to the main house. They weren't moving. When two of them saw light at the main house and started to move in that direction, Jeffrey grabbed Jakob by the upper arm and shouted.

"Wait until they pass," he said, "then do as I asked."

Those words said, Jeffrey leaped out into the open.

"Oi!" he shouted. "You, there."

The creatures snapped their heads in unison and moved in Jeffrey's direction, as if they were ants invited to a picnic. Jeffrey was soaked from the unrelenting rain, whipped by the punishing winds, and confused by the ever-shifting fog. Were the beasts close? He couldn't be sure, as one minute they could be seen clearly, and the next minute they couldn't be seen at all.

Jeffrey backed away, his gun, empty of ammo, slung over his shoulder. His eyes darted left and right in a fretful search of any other creatures. He continued to move backwards, hoping to be able to tell when the beasts passed Jakob and the others. When he felt sure, he shouted to Jakob, "Go, go!" and waved his arms. The noise he made only served to agitate the creatures coming his way with greater malicious determination.

Jakob and the crew from the barracks crouched among the tall hedges alongside the building and saw the beasts slip by, drooling and snarling as they did. When he heard Jeffrey shout for them to go, Jakob led the others out into the open and crept their way up to the main house. When he got halfway, he turned. He waited a moment until the winds split the fog like Moses did the Red Sea. He was able, if only for a few moments, to see Jeffrey fighting like a madman, swinging his empty rifle as a cudgel, splitting heads, and knocking down all that he could. In another moment, the scene was lost to the fog, which swallowed whole both Jeffrey and the creatures he fought.

Jakob would later swear that Jeffrey was smiling as he did battle.

CHAPTER 23

A DESPERATE GATHERING

Lightning cleaved the sky, the resultant thunder as loud and menacing as Thor's hammer. The rumbling boom reverberated up Main Street in Blackpool, marching its way from the marina like a thousand jackboots striking cobblestone. As if in unison, the buildings that flanked its curved climb towards the Royal Oak Pub shook with a wild tremor.

Bryan quivered from the after-effects of the bellowing sky. He looked around and was worried about the stream of refugees now finding asylum in his pub, to say nothing of his emotional anguish concerning his still-missing daughter. He hadn't heard anything of her whereabouts and he was near mad with concern. Was she stranded somewhere? Was she dead, sprawled out on a rain-soaked field, unable to feel the pinging drops of rain that would pepper her tender face? Many of those rushing into the pub carried stories of cringe-worthy horror: finding neighbors splayed and gutted, gnawed upon by God knows what, and seeing visions of alien-like beings wandering the countryside. If only half of what they said was true, Bryan had ample reason to be frantic with concern.

The two men Robert had previously assigned to monitor the front entry were still at it, Bryan saw. Every once in a while, they'd split the opening just enough to scan the outside area in search of wayward souls seeking shelter. Over the clamor of the storm, they grabbed snippets of the horror stories coming in, which made them extra cautious about opening the door at all.

The first beast arrived with a wicked flash of unexpected lightning. Jeff Watson, one of the men at the door, let out an audible gasp.

"Did you see that?" he asked of his partner, Scott Mitchell.

"See what?" asked Scott.

Bryan overheard the conversation and interjected. "What is it, lads? What's out there?"

"It looked like a person," Jeff said. "Only bigger. Down the road, towards the marina."

Scott peered intently into the vortex, with Bryan leaning over his shoulder. The intense rain and intermittent fog obscured most of what they could see, like peering into a coal-black cave through a dirty glass.

"I don't know," Scott said, squinting his eyes and straining with effort to see better. "I can't really see much of . . . ." The lightning struck again with rapid, successive flashes, like a photographer taking multiple pictures of the same horrific scene, the monster getting closer with every flash. He and Bryan both leaped backwards and slammed the door shut.

"Yes," Scott said. "I did see something. And you're right, it's way bigger than anyone I know."

"Me too," Bryan said, "and I don't want to see it again."

The low chatter behind them ceased, as people picked up on the sudden, tense atmosphere between the three men. Bryan back-pedaled to the bar, but stayed within earshot.

Scott popped the door opened a crack. He and Jeff peered out again, their pupils wide, their optic nerves in overdrive. All they could see were shadows of shadows, negative imprints of death crawling up the narrow lane that was Main Street.

Thunder rolled in like the rising tide, accompanied by flashes of lightning that added to the queerness of the storm.

"There it is again," Scott said. "I saw three of them this time, moving ahead like people dancing under strobe lights, you know?"

Jeff put his shoulder to the door and closed it. He jammed the bolt home and turned to those inside who were staring at him with nervous anxiety.

"They're here," he said. "Lots of them."

A hushed panic embraced the room. Some had guns, but others had come empty-handed.

Bryan felt the need to take charge.

"Jeff, Scott," he shouted. "Make sure all the windows are secure. I tended to them earlier myself, making sure the shutters were bolted, but check again anyway." Bryan then turned to the milling group. "Everyone, listen! Those of you with children will take them down into the cellar. Those with guns, take a window or stand near the door. If any of those things breach an entry, blow their heads off."

A long bleat from a car horn shredded the fearful quiet that had descended on them like a silent, stealthy snowfall. Bryan made an instant decision.

"Open the doors, lads, quickly, now."

Jeff and Scott didn't hesitate. Jeff yanked open the door, and Scott leaned over his shoulder with the shotgun.

"Scott," Bryan said. "You shoot anything that looks like it crawled off the screen of a horror movie. Understand?"

"Roger that."

"There's a car outside," Jeff said. "And it pulled up in front of the pub from the south side. Its high beams are on, and . . . Oh my God, there must be dozens of them things creeping up Main Street."

Bryan rushed to have a look, hoping beyond hope that his daughter was in the car.

The car had pulled down Main Street and parked diagonally across it about fifteen feet beyond the edge of the pub, partially blocking the creatures from getting to the pub door. It hadn't fully halted their progress, merely slowed them down. The beasts began to climb over the engine hood and claw at the car-door windows to get at those inside. The driver and passengers emptied the car on the side opposite the beasts, and ran to the pub's entry. The driver herded them all through the storm and into the pub before the door was slammed shut and bolted solidly behind him. In what seemed like a second, there was clawing and banging on the door, accompanied by shrill, horrific screams.

Bryan greeted the new entries. It took him a moment to recognize the family.

"Jim," he said. "I'm glad you made it here."

Jim and Barbara Cross stood still, hugging their children, David, Paul, and Nicola, as well as another little girl who didn't look well at all. Jim had his arm around the girl, but she didn't appear responsive. Jim saw Bryan staring and said, "I think she's in shock. Our neighbors, the Taylors, didn't fare so well, I'm afraid. Robert told us."

"Robert?" Bryan perked up at hearing news of Robert.

"Aye, and once he did, he went down to the southern village along the coast, just below my place. I would have gone with him, but I couldn't leave my wife, Bryan. I couldn't leave my kids. I . . . I . . ."

"It's all right, Jim, you did what was best for your family."

"I was going to stay put and ride it out to defend my home and family. I know now, that would have been suicide. This wee one showed up at our door, banging away in desperation to be let in. At first, we were hesitant, thinking it was one of those things," he said, pointing towards the door. "Barbara was the first one to come to her senses and ran to open it, and there the poor thing stood, drenched from both the storm and gripping fear. She was able to relate a message.

She said, 'I'm Anna. The man, he told me. He told me to tell you, you must leave. There are too many of them. You must leave.' Then she looked off into the distance and went into some kind of trance. Barbara called it something. What was it again, dear?"

"She became catatonic."

"That's it," Jim said. "She hasn't said a word since."

"Jim, what about Robert?" Bryan asked.

Jim shrugged and lowered his head. Bryan knew in his heart that his old friend was gone. He didn't need any further testimony or proof. He could feel it in his gut, a sour, sick nausea that wafted over him. With a tear tracking its way down his face, he said, "Okay, Jim. Send your family down to the cellar. We're going to need you up here, though."

Jim nodded to Barbara, who took all the children down to the basement. Barbara paused at the door and looked back. She blew her husband a kiss and was gone in a blink, her children and the little girl Anna in tow.

Everyone in the room spread out and took a position at one of the entry points in the wide pub, either at one of the boarded-up windows or at the door, lending support to Jeff and Scott. Bryan asked his bartender to gather up whatever guns and ammunition he possessed and tried to hide his grief and sorrow. Robert wasn't just his friend. He was his brother in spirit, his closest comrade. He was the one Bryan could always confide in, someone with whom he could share his most private thoughts, without judgment, but always accompanied with sound advice.

As far as he knew, Bryan was the only one who was aware that Robert had been a war hero. He had found out quite by accident one day, when he and Robert were delivering supplies to a sick friend. While Robert loaded the truck, he asked Bryan to fetch his keys, which he had left in his bedroom. While pulling out drawers on the nightstand tables, Bryan noticed the medal. It shocked him that such a thing was kept a secret, but on another level, he understood. It was one of those things you thought of as your duty, not something you boasted about. He then saw the keys had been tossed onto the bed. Since Robert never told him directly of his war exploits, Bryan had always kept that information to himself.

"What now, old friend?" Bryan said. "What in God's name do we do now?"

Bryan attempted to busy himself with the threat they were all facing in order to not dwell on his suspected loss, but it was no use. He tried again to use his cell phone in a futile attempt to reach his daughter, but it didn't connect. He froze at the thought of never seeing her again. He stood there, speechless, and began to shake. It started with a small tremor, but before he could control himself, he was quivering like a willow in windstorm. The tears came next, falling in cadence with the rain outside. He believed, with a certainty that comes from trusted intuition, that the two most important people in his life, Robert and Marie, were dead at the hands of those creatures. Who knows what unspeakable horrors they met at the end of their lives.

Bryan looked up. He heard something. He doubted himself, at first. He cocked his head and yelled for everyone to be quiet. "There's more shooting," he said.

A steady beat of muffled pops could be heard coming from outside. Everyone raised their guns in a reflex reaction. Bryan walked over to and behind Jeff Watson. He tapped Jeff on the shoulder, who then leaned forward and cracked open the door. All three gazed into the storm once again. Another car had joined the previous one that served as a barrier to the creatures, adding an extra wall of security for those inside the pub.

"I see two more vehicles," Bryan said. "What about you mates?" Both Jeff and Scott nodded in unison.

A pair of men were out there, leaning over their engine bonnet, firing at will. Some of those shots rang true, the screeches of a dying beast a testament to their accuracy. Many sailed through the mist, dancing to a tune called by the ever-shifting winds, resulting in too many missed hits. A cluster of others ran for the pub's entrance, dodging around the bodies of dead creatures.

"Fall back," one of the men cried out.

The two raced for the door, a handful of creatures in pursuit, climbing clumsily over the rain-soaked vehicles. They slid and fell on the cobblestones, one of the few tended roads on Crover Island, but it didn't stop them from coming. Jeff and Scott slammed the pub door shut after the duo entered, with little room to spare.

Jakob and Emeryk from the MacDonald estate were the ones holding a gun, and therefore the last to come inside. Drenched from the storm, Ella MacDonald and the other MacDonald workers who preceded them, all stood still and dripping on the floor, as if they were awaiting orders. Ella MacDonald turned to Jakob, got within inches of his face, and said, "If we survive this, you and I are going to have a reckoning for leaving my husband behind. Now, give me your gun."

Jakob, stung by her rebuke, handed his gun over to Ella and said, "Mr. Mac is a strong man, Mrs. MacDonald. You must have faith."

"Hmmpf," Ella said and marched over to Bryan.

"Where do you want me?" she demanded.

In response, Bryan addressed the crowd. "New arrivals, listen up. Form a second tier behind those at the windows and door. You can replace them in that position if they . . . well, if they should fall or run out of ammunition."

Ella MacDonald walked over to one of the windows and grabbed its defender by the shoulder. "Move back," she said. "I'm taking your place."

Gerald Butler, a burly farmer, turned and looked into her eyes. "Yes ma'am," he said and backed away.

Jack Brodie and Angus McCleod approached Bryan. Before they could speak, Bryan poured them each a dram, then handed the bottle of Scotch to his redheaded waitress, Susan. "Here," he said. "Take this bottle around and give a drink to anyone who wants one. There's more on the shelf when you need it."

The tense atmosphere was as thick as oatmeal.

"Bryan," Jack said. He put his hand on Bryan's shoulder. "Bryan, where's my wife and kids? Where's Emily?" The spark of human touch moved Bryan to focus on Jack.

"Sorry, Jack, I've been distracted. She and the children are safe and in the cellar."

Jack, raced to the cellar door. "I'm going to check on them first. I'll be back to join you shortly."

"Receive bad news, old friend?" Angus asked. "I can see it in your eyes."

Bryan was reluctant at first, but then grateful for the opportunity to unburden himself of the overwhelming sorrow that now encompassed him. He shared the reported news of Robert's death, and his growing fears for his daughter. Angus grabbed Bryan by the shoulders and looked him straight in the eye.

"Marie is one of the toughest people I know. She can withstand anything, and I have no doubt she'll persevere. Have hope, my friend." Angus then took a place near the front entry.

"Why does it always storm at night, eh mates?" Angus asked those manning the front door. The question caused a bit of chatter, at first. Frenzied thumping and scratching at the Australian hardwood doors and front windows soon hushed the room.

"I guess they climbed over the parked cars," Jeff said about the constant scratching.

"I wonder how many are out there?" Scott said. The half-hearted question made Angus think.

"Bryan?" he asked.

"What is it?"

"Has anyone gone upstairs to look out the guest room windows?" The vacant looks gave him his answer.

"No," Bryan said. "God, Angus, I've been so preoccupied, and events have happened so fast, I never gave a thought about it. I have a pair of binoculars over on the desk. Help yourself to them and let me know what you see from up there.

Angus grabbed the binoculars and rushed upstairs to a room that faced the front of the building. He gaped at the surreal scene below. Through the deluge that poured from the sky, and the roaming mist that cradled the earth, he could barely see the tall, outlandish figures that trudged up Main Street, stepping over the dead ones that lay where they fell. Some were climbing over the jammed vehicles that blocked their way. Others already had, and were gathering at the front of the pub, pounding on the windows and door. Angus rushed back downstairs.

"Bryan," Angus said upon returning to the pub. "I've noticed a few things from up there."

"Go on."

"Those creatures are coming from the northern coastal road."

"So?"

"So, we all came down the Central Road that feeds into the back of this building. Once we got past a certain point on Central, we didn't see any creatures. What if the ones we passed eventually do come down that road? Can they get into the pub from the rear?"

"There's no other door, no, but there are a set of Bilco doors to the supply storage area in the very back of the cellar. But, there's no need to worry, they're made of thick steel, and I have them heavily chained and locked on the outside. There are only two people with a key to that lock. Me and . . . me and Marie."

***

Those in the basement, shivered in fear at every shriek and thump that echoed from above. Mostly the younger ones, but also more than a few adults, were openly shedding tears. The stink of fear permeated the room, wearing out their patience and whatever stamina they had left.

Emily Brodie and Barbara Cross huddled near the edge of the dank, open space, each resting on an upturned cart. Barbara had Anna, the waif who warned them of danger at the behest of Robert, nestled in her lap and pulled tightly to her bosom. Her children and Emily's, each in turn, clung to an arm of their mother, the mere touch a talisman against the horror outside that was fighting to get in.

"Do you hear that?" whispered Emily, leaning into Barbara's ear so as not to disturb the children. Barbara shook her head no at first, then tilted her head as a dog might when its owner makes an odd sound. Soon, recognition swept her face, and she nodded affirmatively.

"Keep an eye on the children, while I go and investigate." Emily told her kids to mind Mrs. Cross while she went to check something.

"Mama nooo," wailed her daughter Nicola.

"It's okay, sweetheart, I'll be right back."

"Come dear," Barbara said, "I'll stay right here with you and your brothers." Nicola moved next to her, unsure at first, then grabbed an arm and laid her head on Barbara's shoulder.

Emily had heard movement of some kind in the rear of the basement. It was muffled by the rain outside and the stacked boxes of liquor and scattered shelving. She moved to the rear of the cavernous cellar, negotiating her way over carelessly tossed empty sacks and crates, shifting herself around overstuffed shelves full of snack boxes, ale bottles, and canned goods.

It's darker back here, she thought. There were a few broken light bulbs and a few missing ones, adding to the already nerve-racking experience. She was holding her breath. The small chatter of the group behind drifted off as she continued towards the back of the cellar. The sound she previously heard got louder with every step she took.

The whirr of a refrigerator made her jump. Once she realized what it was, she laughed silently at herself. She was about to return to her children when there was a sudden clatter to her right. She rounded a tall shelf and saw the rear stairs rising to a set of Bilco doors. Something was tugging on them. She heard a chain of some sort being dragged across the doors, followed by one door being flipped open.

Emily yelped, turned, and ran back to the others, leaping over the boxes strewn about. She got back to the group and shouted.

"Everyone, move upstairs. Now. Quickly!"

Her tremulous voice and the tone with which she delivered that message roused the group in seconds. They scrambled up the stairs and rushed into the pub, Emily slamming the door behind them.

***

"They're inside," Emily said. "Through the Bilco doors. They managed to open them."

"Dear God," Bryan said. "There's no lock on the door to the basement. Step back everybody. If you have a gun, train it on that door. When they break through, shoot."

Parents ushered their children behind the bar and stood in front of them. Everyone hushed to listen, despite the clamor of scratching and pounding on the windows and main entrance. Wet plodding steps could be heard stomping up the groaning cellar stairs. The closed door eased open with an eerie squeal. All eyes were glued to the basement, and rifles were raised.

"Hello?" came a tentative voice as the door widened. A figure took shape as the light shined down on a face.

"Well, now, isn't this is a fine welcome," Marie said.

CHAPTER 24

A TSUNAMI OF TERROR

Bryan rushed to his daughter's side, then hugged and squeezed her tightly. He gazed at Marie through tear-filled eyes, as if she were a heavenly apparition, a mirage that would disappear if he got too close, too fast.

Marie broke from her father's embrace and addressed those following behind her.

"Everyone, come on up and spread out where you can."

Marie then hustled Bryan off to the side and gave him a summary of what transpired at the church, how difficult it was to get to the pub, and how, once here, she took off the chain and reinstalled it on the inside of the Bilco doors.

"We had to kill many of them enroute, Da. They attacked some of the cars in our caravan, and we were forced to stop at various points to do battle. I'm afraid we lost some along the way. Andrew Morrison and Gerard Young are with me," she added. "If it wasn't for the two of them, I don't know that any of us would have made it. Young Bobby

Bruce rode with me and is also here. He fought like a tiger, and he's been through hell. He'll be a welcome addition to our group here and what we're facing."

"Where's Tim?" Bryan asked.

A dark cloud descended over Marie, and the light in her eyes dimmed. Bryan's gut hitched at her look.

"He . . . he went in search of John Stewart and his crew. He came across information on one of those maps you keep in the back of the pub. Information he didn't bother to share with me until we liberated the people in the church. He'd been planning it since we left here, apparently, stashing his diving gear in the back of the van."

Her voice quivered. Tears that had fought to be recognized now flowed freely, until she dropped her head into her father's chest and sobbed openly. Bryan kissed his daughter on the forehead, then held her by the shoulders.

"The lad will be all right," he said with renewed vigor. "I'd nearly given up hope of ever seeing *you* again, and yet, here you are. Tim is made of tough stuff. He'll make it, you'll see. For now, we have to focus. Those doors and shutters are strong, but they will not stand forever. We're going to have to mount a solid defense of some kind, and soon."

Bryan could see the change in his daughter, almost instantly. The steel that was in her blood quickly rose to the surface. Marie wheeled around, grabbed a stepstool, and stood on the top rung.

"Everyone, listen," Marie said.

The nervous chatter that permeated the room gave way to the ceaseless beating and scratching on the solid wood doors and shutters.

"Andrew and Gerard," she said. "Take a crew upstairs to the front of the building and use the windows on that side to fire down on them. Pick your targets carefully, we don't have an unlimited supply of ammunition. Bobby Bruce, take a group downstairs and defend the Bilco door entrance, where we came in. The chain and lock should hold, but if not, do not let any of those creatures in. Children and parents, back downstairs, you'll be safer there, at least for now. The rest of you, pick a spot and defend it with your life."

"What about the rear, the way you came in?" Bryan asked.

"We'll keep checking it, but those things we passed on the Central Road on our way here are a distance off, yet."

Shots erupted from upstairs. Marie ran up the steps and found Andrew moving from room to room, checking that all windows had a gun at the ready.

"What's happening?" she said, over the sound of the gunfire.

"We're picking off the ones nearest the pub, those inside the perimeter of that car blockade. There seem to be many more of them coming up Main Street, but it's hard to tell with the wind, rain, and fog."

"I just had an idea," she said. "Maintain focus on those that are inside the car area and shout down to me when that area is clear of the filthy beasts."

Andrew smiled, with a look of understanding.

Marie ran down the stairs in a rush. She grabbed her father's arm and whispered, "I have a plan." She latched on to a nearby stepstool and called for everyone's attention. "I need a few brave volunteers," Marie said. "Those in the upper rooms are shooting the beasts just outside our door. When I get the signal from Andrew, I'll lead a small group out to the street. We'll use the cars as a barrier and shoot the creatures down as they come up Main Street. It won't be easy due to the wicked weather, but we may put a serious dent in their numbers by taking the fight to them. Who's with me?"

Marie was met with a huge chorus of "Ayes." Everyone, it seemed, was in the mood for taking the offensive. Marie smiled at the thought.

"Jeff Watson and Scott Mitchell," she said, "please continue to man the doors while we do battle. We may have to dash back in a hurry and we'll need your help to get everyone back inside safely. The rest, get ready."

Ella MacDonald shoved her way to the head of the line. "I'm going to kill as many of those bastards as I can, so don't anyone get in my way."

The attacks on the door and shutters diminished with the increase of fire power from above. The crowd huddled nervously, but they were a determined bunch, ready to rush out into the elements to do battle with the creatures overrunning their island. A few more shots, then silence. Footsteps were heard running along the upstairs hallway. At the upper landing, a voice called out.

"Go, go, go," Andrew Morrison said.

All eyes were on the entrance to the pub. Jeff Watson cautiously pushed open the door, Scott Mitchell poised and ready to shoot just behind him. The fog cleared for a moment. Scott stood aside, and the crowd, led by Marie and Ella MacDonald, dashed into the gale, charging toward the creatures on the other side of the parked cars.

***

The shooting, the shouting, the noise of the crowd in the middle of a donnybrook conspired to stir Henry Knox. *Where am I?* he wondered. He sat on the edge of the bed, his head still aching, and listened to the commotion outside his door. *People are yelling, barking orders to one another and, what was that? Shooting?* Henry stumbled to the door of his room and jiggled the handle. It was locked. *Who did this to me? And why?* Henry put his ear to the door and listened intently. He heard bits and pieces of conversations from those taking orders and those giving them. It was hard to make out everything that was being said, but it was clear as a bell with whom they were doing battle. He heard them mention several times the word "beast." And to Reverend Henry Knox that meant only one: *The* Beast. Lucifer. Satan.

"No, my friends," Henry said. "You're doing it wrong. You'll not defeat him that way."

He pounded on the door, but he was still weak and he doubted anyone could hear him over the sound of the gunfire. He panicked as he paced around the room muttering to himself. "Lord, my Savior, what do I do? Let me be thine instrument. Let me save my people and drive the Evil One back to hell, from whence he came."

Henry fell to the floor next to his bed and knelt in prayer. He clasped his hands together and recited the Lord's Prayer in earnest. His voice quivered, and he perspired as if he were at heavy manual labor for hours without pause. God would answer him, he was sure. He had to pray harder, harder than he ever had before.

But when no answer came, he despaired. "Why have You forsaken me?" he said.

Henry arose slowly, depressed and in tears. When he finally stood tall, it came to him like a hammer to the head. He knelt once again, and loudly recited Romans 15:13. "May the God of hope fill you with all joy and peace in believing, so that by the power of the Holy Spirit you may abound in hope."

This time when Henry stood, he was filled with a purpose he would only describe as heavenly inspired. Now that he knew what was expected of him, it filled him with great joy.

***

Once outside the pub's entrance and in the bloody mess outside, Marie and those who followed her took no note of the beastly body parts and lacerated carcasses that lay strewn across the slippery road-way. They were motivated by a singular objective, and that was to add to the creature body count. The intense rain that continued to fall created a raging river of blood, water, and physical ruin, one that gushed down Main Street towards the marina. Lightning still flashed periodically, but gave little recompense to the darkness and fog that surrounded them and served only to obscure their vision further.

Nonetheless, they bravely lined up behind the silent row of cars that blocked the road and fired at anything that advanced up Main Street. The loud, anguished beastly cries of wounded animals that echoed in the night told them they were hitting their mark. Although their numbers seemed to have thinned, the beasts kept coming. The death of so many of their kind did not affect them in the slightest. They crawled over their fallen as if they weren't there, a mere obstacle in their quest for new meat. They were a brutal, ruthless killing machine, tramping forward in a fever of relentless terror, trying desperately to get to their catch. Their blind determination pushed them ever forward, putting pressure on the group from the pub to take more careful aim and conserve their ammunition. It was difficult enough to see their targets in the pitch of the storm, but the mysterious fog that accompanied it made it ever worse. It gave the creatures a blanket of cover. So much so, that some were able to get close enough to kill.

One person, Timothy Wilson, slid over the bonnet of Jack Brodie's Subaru, filled with the adrenaline that pumps one during battle, causing the fighter to think it was enough for he and his comrades to win the day. He charged ahead through the mist, wind, and rain, pausing after ten paces, only to realize no one else shared his vision of what could only be called a reckless strategy.

"Come on," he shouted to the dark, unable to understand why he was alone. "We have them on the run."

Out of the fog came a figure, not two feet in front of him. Wilson's head separated from his body in a second, flew across the vehicles, and rolled to a stop halfway to the pub's entrance. When those on the front line looked up, they saw a specter emerge from the alley between the pub and the shop next door. The fog dissipated with a wind gust, and Reverend Henry Knox emerged on the creature side of the cars.

"Dear God," shouted Angus McCleod. "What's he doing there?"

***

At the time Ella MacDonald and Marie led the assault out the front door, Reverend Henry Knox had tied two sheets together, anchored them on the bed's headboard, and draped the line out the bedroom window towards the rear of the pub. He climbed down to about five feet above ground and dropped, landing safely without injury. Central Road, accessed from behind the pub, ran up to Robert Campbell's house. Two miles beyond Campbell's house, South Shore Road blended in to connect with Central, which came all the way down to the back of the pub. It then veered south and continued around the general store on that side of the pub, tying into the top end of Main Street.

When Henry climbed out the window, he thought he saw the devil's minions coming down the hill from Robert Campbell's, but in this storm he couldn't be sure. He turned to his right, passed the pub's Bilco doors, then turned down the alley between the pub and barber shop, to the north side. At the end of the alley was a thin wooden gate with a latch. He unhooked the gate's latch and walked out onto Main Street, a few feet beyond the car barrier, and witnessed how one of his parishioners lost his head.

Momentarily stunned, Henry flinched at the site. The rain saturated him from head to toe. The sliding fog confused him, causing him to be disoriented. Wind buffeted him, shoving him forward, despite his reluctant feet. He took it as a helpful sign from God, a divine push forward. He clutched the worn Bible he had fetched from the bedside table and began to shout biblical passages and their citations over the racket of the storm, in a steady stream of consciousness.

"'Resist the Devil, and he will flee from you,' James 4:7. 'The Thief comes only to steal and kill and destroy,' John 10:10. 'Your adversary, the Devil prowls like a roaring lion, seeking someone to devour,' Peter 5:8."

Knox stumbled out of the shadows and into the middle of the street. He could hear a few of his parishioners, along with Ella MacDonald, screaming for him to come back and get behind the cars. Instead, he smiled at them and moved down Main Street towards the marina. He would show not only Satan, but also his parishioners, what the power of his Lord could do. After a few tentative steps, a patch of fog cleared, and the reverend found himself standing in the middle of a pack of the vicious beasts. The two on the edge of the pack moved around him to encircle him and close off any attempt at escape. Those behind the car were reluctant to shoot. They were unable to get a clear shot through the shifting storm and didn't want to hit Knox by mistake. The reverend smiled again and turned his face to the sky. A warmth of righteousness spread throughout his body. He'd never been surer of anything in his life. The fear and weakness he'd previously felt dissolved with the rain. It cleansed his soul, washed away his sins, and filled him with God's purpose.

With his right palm open and his left holding the Bible to the heavens, he shouted at the top of his lungs, "The Lord will shine his light down on thee and smite thee to hell, foul beasts!"

The world as he knew it appeared to cease at that moment. It was as if the earth, for a few seconds, was entirely silent. No one behind him could speak. The monsters stood and stared, dripping with rain, saliva, and blood from their pointy teeth and sharpened claws. With a solid belief in his mission, Reverend Henry Knox was finally at peace.

Slowly, methodically, Knox began to recite his favorite psalm: "'The Lord is my shepherd; I shall not want. He makes me lie down in green pastures. He leads me beside still waters. He restores . . .'"

The creatures pounced. They ate with voracious abandon, tearing off limbs while the reverend screamed in agony. They continued biting into tender flesh, ripping off chunks of muscle, sinew, and bone, as Knox whimpered for salvation.

Marie and the others, momentarily shocked by what they saw happening to Reverend Knox, hadn't noticed how close other beasts were to the vehicles.

"Back up!" Marie said. "Keep shooting, but back up!" The creatures were climbing over the cars to get to them.

"They're behind us as well now!" Angus said. "Run for the pub, everyone."

A contingent of creatures was coming down Main Street after rounding the general store on the south side of the pub.

"They must have come from Central Road," Angus said.

"Get these people inside in a hurry," Marie said.

The group raced for the door. Marie, Ella, and Angus, still shooting, pulled up the rear, ensuring everyone got inside. They made it with only seconds to spare. One of the creatures reached out for Angus, but Jeff Watson stuck his gun into its face and blew it to hell moments before the door slammed shut. The pounding and scratching on the wooden shutters and door began anew, and the creatures were finally getting results.

We have a hole here at the door," Scott Mitchell said. "And it's getting bigger."

A tiny hole appeared in the center of the door. Not a large one, but one large enough to serve as a breach the creatures could pick at. The same thing was happening at the shutters.

***

In the basement, Bobby Bruce organized a group to move some of the storage shelves in front of the Bilco doors.

Something was tugging hard on the outside trying to get in, and it was causing quite a racket. As of now, the chain was holding, but Bobby was not sure it was going to last. The gap between the doors kept getting larger. Large enough for a claw to get through and swipe at the chain itself.

He'd seen these things up close and knew what they could do. He was beyond fear, though. His battle at the church, the death of that old man, Keith Argyll, and the thought of what they would do to the children if they got through put him way beyond fear. He was now fiercely determined to rid the world of these creatures or die trying.

A harder tug was accompanied by snarls that would straighten the hair on a poodle. Sharp claws reached into the growing space between the two doors, grabbed the inside of the doors and pulled. It didn't take them long to figure out how to pry the doors open. The chain was in danger of snapping, and then they'd have free access. Bobby tugged the shirt of a person next to him, Tom McGann, and gave him some quick instructions. He, in turn, snatched two bottles of vodka and ran upstairs.

Bobby knew he had little in the way of ammunition left. The door gap was widening, and the noise now spread throughout the basement, scaring those gathered there. The children were shuffled over to the staircase, while able-bodied parents formed a barrier between the Bilco doors and their offspring.

"They're breaking through," Bobby said in a controlled panic.

The parents gathered behind Bobby tensed at the news. Some grabbed a bottle off the shelf and smashed the end on a crate to create a jagged, impromptu, last-resort weapon. One of the parents at the top of the stairs peeked out into the pub, with hopes the children at least could be moved to that floor. Unfortunately, the situation up there was not any better. The main door and window shutters were being torn to shreds. Whole monstrous heads could be seen. Creatures were fighting with each other to be the first inside. The cannibalistic brawl that ensued resulted in blood spurts coating the ever-widening holes. Those inside the pub were shooting through the large cavities in a futile attempt to stop the beasts' progress.

Bobby Bruce wasted no time. He didn't give any commands. It wasn't necessary. He put his head down and charged, pulling out the large knife now sheathed on his side. He fired one more shot into the broad gap, then sliced two creatures low on their bodies before stabbing them once more in the head as they fell. Those behind him followed suit. As Bobby dove low to slice the beasts below the knee, they raised their guns and shot into the vicious tumult above him.

It was at that moment Tom McGann, the man Bobby had sent upstairs, leaned out a rear window and threw a Molotov cocktail behind the crowd of beasts fighting to get in. He hit his target and the bottle exploded, spreading liquid flame and burning beasts in every direction. Bobby and his mates attacked those that remained near the Bilco doors in hand-to-hand combat. There wasn't much space to maneuver and one of his mates tripped on the staircase trying to get to one of the creatures rushing towards him. He fell into its embrace, and the monster dug its razor-sharp digits into the exposed flesh of his back and tore out his spine. Bobby dug his knife into the lower belly of the beast and thrust upwards, tearing a seam up to its gullet, spilling its innards over the basement stairs.

Someone grabbed Bobby from behind, yanking him towards the group of frantic parents. Others managed to shoot two remaining creatures attempting to enter the basement, while two more jerked the doors shut, then drew the chains through the handles and secured them as best as he could with a metal bar.

After throwing his handmade bomb through the back window at the beasts below, Tom McGann raced to the front of the pub, elbowed his way to an opened window, and lit and threw another cocktail. He concentrated his toss on the creatures outside the main entrance. The fire ignited at least five of the beasts that ran amok in the aftermath of the inferno, sputtering to a stagnant, crispy pile in the street as the rain gradually put out the flames. Tom looked down Main Street towards the marina and what he saw was not good news. Perhaps it was a trick of the shifting fog, or the sporadic lightning, or a combination of both, but it appeared as if many more of the creatures were finding their way up the hill towards them.

Those on the main floor of the pub would soon be out of fire-power. The last rounds of ammunition were handed out with dire warnings to be sure of a shot before taking it. Anyone without bullets was told to fall behind those with ammunition and prepare for close-contact, hand-to-hand fighting.

"Marie," Bryan said. "We're going to need help down here. Please go upstairs and send everyone down." He looked at his daughter through tears. Marie nodded and proceeded to the stairway. Bryan grabbed her arm as she passed him. His look was one of fatigue and failure. He was giving up and conveying to Marie that no one was going to survive.

"I know it's probably useless to suggest it," Bryan said, "but I'd like you to stay up there. This will be our last stand against these things, and I don't think it will end well for us. If it comes to that, you might be able to slip out a back window, lower yourself to the ground, and make a run for it."

At first Marie was shocked. The thought of doing such a thing—trying to save herself while everyone she knew and loved was fighting to the death—never entered her mind. She then saw the pained look of a father trying to avoid witnessing the violent death of his only daughter, and she softened.

"Well then," she said, "as long as you know it's useless." She smiled, kissed his forehead, and ran to complete her task. A few moments later, everyone upstairs had come down to join the others.

The tearing mania at the shutters and doors continued unabated. The din that accompanied the mad rush to kill the beasts outside of their refuge gave way to an eerie silence. A strange melancholy descended over them all, born of a tacit acceptance of the fate that soon awaited them. No one breathed a word. All that could be heard was the unceasing pecking at their splintering fortress.

Gerard Young shouted to the crowd. "I guess this would be a bad time to put my bagpipes into service, eh?" He received a few chuckles for his effort at humor.

Ella MacDonald was quick to respond. "Do you all know why pipers walk while they play?" she asked.

Met with a wall of attentive silence, she responded, "To avoid the noise."

A silent moment in time was followed by uncontrolled laughter.

When the laughs ebbed, Ella looked over her fellow islanders and swelled with pride at the exhibition of such bravery in the face of certain death. She smiled and said, "What say we give these filthy beasts a taste of who we are here on Crover Island?"

The room erupted in booming cheers that drowned the manic tearing that occurred at the door and shutters. Their laughter brought them courage, and their courage was showcased by their determined battle cries.

As the long night finally waned towards dawn, and they readied themselves for their last battle, no one took notice that the winds and rain had suddenly lessened in intensity, and the strange, ghostly mist that accompanied the storm was dissipating. It seemed in that moment that superstorm Nora had dramatically slackened, rapidly fading from the brute force of her initial introduction to a sputtering farewell at the crack of dawn.

The group was, instead, pre-occupied. They were about to fire their final rounds of ammunition as they raced headlong into certain death when they heard something. It was a gunshot, just outside the pub. The attention of the creatures was drawn from the fractured shutters and splintered door. Marie ran to an opening at one of the shutters and looked out. The vehicle outside was blowing its horn and someone had leapt from the passenger side, firing his weapon.

"It's a van," Scott Mitchell said as he glanced out the picked-at hole in the door.

Scott spun back around in time to see his friend, Jeff Watson, yank open the door and race into the outside fray. Scott didn't hesitate. He tore into the brawl after his friend. Others from the pub quickly poured into the street, grabbing whatever they could lay their hands on that passed for a weapon, from mop handles and broken whiskey bottles to the butt of empty guns.

Bryan opened the doors to the basement.

"Barricade this door," he shouted. "Everyone stay here to protect the children. We're making a last stand."

Before anyone had a chance to follow through with that order, Bobby Bruce sprinted from the rear of the basement, jumped the staircase, and burst into the pub in time to see Marie join the others in a dash to the street in front of the pub.

Rivulets of red blood flowed freely down Main Street, like wavy stripes of ruby-red ribbon, long, stringy fingers stretching for the distant and dark marina at the bottom of the hill. The overlay of pink-tinged innards the color of raw ham spilled over the cobblestones, causing people to slip and fall as they fought for their lives. An overwhelming, pungent stench crept over the entire area. It was an evil-smelling putrescent effluvium, like rotted mammals decaying in a roadside ditch. As the winds diminished, the loathsome smell hung in the air, thick enough to touch.

Bobby Bruce made good use of his well-seasoned knife, crippling and gutting creature after creature without pause. He was covered in so much blood and gore as he rolled across the road it was impossible to say if any of it was his. His weapon was a lethal appendage, whipping in all directions at once, craving death as its only reward.

Andrew Morrison and Gerard Young fought side by side, swinging empty shotguns and dodging sweeping claws. Andrew would jam his empty weapon into the kneecap of one of the beasts, while Gerard would then slam his down onto the skull and finish it off. When the stock on Andrew's weapon broke, he used the barrel of the gun in a similar fashion, dispatching beast after beast after beast.

John Stewart had been the first to jump from the Ford Transit van. He pumped the weapon Tim had handed to him on their way to the pub and fired away, gunning down several creatures at once. He immediately jammed two more shells into the chamber and cut down several more. Some of the passengers who were still in the rear of the Transit, especially those with children, were guided into the pub. Everyone else who could fight grabbed a tire iron, a car jack, or anything they could use to club the beasts.

Andrew Morrison fought like a man possessed. Blood and spittle flew in all directions as if he were unhinged. He whipped his head around and noticed that his friend, Gerard, was no longer behind him, but was charging after a beast he had wounded. He was about to ram the creature with the gun he carried when the monster, falling from its own wounds, turned on him and swiped his chest, leaving a trail of bloody ruts from his neck down to his abdomen. Gerard stood in shock for a moment, his face as white as lamb's wool, holding his bowels in his hands and staring at them as if he could wish them back into his now-empty cavity. They slipped through his fingers and fell to the earth with a sploosh, and then, so did he. Andrew screamed and raced after and beat the falling beast until it lay in a heaping, smelly mass of gore and tissue.

The last passenger to emerge from the rear of the van was perhaps the only one without a look of fear. He jumped to the cobblestones below, scanned the bloody scene unfolding before him, and strode to the one person who gained his focus. He grabbed Ella MacDonald and spun her around to face him.

"Mac!" she said. "It's you!" Ella fell into his embrace as they stepped back, away from danger.

"No time to explain," he said. "I'll tell you all about it later. Right now, let's finish these things off."

Jeffrey MacDonald, given up for dead and with tire iron in hand, fought bravely aside his wife, both battling with renewed energy.

Marie rushed into the brutal struggle at the precise moment Tim jumped from the front of the van. He looked up to make eye contact, then bolted to her side. He kissed her quickly, but passionately, then darted back into the upheaval. He took two steps and noticed something was wrong, or perhaps troubling. His background and training, nagging at his subconscious, were trying to tell him something. Something that was strange and different. Something unpredictable, but important. The rain had diminished to a fine spray, and the wind had faded to a soft whisper. The sun, now rapidly rising in the east, replaced the storm of the night before and steamed the mysterious fog into a gauzy, fading nightmare.

Nora wasn't completely through with them yet, but this time she was giving the island inhabitants an unexpected gift. She was ending her violent path of destruction earlier than anticipated, giving the so-called weather experts one more reason to scratch their heads in disbelief and wonder. By doing so, she removed the umbrella of protection made of rain, wind, and fog she initially provided the creatures that roamed the island. The beasts that plagued them throughout the night had survived for millennia in deep and dark water, protected from the heat and harmful rays of the sun they saw only through muted waters. They had lived in an all-encompassing moist locale, but were suddenly freed by a twitch of the earth and encouraged to explore the island in the shadow of the deadly storm that was Hurricane Nora. As the sun regained control of the sky and its bright flickers of light warmed the land once more, the creatures of Crover Island dropped to the earth in droves, practically liquefying under the sun's burning beams of heat and light, leaving nothing but whisps of smelly smoke in their wake. For the first time during their terror-filled nightmare, the island's dazed and exhausted residents felt the possibility of survival was within their grasp.

CHAPTER 25

REVERBERATIONS

The *whump, whump, whump* of helicopter blades sliced through the warm air of late summer, disturbing the stillness that was now a rarity on Crover Island. Four PUMA helicopters cut through the clouds, zipping across the sky on their way to pre-established military bases. One month had passed since the horror that was Hurricane Nora, and the island was never busier. Since the sun had made an early appearance on that last day of battle during the storm and hastened the demise of the Crover creatures, as they had come to be known, the island had been inundated with military and scientific personnel. While their primary mission was essentially a science-driven endeavor, the military exercised a strong role in maintaining safety, security, and the shielded transportation of officials around the island. And, of course, was quietly overseeing any weaponizing possibilities of the research that was uncovered.

While clearing the creature carcasses (at least what was left of the gelatinous beasts), and burying the island's dead was of paramount importance, their primary task after the event, as they referred to it in their reports, was to create rapidly built military bases, or RBMBs, in secure and strategic locations around the island, mostly at or near the largest lochs, as well as along the western coast of the island. Using maps provided by the Royal Scottish Geographical Society, the National Library of Scotland, and Bryan Brown at the Royal Oak Pub, the military brass had done a quick survey as to which areas of the island would provide them the best opportunities for possible creature discovery, apprehension, and study. That is, if there were any beasts left to be found. To date, after twenty-four-hour shifts of work, seven days a week, they were simply coming up empty, finding no further trace of the creatures on the island. Those bases were manned by a significant array of scientists and university faculty, but all were finding it increasingly difficult to justify their continued existence due to the lack of viable specimens.

"What do you think will come of all of this?" Marie asked.

Marie, Bryan, Tim, John Stewart, and Andrew Morrison were sitting at a table in Robert Campbell's house, which Robert had willed to Bryan. The Royal Oak Pub had become ground zero for the handful of military and science brass that were responsible for any key decision-making related to their respective missions, so, when a modicum of secrecy or discretion was needed by the locals appointed to assist with civil matters, the house was where they met.

"I'll start us off with some good news," Bryan said. "Jeffrey MacDonald, as you all know, is alive and well. I've come to find out he's a bit of an island hero again, but wants no recognition of that fact. Nevertheless, he saved his work crew by drawing off attacking creatures so they, and Ella, could escape. Backed up to a cliff, he jumped off and landed on a small ledge. From there, he climbed his way across the outcrop to a dirt path leading to the back of his house. He managed to get to Central Road and was eventually picked up by Tim and John."

"That was a sight, I can tell you," John said. "He was strutting along the roadside in the midst of a hurricane as if he were out for an evening stroll."

"Oh, and he saved his workmen a second time that evening," Bryan said with a chuckle, "by stopping Ella from throwing them off the cliff for leaving her husband to fend for himself. And then," Bryan continued, "there's the wee girl, Anna, who delivered Robert's warning to the Cross family before . . . before going silent. She's being cared for by Jim and Barbara Cross, along with the enthusiastic approval of their own children. They wish to adopt her and get her the help she needs to fully recover. Jack and Emily Brodie, Angus McCleod, and many other local families have elected to stay here on the island to repair and rebuild. It's the only home they've ever known, and they're not about to let anyone tell them they can't stay. Many others have already left, or . . . or are buried here."

"After the initial horrific end to our collective nightmare," Tim chimed in, "I'm afraid there isn't much I can tell you in the way of good news. Not after the military put a clamp on sharing official information. The world knows what happened here, of course. There were far too many people involved for that information not to get out. But all research and related information is top secret at present." They all knew Tim was often called upon to meet with the scientists, given his background and up-close interaction with the Crover creatures.

"I *can* tell you, however, that the military is losing interest quickly. Besides the perennial issue of budgetary constraints, they can't seem to find anything substantial that would give them a reason to stay on here. Even some of the academics are starting to pack up, although they, along with a reduced military presence, plan on leaving a skeleton crew here to do further research. And I've been asked to head the team from the University of Edinburgh," he said with a smile towards Marie.

"That's great, Tim," Bryan said. "It'll be grand to have you here longer. And you, Andrew. Anything to report on the church?"

"Indeed. We had a recent gathering at the church site," Andrew said. "A celebration of sorts, to break bread and reach out to one another. After eating and talking, we assembled in prayer, giving thanks for the lives we saved, and for those who lost theirs while saving ours. People like Maureen Murray, Keith Argyl, and Thomas Thomson. We said a special prayer for Reverend Knox, who we all believe martialed his faith to fight the evil we all confronted. It was as if he could see this coming and told us that God would take a hand in ending it. For that, we decided to honor him by rebuilding the church further inland, near a spot he desired it to be, and renaming it The Reverend Knox Chapel." After a moment's pause, he added, "We thought he would like that, to know that in our moment of need, both spiritual and corporeal, he came to our aid."

"John," Bryan said to John Stewart. "Catch us up on your news."

"As some of you know, I went back to Loch Crover and, with Tim's help, I was able to retrieve the bodies of the elderly couple, Allan and Margaret, who were part of my tour group, and I saw to it that they received a proper burial. We did the same for another member of our group, a man named Charles Clark.

"Thanks to Bryan, we've all been made aware of Robert's sacrifice in Korea and the medal he received. I'm thrilled to be able to tell you I've already contacted the press on the mainland about his achievements, and they'll be publishing it in the papers. I've also contacted a monument company on the mainland, and they are already making the memorial we requested, which, when finished, will be the first thing visitors see when they arrive on the island at the marina. After the military lifts the travel ban, the travel business will resume, strangely. I've heard from our tour agent that people are clamoring to come here and see the site for themselves. Lastly, my mate Michael and I decided to rename our boat, The Billy Thomson."

John choked up on that last bit of news to the group. He had been fond of Billy and wanted to do something concrete to honor his memory.

Their meeting over, Tim and Marie went for a walk, while the others stayed behind to enjoy a quick supper followed by several rounds of good scotch and soft laughter that would echo throughout the night. Their voices carried through the opened windows, trailed by the dim house lights that fanned across the lawn outside. Tim and Marie sat on a wooden bench that overlooked the sprinkled lights of Blackpool below.

"I'm glad you're staying, Tim."

The silence between them embraced them both, until Tim grabbed Marie, pulled her in close, and kissed her with a passion reserved for those falling deeply in love.

***

Inverness was quiet as the tourist season slowed. The setting sun cast its last reflection on the Moray Firth to its north and the Loch Ness to its south. Heavy clouds quickly rolled in, and the developing cool, wet breeze drove those in search of a festive evening indoors to enjoy the conviviality and camaraderie offered by the many restaurants and pubs that lined the shore along the northern edge of Loch Ness. One such pub, The Nessie Inn, was enjoying a late-season packed crowd due to its enviable location on an outcrop overlooking the shiny mirror that was the Moray Firth to the north. Its fireplace was ablaze, warming those in search of indoor food and fun on this damp night. Laughter and friendly conversation wafted over the water's surface, now dolloped with the light raindrops that were beginning to fall.

The puckered, reflective water surface suddenly broke with the force of a torpedo. A lone figure stood like a sentry, silent and stoic. Then another appeared to its left, almost immediately. And still another to its right. They breathed in the atmosphere that fell from moisture-laden rain clouds and looked to the lights on the hill, attracted by the life and laughter within. The three creatures flexed their sharpened claws and moved to the shoreline that rested below *the Nessie* Inn. They made their way up a dirt path that skirted a carpark and led to a side entry to the restaurant with but one driving biological imperative.

Hunger.

ACKNOWLEDGEMENTS

With heartfelt thanks and recognition to Helga Schier. She has aided countless authors over the years, myself included. Helga was always available for a consult on developing a character, discussing a plot point, or suggesting changes to a manuscript. I count myself fortunate to have benefitted from my relationship with her, and her recent passing has left a large hole in the writing community.

Some weather expertise was needed to provide a plausible direction for Hurricane Nora, a major plot point in my story. I received it gratefully from the following:

Dr. Hun Bok
Associate Professor and Department Chair
Department of Earth and Environmental Sciences
New Jersey City University
Jersey City, New Jersey

Bob Harrigan
ABC7's Chief Meteorologist
Suncoast 7
Sarasota, Florida

Please note that any meteorological errors are mine alone.

I am also indebted to my new team of experts at Publish Pros, especially Mary Hall and Rich Carnahan, for their help in guiding me over the finish line and beyond.

Lastly, I have always benefitted from the love and support of my wife, Bronwen, my children and their spouses, Peter and Anna, Alex and Kayla, and Brianna and Phil, and the light that shines in the eyes of my grandchildren: Nora, Wesley, Lucas, Nathaniel, Bennett, and Colbie. Your Boompa loves you.

ABOUT THE AUTHOR

Before retiring, J.M. Kelly was a middle school teacher, a vice-principal, a principal, a consultant for the New Jersey Foundation for Educational Administration, a board member of the Global Learning Project, and president of the Morris County Association of Elementary and Middle School Administrators. He has received numerous education awards, including the New Jersey Governor's Teacher Award, two Geraldine Dodge Foundation Grants, and the New Jersey Principals' and Supervisors' Association's Principal of the Year Award for Visionary Leadership.

Kelly has authored two professional books: *Student-Centered Teaching for Increased Participation* and *In Search of Leadership: Sailing with Roland.* He has also published two middle school horror books in a series, *The Lost Treasure* and *Monster on the Moors,* and a humorous mystery for adults, *Tommy Ails: Good for What Ails You.*

Kelly divides his time between Sea Girt, New Jersey and Sarasota, Florida, with his wife Bronwen. They have three grown children and six grandchildren.

BOOKS BY J.M. KELLY

ADULT FICTION

Crover Island

Tommy Ails: Good For What Ails You

MIDDLE GRADE FICTION

The Lost Treasure: A Bobby Holmes Mystery
(Book 1)

Monster On The Moors: A Bobby Holmes
Mystery (Book 2)

NONFICTION

In Search of Leadership: Sailing
With Roland

www.ingramcontent.com/pod-product-compliance
Lightning Source LLC
Chambersburg PA
CBHW061058100726
47911CB00012B/287